For ... ...
hour and the place of
zombification's incarnation.
That dubious advent.
From the Fowl Duessa
                April, 1995

Zombification

Books by Andrei Codrescu

Zombification
Stories from National Public Radio

Andrei Codrescu

Picador USA ❧ *New York*

Picador ® is a U.S. registered trademark and is used by St. Martin's Press under license from Pan Books Limited.

Design by Jaye Zimet

Library of Congress Cataloging-in-Publication Data
Codrescu, Andrei
    Zombification : stories from NPR / Andrei Codrescu.
        p.   cm.
    ISBN 0-312-11933-X
    I. National Public Radio (U.S.)   II. Title.
    [PS3553.O3Z44   1995]
    814'.54—dc20   94-46554
                                                        CIP

First published in the United States by St. Martin's Press

First Picador USA Edition: April 1995

10   9   8   7   6   5   4   3   2   1

Contents

Part II—Confessions of a Video Vigilante

Part III—The PC Age,
or How to Spank Three Presidents

Part IV—Trouble at the Cultural Cantina

Part V—From Euphoria to Depression in Three Years, or From the Suicide of Communism to the Rebirth of Fascism

Part VI—New Orleans Doesn't Rhyme with Rice and Beans

Part VII—Places That Are Not New Orleans Reached by Dawg and Bird

A Foreword to Days Past

The pieces collected here are a record of private and public life between the years 1989 and 1993. They were written for the radio and broadcast weekly on NPR's program "All Things Considered." In retrospect, these four years turn out to have been inordinately dramatic. It was, as a reporter put it, as if someone pushed the fast-forward button on history. In 1989, the shape of the world changed radically when the Soviet Union disintegrated and Eastern Europe left the imperial matrix. At first, this change was welcomed euphorically ("the New World Order," alas!) but soon enough the euphoria turned into despair as it became apparent that fascism rose from the ruins of red totalitarianism. The "velvet revolution" of Prague turned into the "ethnic cleansing" of Bosnia. During this time, the United States, winner of the cold war, bombed Baghdad in an impressive video display of high-tech killingry. And in 1993, American voters ended decades of Republican rule and cold war rhetoric.

I was fortunate enough to have a personal stake in the unfolding events because Romania, where I was born, was briefly at their center. I returned to "cover" the situation for NPR in December 1989, and wrote a troubled and sad chronicle called *The Hole in the Flag*. My private life merged for a short time with the public drama. My incredibly generous and supportive friends at NPR, Art Silverman, Michael Sullivan, Noah Adams, and Melissa Block, encouraged my curiosity and indulged my excesses. The exigencies of writing weekly kept me on my toes even as I rode an emotional roller-coaster. At the same time, I tried my best to continue being an American, to travel with my eyes open in my adopted country. I wrote a movie (and a book), *Road Scholar*, about America. Paradoxically, this helped my Romanian side recover.

What you have here then is the still-smoking matter of the mad rush of the last four years, which have gone, like in a fairy tale, in the blink of an eye. The passing of the old world order, three presidents, thousands of miles, are herein presented simultaneously. Speed abolishes time, as the physicists tell us, and here is a bit of proof. If you were living during these years you should have no trouble knowing what, where, and when. And, hopefully, re-experiencing the adrenaline.

Not so hopefully, the world has become more indifferent to suffering during this time. We have become inured to the faces of dying children, whether in Sarajevo or Washington, D.C. Our televisions have turned us into mute extensions of their shadow worlds. This is what I call "zombification." For some people, it may be an understandable psychological defense. But as the heart-dead zombies multiply among us, our governments reflect the process. Our lack of heart and failure of nerves are eerily reminiscent of the last "zombification" of the world, just after 1933.

—New Orleans
January 2, 1994

The Hours We Keep

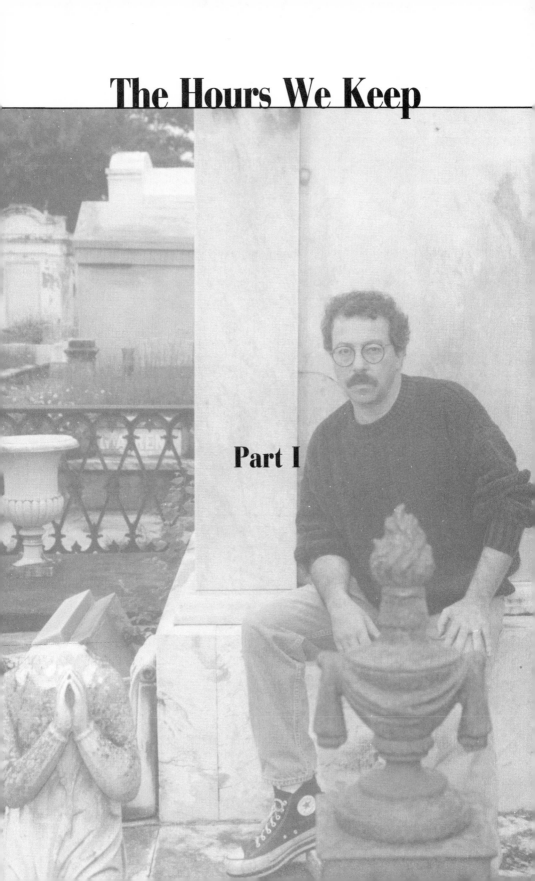

Part I

World Without Onions

Imagine a world without onions. Impossible? Hard as it is to believe, the onion didn't arrive on these shores until the mid-1700s. What did the natives do without the full-skirted comfort of this most generous vegetal? Yes, vegetal, not vegetable, like an eggplant or lettuce. The onion, in its manifold glory, is more of a fruit than a vegetable, in fact. There are entire cultures—like the one I come from—that would be inconceivable without the onion. A single onion, sometimes accompanied by a hunk of black bread, was my entire breakfast for the whole of my childhood and adolescence. I would balance my single onion on the top stair of the school and bring my first down with a *blam* on top of it. I would then extract the sweetest part, the heart, from the elegantly smashed body, and delight in its succulence until the bell rang. Tearfully, we lined back up to go to our classrooms, hundreds of little hearts powered by the pungent queen of veggies.

I would have continued late into my extensive youth if I hadn't been made self-conscious at Soho parties. Anyway, it appears that in addition to its having come to these shores late, the onion is in danger of being denigrated to second-class citizenship in cooking, since many cooks these days prefer, it appears, such onion simulacra as chives and scallions. Even if one disregarded for a moment the execrable taste of someone who would chase the onion out of the kitchen, the loss is incalculable.

An onion isn't just an onion: it's a metaphor. The earth is an onion. The moon is an onion. A person is an onion. The more sophisticated a person, the more onionlike he or she is. The more layers of mystery wrapped around the simple soul we are all born with, the more interesting we are and the more interesting the world becomes. In other words, no man or woman resembles an onion until he or she has earned the layers.

Understanding a person is like unwrapping an onion, layer after layer of transparent experience until, at last, the Zen nothingness beams from everywhere. I beg you: do not let them take away the onion. If they do, you'll be next.

Secrets

It is important to have secrets. It is important also, as Ted Berrigan said, "to keep old hat in secret closet." A friend of mine recently told me a story that she said she had never told anyone before because she didn't think anyone would believe it. Many years ago in Amsterdam she met a man who took her to a house completely filled with broken music boxes. This man lived in the narrow tunnels made by these boxes, which he constantly fixed. As soon as a box was restored he would set it to work until it broke again. The whole house chimed and hummed and sung, and my friend, crouching in there with the strange man, experienced a kind of time lapse to the Victorian Age. She had kept this story secret until now because it made her feel good to have a secret point of reference that didn't seem to partake of the reason of the daily world. But now she's told it, and it's a terrible thing because I'm telling it to you and it's no longer secret. The fact is that we all know that there exists in the world an order different from that in which we pass our days. If we reveal its existence people think that we are crazy. But secrets do not have to be extraordinary to be important. Our secrets, odd or not, are the pins that keep our inner life in place: they inform our psyche with meaning.

America is now in the throes of a confessional crisis that will transform human beings into mere shadows on a television screen. People will tell Donahue, Oprah, or Codrescu anything. "Yes, I strangled a nun. I am a nun strangler. There are many more of us than you think." The media has become our electronic absolver, a giant confessor that wipes the slate clean. Having confessed, we can now go empty into the world, believing that the extraordinary has been banished. But our secrets, spilled into the maw of television, become the collective property of an inhuman force that holds us all hostage. Emptied of secrets, we are playthings of the world. Once upon a time, we thought that we were different from animals because we were intelligent. That fact has been disproved. Our only claim to difference may be our ability to keep secrets.

Do tell me, will you?

Nymphettes

I panicked when they asked me to do the introduction to Nymphette Night at the New Orleans Film and Video Festival. They were going to show *Lolita* and *Pretty Baby* at the Joy Theater, and I'd been tapped. Why had I accepted? Neither a purveyor nor a surveyor of nymphettes myself, I am barely conversant with the genre. I prefer a face stamped a bit with wisdom and experience, which makes, I believe, for character.

Nymphettes, as I understand it, have their flowering about the age of thirteen, only to fade into ignominious nymph-hood or oblivion by fifteen. Some of my students, it is true, have the oblivious faces of children untouched by either thought or learning, though their bodies wiggle in that peculiar and blind fashion that makes all things in nature quiver and get marching. But I'd never—beyond an occasional involuntary pro forma leer—deigned to acknowledge such wiggling as any more than bio-automatism. And now here I was, nymphette-specialist about to introduce two classic tales of gray whiskers and bubblegum.

In the student bar later that night, I took my questions to a table full of nineteen-year-olds. "What is a nymphette?" I asked the one least likely to have gotten in the door without a fake ID. "Oh," she said coolly, "that would be my sister. She's only fifteen, and gets into every bar in New Orleans, is man-crazy, and nobody can stop her." "Were you ever a nymphette?" I continued. "*I* was," perked one of her friends, "I went to dinner with my boss and his secretary and I played with his leg right under the table. We've been going steady since." "How long ago was that?" "*Three months,*" she replied. Clearly, the boundaries of age were slipping perilously. Aware at this point of the immensely sexist gulf opening beneath my feet, I turned to one of the boyfriends. "Are there boy nymphettes?" I asked him. "Sure," he said, "I go with older women alla time." When the giggling subsided I said, "So what's the attraction?"

They all started talking at once. "Older men," one of them said, "they worship you. 'Cause they're married and everything."

That was as good as it got. Enter Humbert Humbert, ladies and gentlemen.

The Exhibitionist

There he was, stark naked on his balcony. He looked as if he'd just gotten up and come out for a breath of fresh air, soon to retire to the safety of the room. I paid him no more attention and started working. An hour later I looked up, and there he was, stark naked, still on the balcony, still looking like he'd just come out for a moment, but there was a difference, a big, er, difference. Now this had nothing to do with me, since he was looking at the street, I realized, at people in cars. His attention was entirely absorbed by passing cars, the drivers of which, should they look up, would be, no doubt, terribly startled.

He was young and good-looking, and completely absorbed by his activity. I chalked it up to a passing kink, but four hours later he was still there. It disturbed Alice when I pointed him out to her. She didn't want Tristan, whose room also faces the naked man's balcony, to see him. I could see her point, especially since the naked man, now flaccid, now erect, was definitely, as the day wore on, becoming bolder and more active. I hate to turn in my fellow humans for being naked, but Alice insisted. He wasn't just naked on the beach or in his bedroom with the lights on, he was displaying himself to passing automobiles and children, and would continue to do so until somebody stopped him.

Now, the Mardi Gras season isn't far off, and exhibitionism is one of *Carnival*'s favorite pastimes. In a few days it would be perfectly acceptable, even encouraged, but only in certain areas, and this wasn't one of them. Well, at her insistence, I called the cops. Told them a naked man was posing for motorists. They said they'd send someone. I don't know if they did or not, but next day there he was, the naked man, showing himself to passengers in their cars. And there he was, every day after that. Friends started to come over to watch him. Showtime from three to six. We started charging. Made hundreds. And there he was, nude for no good reason, charging nothing, incredibly serious, concentrating on the job.

Heavy Breathing Goes Legit

In the space of three minutes there were four 976 commercials on TV. 976-RAPP. 976-LUVV. 976-PARTY. The calls cost from ninety-nine cents to three dollars for one minute. Hired party prompters get sex talk going until you run out of breath or cash, whatever comes first. The new phone sex is the old obscene phone call gone legit. Heavy breathing authorized. It is also the sex of the coming decade, sex in the age of AIDS.

We had a big, black phone when I was a kid. Only a few people in town did. Only bad news came through it. It never rang frivolously, nobody ever chatted on it. It existed solely for weighty news, a heavy bird of ill omen. It fascinated me. I picked it up once and rang a random number. A woman answered. Holding my breath for what seemed like infinity, I trembled as I said these fatal words: "Cream cheese." I immediately hung up, my heart pounding, my mouth dry, my whole being unsettled.

I have difficulty speaking on the phone: I find it both intrusive and impertinent. I even wrote a book called *Why I Can't Talk on the Telephone*, enumerating the reasons. Still, it is an undeniably sexual instrument, capable of carrying words like *cream cheese* directly into the heart of an unsuspecting ear. And sooner or later someone was bound to market it.

The old obscene call was a nasty, criminal thing to do. We punished heavy breathers. But now they have gone middle-class and we have found a way to charge them. It is the job of the market to turn the base material of our emotions into gold. Just when I thought that we had nearly run out of marketable desires here comes a new one. Even without AIDS, face-to-face encounters between the hassled beings of our age have become exceedingly difficult. Sex phone arrives just in time to seal us from one another in pure electronic/fantasy space. Going home to a phone orgy and a hot bath will now become the dream of every working stiff. People who will never meet will have phone marriages and will take phone honeymoons to imaginary places. They will have imaginary children, one for every phone on hold.

Wreck of the Vampire

There is honor among vampires, but enough is enough. When the parvenus mass on the ancient blood banks, it's time to bat your wings! Anne Rice, the current vampire queen and a neighbor of mine here in New Orleans, the Vampire Capital of the New World, is fooling with the clockworks of the Immortal One. Her books, particularly the last one, *Queen of the Damned*, have seized the American imagination, if the *New York Times* best-seller list is right. One of my students, whose imagination was most definitely seized, wrote that she would submit to a vampire without questions if she could be made even a little immortal. I didn't ask how one could become a little immortal. Perhaps the same way one could become a little pregnant.

In any case, the degree of penetration effected by Ms. Rice's vampires is sufficiently deep to warrant my speaking out. In short, Ms. Rice has wrecked the vampire. Originally a Transylvanian gentleman whose considered bites made Victorian maidens swoon slowly into an ecstatic state after many nightly visits, the transformed new breed is a one-bite worker. Instead of the slow seduction of a dark, old-world aristocrat threatening the thin ice of Anglo-Saxon womanhood, we now have a hustler biting anybody anywhere, a deritualized quickie better suited to a peep show than a palace. And there is no longer a single vampire, Dracula, with his suitably low-life assistants, but whole slews of vampires roaming the cities like cyberpunks from a suppurating back lot. Worst of all, the vampire, thanks to Ms. Rice, is no longer from Transylvania, whose original dirt he once carted in splendid coffins all over the West, but from New Orleans.

Don't get me wrong: I do believe that New Orleans is ideally suited for vampires, and that many do, in fact, live here. Why, right around the corner . . . but that's another story. No, I don't object to their finding my city hospitable—after all both Anne Rice and I live here—but I do mind them having their *Headquarters* here. After all, you can mess with anything, but not with the original creative insight, that deep satisfying first bite that Dracula the Transylvanian took out of the neck of Europe.

Your Sons Can Defend Themselves

I heard the thwack before I saw the impact, and next thing I knew my youngest was sporting a shiner the size of an old dollar. They should have disqualified the thug that thwacked him but they let him stay, so my tyke lost the fight. "Unfair!" I screamed, but it was too late. Everywhere hundreds of martial arters resplendent and sweaty in their colored belts thwacked each other for trophies in the big Southern Chop-Chop conference. When older son got on the floor his mom cringed and swept the arena for the doctor, who was bending over a broken nose a mere two feet below.

Older son, a brown belt, disposed of two adversaries in short order. Then a third. A fourth. A fifth. He swept to first place in his belt class and a great swelling of pride overcame his mom and dad, who could now look with kinder eyes on the organized bruising before them. Father was a confirmed hater of things organized, including organized sports and organized religions. As a child, his major sporting experience consisted in walking the wrong way up a street jammed by the soccer fans of the losing local team. And he wore glasses and had a book under his arm. In those days, guys with muscles beat up guys with glasses. It was the form. The mother, who was American, made no such distinctions. She'd played baseball and her brother football and she'd also read a book or two. America, it seemed, was not overtly adverse to the harmonious functioning of mind and body together, though when the chips were down the football team got the money and they cut back on philosophy. If it came right down to deciding between keeping the quarterback and dropping Nietzsche, there was no question which Fred was kept. But so what? It's a healthy country and the healthy are partial to the healthy.

In any case, here was the older son, trophy in hand, having out-chopped the best. "What kept me going," he declared in a later interview with his elders, "was that shiner my brother got. Every time I needed some anger I thought of that shiner. And I got sharp." The father, who'd had no brother, felt warm inside. As a child he'd been angry too, but there'd been nobody right there to take it out on. So he became a critic and gave it to the whole world. Fred Nietzsche put an arm around his son. Perhaps health wasn't such a bad thing after all.

My Checkup

I'll go to a cemetery before I'll go to a hospital, but the other day, despite better considerations, and for the sake of my loved ones, I went to get a checkup. I took very shallow breaths in the hospital lobby because it is my deeply held belief that you can get sicker in a hospital than just about anywhere else on earth. The great concentration of sick people breathing near each other creates malevolent viral clouds that swarm about the innocent. The innocent, in this case me, was made to fill a vast yellow folder of personal history that went way beyond the reasonable bounds of memory. How in the world am I to remember the year of my immunizations? Or the fate of my tonsils? Or even whether I have an appendix or not? These are my mother's memories, not mine. Not everyone in their forties still goes to the hospital with their mother, though it's a splendid idea. Still, these were understandable physical questions, mere facts compared to what came next, things like, Do you like your job?, Are you happy with your life? It took Kierkegaard and his ilk thousands of pages to avoid those questions. The yellow form was as nothing, however, compared to what came afterward. "Please undress and wrap this sheet around your waist," the nurse said. "The doctor will be with you shortly." I stood there naked, shivering, like a forlorn gladiator among gleaming steel blades and hooks, while somewhere out there, a doctor was being slowly born. At long last, he entered. Tall, imposing, manly, with no-nonsense manners, he counted my heartbeat, shined a bright light in my eyes, and then, how shall I say it, humiliated me with his rubber-gloved finger. Well, I'd rather not talk about it.

My question is, Is all this necessary? Every day we hear of wondrous advances in medicine where Dr. McCoy—type devices will tell us what's wrong by being merely dangled over the body. And yet, we still have to submit our persons to unimaginable probes in little neon-blasted offices, and our minds to equally probing tests on bright yellow paper. This is not a complaint, mind you. It's only the astonishment of a relatively healthy person before the vast humiliation of possible illness. If they told me that I could live forever if only I lived in a hospital I'd tell them where to get off. That kind of immortality is a hell of a lot worse than croaking at once in a low-life dive on some stormy night.

New Year's Resolutions

Mr. Philip Morris and Mr. Smirnoff get the blues this time of the year. So many people resolve to give up cigarettes and drink, they teeter on the edge of ruin. Luckily, most of them forget their resolve at the first opportunity. I could only think of two new resolutions for the new year, and neither one involves giving up anything. I decided to watch more TV in 1989,* so I'll know what most people talk about when they talk, and what my students are saying when they're saying things. And I also decided to change my mind about everything I've been sure about last year.

This is both a health and a safety measure, and it anticipates the world proving me wrong. For instance, I made light not so long ago of the raging epidemic of humorlessness in this country concerning such mumbo jumbo as Satanism. Sure enough, two days later I found a stiff dead cat on my steps. Next day, two teenagers explained to me that the recent murder and rape of a ninety-year-old woman in New Orleans was the work of Satanists.

I met a teacher who knows for a fact that many of her students are involved in drug and death cults, and as proof she offered me a little essay, written by one of them. I quote in part: "I sit in my room, I stare at the walls and decay. I feel my self rotting deeply inside . . . my room is my dungeon, my grave." At the bottom of the essay is a skull with a dagger through an eye socket. Another teenage informant assures me that one of her friends digs up things in the cemetery for cult practice and has hairy skulls in the trunk of his car. I try to understand, but I'm a little baffled. Adolescents have always freaked out their elders with appropriate symbols. But there might be something to it. This year, I'm

*And ended up, instead, being on TV, when I got to cover the bloody events in Romania in December 1989.

— 20 —

willing to give even Satan the benefit of the doubt. Tolerance is the only virtue I hope for. Failing that, I think I'll just sit here, getting the blues with Mr. Morris and Mr. Smirnoff. Most people's resolutions involve giving up something that's not good for them, which is very bad from an economic point of view. If all the people who resolve to quit drinking, smoking, and eating actually did so, the market would be in trouble. Luckily, most people forget their resolve at the first opportunity. I don't want to ruin the country, so I'll resolve to increase consumption instead. I'll watch more TV in 1989. That way I'll know exactly what people are talking about, and I will be able to communicate with my students as well.

Satan

One of my friends swears that prayer in the schools is a satanic rite. She argues that children use prayer as a kind of magic, an incantation to get what they want, and to make the teacher's hair fall out. Even the ones who just mumble the words do it as slowly as possible in order to shorten the school day.

"Okay," I say, playing the devil's advocate, "what's wrong with a bit of magic at the start of each day, a little mysterious chant to the deity, a low hum, a vibratory rite, setting in motion the invisible forces? Is a bit of bit of voodoo, mantra, chant, prayer, and magic truly dangerous? And Satan, really! Everybody knows that Satanists pray backwards! They are not like us, though they do watch TV the right way, from the couch!"

"You can make a joke out of it, if you want!" My friend was angry. "But Satanism is no joke."

She has a point. These are satanic days. Near Washington, D.C., two teenage girls scrawled Satanist symbols on things and then killed themselves. One of them had reputedly said that she "couldn't wait to meet Satan." In southern Louisiana teenage suicide is up, and so are Satanic graffiti. At the Occult section of my bookstore, a boy with shaved head and one swastika earring tells a Catholic high school girl still in her uniform, "Don't ever look at these books without me!" And she looks at him completely trusting, and totally scared. On television, a priest is having an orgasmic experience with a horned dwarf in *The Exorcist, Part 72*, simultaneously keeping the family nailed to the couch with the double nails of suspense and terror. In Congress, there is new testimony about Satan living inside rock and roll played backwards, and as soon as the names of the satanic records are released, all the teenagers start playing them backwards. Which is how they would also pray, no doubt.

So who is Satan? Well, I have a hunch. His real name is Mumbo

Jumbo. He lives in an empty house, crying for attention. He wants your prayers but only if he can't have your affection. He gets mad if you won't play with him. He wants your eyes shut tightly at the beginning of each day so you can listen to heavy metal in your head. He wants you to stop thinking so much and to watch more TV, where he also dwells most of the time. He doesn't want you to kill yourself so that you could meet him, because you meet him every day, chewing gum and staring into the empty mirror at the shopping mall. But he does want you to draw stick figures all over the walls and tattoos all over your skin so you could look more interesting. He relieveth your boredom and leadeth you through the shadow of the Bomb. He has a cute behind.

Godscams

News of God hasn't been good since they razed Jimmy Swaggart's Motel on Airline Highway. The latest twist involves millions of dollars squeezed out of the faithful by businessmen working with the Scriptures. An oil and gas company was stopped by Massachussetts and Missouri authorities from selling stock to wells drilled in accordance with instructions in the Old Testament. Divinely inspired investment advice is snowblowing through the land. Bible-propelled precious metals, coins, real estate, and oil are getting the attention of the faithful. People of every faith are falling for it: Black Protestants, Greek Orthodox, Hispanic Catholics, Mormons. The only people immune to it so far are adherents of the Church of the Subgenius out in Texas, who conduct their investments strictly according to the weather. If it rains, buy, if it's sunny, sell. Since most of them have no money to speak of, they always come out ahead.

There was a time, correct me if I'm wrong, when God seemed to be against greed. I'm not sure exactly when this was, since there is nothing in the history of any church to prove it. It seemed to be more in the nature of a folk belief based on the poverty of Jesus and his pristine hatred for the rich. That time was long ago, probably in the sixties or something. In any case, anyone propounding that theory today would be laughed out of the pulpit or shoved off the soapbox. Looked at in another way, greed may actually be the one thing to end the schisms and arguments between creeds, faiths, or religions. Instead of arguing points of doctrine, the faithful could trade beliefs the way people trade systems at the track to see what works: one bread-and-fishes miracle for a camel-talking-in-the-desert, one icon for a Psalm, a lamb for a goat, and so on. You can adopt whatever system yields the most gain. It would be the end of foolish argument, and there could be the much-sought-after way to measure the immeasurable. Trust me, it's a good deal. We'll trade in my brand-new church.

The Extra Second

The year 1990 has an extra second in it. Watch out! The U.S. Naval
Observatory, which is in charge of time, says that clocks are too accurate
and the earth is too slow; 6:59 P.M. today will be followed by 6:60 then
by 7 P.M. The extra second will come in handy to those of us who need
another second to figure out what went on in 1990. How often have we
heard the cry "Wait a second!"—uttered by lovers, workers, and plain
schmoes like ourselves. We've said "Wait a second" to guys making
estimates for repairs, to employers who said no to requests for pay raises,
to fast talkers who shook hands before we knew what the deal was, to
news reports that didn't make any sense, to children who were out the
door before you could tell them when to come back, to crooked scorekeep-
ers in Little League games, to presidents who sent us to war before we
had a chance to ask why, to lawmakers who slipped things we didn't
know into bills we barely had time to read.

You could say that we've said "Wait a second" to most things in
this life, which—like the clocks—have been going faster than the
earth that we are on. And nobody waited a second, not the news events,
not the children, not the neighbors, and not the people in a hurry
everywhere whose job is to move their hands faster than the eye can
see. The whole world is a shell game, Marge, all on account of that
missing second. Those of us who know know that everything happens
in a split second. Between life and death there is only that split second,
half of it in life and the other half on the other side. We don't know
what splits it, we don't even know where it went. Only advertisers, for
whom seconds mean cash, know what and how much a second is worth.
But most of us are not advertisers, we are only consumers. You can't
kill time without injuring eternity, says Thoreau, but somewhere along
the way someone's got away with the most important second in our
lives. And now we have it back for a second, so let's use it to clear

up our baffled and hurried lives. 1991 won't have an extra second, and it's a dyslexic year as well; it reads the same backwards as forwards.

Yo, as the dyslexic rabbi said.

Utopia Is Here

Any day now I am going to discover It. Capital *I*, *t*. I will be sitting quietly at the kitchen table stirring an absentminded cup of coffee with an indifferent spoon and it will be right there: It. Attempts to duplicate the experiment will fail or succeed, it doesn't really matter. It will have been done, cheaply, efficiently, and incontrovertibly. It will be the last discovery in the series that began with fusion in Utah. Last week, scientists in Louisiana announced that they found the cure for cancer in crawfish shells. They contain a protein that feeds on cancer cells. I almost discovered that protein myself because it always seemed to me that the stinking mounds of shells left over after a crawfish boil are just too powerfully pungent to be simply rotting. There was an intoxicating extra something in the stink that belonged to a different order of reality, particularly on a hot day.

The same with fusion. Every high school student left alone in the chemistry lab with a couple of test tubes must have noticed at one time or another that more energy came out than was put in, particularly if his or her mind was elsewhere. This is important. Every important discovery was made while the mind was elsewhere, as far as possible from the business at hand. The apple that hit Newton was to make him pay attention. He did. All great discoveries come in threes. Fusion and the cure for cancer are fundamental discoveries awaiting the third: the discovery of It. When this trinity is in place, we will be living in utopia. No more cold, no more hunger, no more disease. We will occupy ourselves with discovering more and more things. We will discover birds, for instance, if there are any left. If there are no more, ornithologists can always collect bird *names* and through those, somehow, bring back the birds. In fact, ornitholinguists, lepidepterolinguists, herpetolinguists, and all other varieties of zoolinguists will use their semantic skills to rediscover nature in all the classifications that obscure living things now. It won't be long now; every next cup of coffee could be the one.

The Ultimate Deadline

I'm up against the deadline. Not just one deadline. Several deadlines. If you cross this line, you're dead. It's the line of death. The world's on a deadline: hand up the goods or die. The doomsday clock is working against time. The dead say: our deadline was yesterday. That's the line on the other side. There is still a Party line even if you don't see it. It follows the hemline like the market. The market has a five-o'clock deadline. The bluelines arrived past the deadline and everyone was gone. There were deadlines between the lines. I can read between the lines because I've been up against a thousand deadlines and made it in the nick of time with nary a crease more in my lined forehead.

Looking at my lifeline, the palmist said, you'll live up to here, where the line ends. I looked down from the plane and saw all the neat lines. It's not a country, it's the Cliff Notes. The Polish refugee next to me opened the Polish paper: see, it's my byline, he said. Before the revolution you had to wait in line for everything except the newspapers, which were full of meaningless lines. After the revolution you have to wait in line for everything, including the newspapers, which are now full of too many lines. A line is a lie with the lead *n* in its belly. A deadline is a fishing line caught on a root. You have to get to the root of it to meet the deadline. I was ahead of my deadline so I watched "Flatliners," about some serious deadliners with a headliner complex. It's not a linear world, my cosmic adviser told me, but you have to toe the line as if it were. I fired him: gave him a deadline to improve his line. These are the *liner* notes of a man lying flat on his back on the deadline he isn't going to meet.

The Light Is Changing

It is no more than a hint, but it has come. Light has a richer golden hue and it lingers longer on the trees. It is an oblique and burnished light, still full of summer. But you can see the shadow growing in it. I don't know about you, but these preautumnal days, when fall sends its advance emissaries of shadow through the lingering heat, tear at my heart. This is the omen before the fact, the sign before the event, the season of overly sensitive souls: poets, migrants, gypsies, exiles. Autumn, the time of plenty, isn't yet pouring its melancholy wine into the metaphysically drunk soul. There are only drops, creating an intense thirst.

The urge to disappear and the desire to move begin stirring strongly now. People want to leave their jobs and their lives and strike for the unknown, while it's still warm. Gypsies start reading the night sky for directions and sending out their boulibashas to bribe officials in warm winter cities. A great desire to smash the old couch and throw the furniture out the window comes unexpectedly over generally placid souls. The S-word rises darkly in the minds of children, a mixture of dread and excitement.

Personally, this is the time when projects hatching in me since the beginning of the year are beginning to call for release. Whole novels sprout from the nutshells of skimpy ideas, and the eggs of casual observations are cracking to allow enormous essays to dream themselves into books. My friends also are becoming ready to reveal the things they have been keeping bottled inside. An urge to confession breezes through my world.

Many years ago, on a preautumnal day like this, an old French dwarf named Louie who used to manage my apartment building in New York emerged briefly from his musty hole beneath the boilers to announce to his tenants, *"Il s'en va, comme le vent."* It is going, like the wind. He didn't know, nor did we, what it was that was going like the wind, but it was, and it is, and we feel it in us.

Nostalgia for Everything

This time of the year for some reason I get filled with nostalgia like a Jules Verne balloon. I'm like Marcel Proust, who smelled a cookie and couldn't stop remembering. Wood fires are my cookie. I remember walking through an old square in my hometown in Romania, late fall 1958, kicking leaves with my feet and feeling as nostalgic as I do now for something I remembered then. I remember sitting on the steps of the Santa Maria Maggiore cathedral in Rome in 1965, eating an apple while everything turned to nostalgic gold around me. I sat in a steamy café by the Spanish Steps later with a bitter, hot espresso, looking wistfully on the fashions of the year 1965, miniskirts and polka dots, and feeling so terribly young and alone. I remember the wind whistling with snowflakes in it down Woodward Avenue in Detroit as I looked for a warm place to sit and contemplate the future year 1967, for which I already felt nostalgic though it hadn't even happened. I remember the Blimpie's on the corner of Sixth Avenue and Ninth Street in New York across from the long-gone Women's House of Detention where I sat writing nostalgically in my diary about the incredible year 1969 that was just around the corner. I remember the back porch of Gabriel's hilltop apartment in San Francisco in 1970, looking on a pastel blue and gold city and wondering where winter was. I went looking for it in Golden Gate Park, wrapped in its cocoon of eucalyptus and ocean salt, and rocked like a baby listening for hints of 1971. I remember the mists swirling above the Knotty Room in Monte Rio in 1974 while Pat and Jeff and I drank Rhoda's bad coffee and looked out to the huge redwood trees bending in an awesome wind announcing the torrential winter rains of 1975. I remember late fall, early winter, at the Mt. Royal Tavern in Baltimore in 1978, when all the lights went out and we continued drinking and talking by candlelight as the world fell apart. And the autumnal littlecafé near Pont Neuf in Paris in 1981, where nostalgia was invented. I'm writing now at the Déjà-Vu in New Orleans at the end of 1992, and I miss this place already.

Autumnal

It's fall. The leaves are already off the trees in the North and the East. Here in the Deep South defoliation is merely internal. The state legislature has stripped the budget for higher education, and programs, teachers, and classes are falling to the ground like so many leaves. My colleagues at the university are buying fishing rods in expectation of a hard winter of subsistence fishing. At least our lakes don't freeze. Through the stark branches of the skeletal tree of knowledge we can glimpse the gilded domes of gambling palaces in our future. Who needs higher education when the only skills needed to survive in Louisiana are dealing cards and fishing? There is a feeling of hope borne along by the cold winds in most of the country, but here we have resigned ourselves to crawling like mudbugs at the bottom of every statistic.

I like to visit cemeteries in this season of unredeemed nostalgia. The dead make me feel better. They've had their higher education and look where it's got them. Hollywood Cemetery in Richmond, Virginia, is perhaps the best place to consider the woes of my deep southern state. Buried here are all the heroes of the confederacy, Jeb Stuart, Robert E. Lee, Jefferson Davis. They rest in their tragic graves overlooking the James River, no longer surprised by anything. The inscriptions on their graves and monuments hint vaguely at loss and mention honor and death. Jefferson Davis, we are told, left the earth "wrapt in the purple mantle of death." Unbeknownst to him, he also left us wrapt in the mantle of purple prose. No such grandeur attends us here in Louisiana in the days of budget cuts at the near end of the twentieth century. We welcome the nip in the air and anxiously check the rusty hooks on our fishing rods. Unlike the majestic losers of Richmond, we get buried above ground here in Louisiana. Even better, we don't have to wait to die before they lay us to rest.

Hunger for Silence

In the small mountain city where I grew up, the first snow of the year wrapped the town in layers of silence. Roofs and spires slept under white comforters. A wisp of smoke from a chimney hung in the air like a fat, lazy question mark, while I rode the bus to school in the quiet of December, warm and safe in the cocoon of my own dreaming. School dragged on monotonously, but the drone of my teachers didn't breach the secret place inside myself where I was hiding. The grown-ups I knew were as remote and mysterious to me as the snowbound peaks of the Carpathian Mountains.

This was a silent age, not just for me but for the entire country. In those faraway Stalinist fifties behind the Iron Curtain, not much of the real world ever reached us. We were protected from bad news by total censorship, and when we had real things to say to each other we spoke them in whispers. There was little to listen to on the radio, unless one had a short frequency band and picked up Radio Free Europe or the Voice of America in the dead of the night. There were no advertisements on the walls, no spontaneous street festivals. Even those who dared to get drunk in the few restaurants and taverns that stayed open past 10 P.M. made sure that they kept their voices down and their thoughts to themselves.

When I left Romania the world exploded in song and color. It was a vertiginous change, like going suddenly from a black-and-white silent into the full-volume Dolby stereo of a Disney cartoon. Radios and televisions blared, people spoke their opinions as loudly as they could, the streets vibrated with traffic and power tools, the cafés shook with dance music. Luckily, I was an adolescent by then and something in me was calling for the ruckus just as it came to meet me. I don't know what I would have done in the quiet world of my mountain town had I stayed there.

I am not an adolescent any longer, and something in me is calling for silence again. I appreciate people of few words, and am beginning to find comfort in shared quiet. Mountain people are generally taciturn, not voluble like the people of valleys and seacoasts. Likewise, people from small towns do not talk a blue streak like people from cities. But what the silent ones lack in cleverness they make up for in strength: the spareness of their words guarantees their solidity. Or so I like to think, knowing full too well that silence sometimes also masks a lack of intensity and thought.

I like too those days when people put down their tools and turn down their telephones and stay out of their cars. I crave the quiet streets of holidays, and dream of snow, relentless, endless snow.

Christmas Wish List

This Christmas give a frog back his life. Don't dissect one. Millions of frogs, snakes, and turtles are ripped open every year in classrooms so that kids can see what's inside. We already know what's inside, so what's the point in looking and looking and killing and killing? Kids can see pictures of what's inside. At LSU where I work we have a cow with a window in her stomach. You can look in the window while the cow walks around and you can see the guts all coiled up and huge wads of grass being turned into beer or something. Why can't the same be done with one frog or one snake or one turtle instead of having to waste millions of them?

Here in Louisiana we have plenty of frogs, and some people eat their legs. We have turtles, too, and they turn up in soup at every restaurant. Only the snakes escape serious eating, and consequently it's like stirring spaghetti sometimes when you're out on the bayou in your rowboat. But so what? I'd rather stir reptiles than eat them.

My attachment to frogs goes way back. My first poem was a school assignment to write about an animal, including the sounds it makes. I spent one whole night by a swamp behind the road listening to frogs. My poem was made entirely of frog sounds and it was so realistic it was eerie. Everybody gave frogs a lot of thought after that. "The Princess and the Frog" would be a very different fairy tale if some high school teacher'd had the prince dissected.

Fairy tales are full of turtles, too, and so are fables and parables. They tell us turtles are wise, patient, and tough. How can we, who have yet to achieve such virtues, eat them and carve them up? And snakes, well, they have a bad rep and people feel justified. But I wouldn't be so sure. I've seen them lying in the sun. They just want to be warm.

Striking Back: The Reptile Defense Fund Newsletter, to which I subscribe, advises kids unwilling to dissect to call the dissection hotline at 1-800-922-FROG to learn about their legal rights if they refuse to slash Kermit. They also sell some really nifty T-shirts featuring intertwined reptiles and amphibians. Give those for Christmas, too.

Weather or Not

I bought a handful of squishy plastic worms from a bin at the Louisiana Sportsmen Show. I liked the colors and they felt just like real worms. I wasn't going fishing anytime soon and I wasn't in a *total* Baudelairian mood, but I was feeling pretty melancholy surrounded by boats, trucks with oversize wheels, hunting bows, fish-cleaning knives, plastic fish hatcheries, and pleasure crafts called *Aw Heck* and *Lucy in the Salt with Daddy*. Somewhere there were blue skies and green water, though exactly where I couldn't say, since it's been raining here since the beginning of time, and snowing elsewhere for as far as people's memories go. I was on the phone with friends of mine who couldn't even speak anymore, they just held the receiver to the window for me to hear the hellbound winds, and I, likewise, held the receiver into the fury of the storm that was shaking the house like a psycho with a rag doll.

This winter, those of us who didn't drown were buried under. It was all relative, of course. In the killing fields of Bosnia people were digging their own graves in the frozen ground. I watched a man train a dog to swim across a puddle in a plastic pool, catch a fake duck, and freeze like a statue upon a whistle. Behind man and dog, there was a suggestion of idyllic pastures and verge-of-sleep summer. I lay in the fields of rye, lulled to dreams by the red poppies. As I wandered past plastic sharks, duck decoys, fearsome examples of taxidermy, men selling deer-jerky marinade, and a swamp family demonstrating homemade turkey whistles, I felt most keenly the narrow confines of my paperbound life. Here were radically different ways to spend time. But who's got time? I used to have time, but something happened to it. I let a guy clean my glasses with a drop of something that, he said, would keep them from fogging. One drop on the mirror or on your rifle scope and you'll never be blurry or miss your target again. I liked that. I clutched my plastic worms and walked out into the rain. I couldn't see a thing.

Spring Is a Dance in the Head

Spring is a dance in the head and the body performs it until it becomes a tree. The tree flowers, becomes heady with perfume, and for a few short moments in most places, it enters the state of intoxication we here in Louisiana experience for a dizzyingly long time. It is possible to jet between regions and catch several springs. Six weeks ago in North Carolina I saw the subtle trembling that overcame the brown land and I touched the tender fuzz on the still bare branches. "It's here," said the natives, "listen!" You could hear the faint rising of the sap in the trees, a steady hum like a bright night sky. To the natives it was the explosive prelude to the main explosion due in the coming weeks. But it was hard for me, having come from the flowering of nearly everything out of deep green to see the too-subtle changes.

In Louisiana, sap doesn't rise quietly; it swells, it gushes, it bends houses, it agitates the light, it makes people walk funny. Three weeks ago, long after spring came to North Carolina, I saw spring come again— in western Michigan. The nights were still cold and a chilly wind came from the lake. A strong, fresh smell of earth waking from sleep was over everything. You could practically hear the new grass pushing through the dirt while flour-white humans pushed out of their parkas into the sun. By this time, spring had left Louisiana, giving way to the humid, hot heaviness of summer that slows people to reptile speed and makes moving a matter of urgency but little else. Instead of humming and whirring, the iridescent landscape sets itself to steadily hallucinating. Like the surfers who keep following the big waves around the world, I could follow spring. Keep going north to the Pole and then switching directions, following the rising of the sap and the expectation of release. I am an addict of hope, and spring is its season. Winter is heavy and summer too mindlessly light. Spring is the critical balance. I leave all solid states to others: I'll take the flux and the change. I want to be there when it breaks.

In the Lusty Month of May

May Day, Workers' Day in Romania, was the day nobody worked. We Pioneers were out of school. Our mothers ironed our little red kerchiefs straight and we went out marching in front of the daïs in the central square jammed full of fat men. We went past them screaming, *"Ura Partidul!"* which means, "Long live the Party!" only *ura* is a funny word in Romanian because if you put the stress on the last letter, it means "hated." So when we got older, we often went past screaming *"Urà Partidul,"* which meant "hated the Party!" as if the party was an actual party, American-style, and we'd had a dreadful time at it. In reality, they could have jailed us for it.

But in truth, everyone had a good time on May Day because it never rained, the sky was always blue, the girls were beautiful, and we all went to the woods after the demo to flirt, eat hot dogs, and row boats with sweethearts in them. When I didn't march in the parade I used to watch it go by, and I was always impressed by the strong girls from the Stella Soap Factory, and the Tractor-Machinist Sub-Engineers, who went by with enormous cakes of soap, engine wheels, and shiny cogs lifted high above their heads, rhythmically chanting production figures that proved that they were way ahead of the Five-Year Plan. "Seven thousand units done! Socialism has already won!" was one slogan that never failed to give me the giggles. We had variants like, "Seven hundred upright weenies! Golden communism's hot!" I know, it doesn't rhyme in English. We were a bad gang of young punks, and May Day was a big day for us because everyone was out on the streets and we could run wild.

Workers' Day still stirs my heart, especially these days when the parades have stopped in Eastern Europe. I liked the fact that nobody worked on Workers' Day, and my first grown-up slogan was "Workers of the world, disperse!" Now that they have, or are about to, we could have a permanent May Day, a lusty one like the medieval English or the

Hungarians who have a May Day feast called "the pinching of the maids," where the soldiers go to the market and pinch the maids. I saw a banner at a May Day Moscow demo recently that said, "Workers of the world, we apologize!" I agree. Every day should be May Day. We've worked enough.

The Promise of Summer

The promise of summer is putting a sweet knot of longing in these weary bones. In New Orleans summer usually shows up in early March, after Mardi Gras, but this year it held itself off until after Jazz Fest, a whole month later. After torrential rains that had all the Noahs in the neighborhood patching their arks, summer's finally here, pushing flowers through the wrought-iron balconies. The gardenias exploded and their sweet scent now makes everyone dizzy as they float around and around in their glazed Chinese bowls. The fig trees are putting out hundreds of leaves a day and the banana trees are shooting straight up into the blue sky full of shattered crystals. Suddenly, all thoughts of death and destruction that gave this winter its bitter flavor seem unreal.

Yes, there is still war in Bosnia. AIDS is raging like a blood-gorged serpent through the dreams of America. A child falls in a hole in front of his father and dies crying out that there are snakes down there. The ashes of children in Waco still drift on the breeze over the uneasy pastures of Texas. All these events, recent and unsettling, coiled about each other like dank demons in the wintry caves of our national psyche, are giving way before the sweet narcotic of summer. The newspapers still flap alarmingly around my chaise lounge, the TV still screams from the open windows of the houses next door, an occasional gunshot still rings from the unpaved streets down the alleys a bit, but the flowers are advancing on the noise and anxiety, determined to conquer all with the help of the sweet breeze that whistles the leaves and unbraids the beards of moss and old men. The music summer makes as it takes over is captured in the cases of instruments still left open after Jazz Fest. The musicians will put away their instruments in that sweet bed of frogs croaking, trees rustling, and flowers flowering, to soak in until we need to be healed again by new music. I deposit my summer longing, lassitude, and forgetting in somebody's saxophone case, too.

Summer

It's summer. Empires are breaking up everywhere, but in New Orleans the dogs lie still on the road until cars just about run 'em over. The alligators sprawl quietly on the bottom of the bayous with sleeping turtles on their backs. The magnolias are dozing, and the girl at the 7-Eleven moves in a dream and holds your quart of milk for what seems like a day.

It's a fine time for Rep. Arthur Morrell, a Louisiana House Democrat, to propose that New Orleans secede from Louisiana and the nation. That would make legal what is already a fact of life. Louisiana and the nation seem as far from New Orleans as Tierra del Fuego. The legislator's reasons are economic— "The city pays the state more than it gets back" —but there are better reasons. A place so deeply sunk in the summer of its Catholic African Creole past is already gone, slumbering along with its sister cities of myth, Macondo, Nineveh, and Salvador Bahia de Todos los Santos in Brazil. Seven golden-winged dragonflies rest on a purple cabbage growing out of a crack in the sidewalk. The shutters of Victorians on St. Charles Avenue are drawn: behind them ghosts are dozing with leather-bound books in their hands. For the past century, I've been sitting at the Napoleon House watching a bottle of Dixie Blackened Voodoo beer give off steam. They outlawed this brew in Texas last week, which is only right. What do they know about magic there? To tell you the truth, I'm waiting for the night. That's when some of the stillness evaporates and people come out on their steps and into the streets wearing mostly their skins and their eyes. In the rest of the world they go to sleep about that time.

And what would we do if we secede? Nothing—just like we are doing now. Everywhere in the world they seem to be doing this or that, but here we revel in nothing, and that makes us different. And when we get our Republic of Summer, our Kingdom of Stillness, what should we do to keep this way? I ask my son, Tristan. "Invite all the pirates back, throw out all the tourists," he says, and takes a long time to take a sip of iced tea through a long, crooked straw that's got an ant sleeping on it.

The New Tattoos

David Graham and I were watching the summer night mobs milling on both sides of the street by Cafe Brasil. A local band with a big following, Tribe Nunzio, was playing in there, and we were getting to listen outside without paying the cover charge. At some point, a brass band appeared out of nowhere on the corner and people started second-lining. My friend Adé, who owns Cafe Brasil, came furiously out the door to tell them to move. It was a fine New Orleans evening with all the funk and craziness we've come to enjoy and expect from our blossomy burg.

David, who lives in Pennsylvania, was pleasantly startled by everything. At one point, he noted the extraordinary number of tattoos that young people were sporting. And not people you'd expect. From the round shoulder of a demurely dressed young woman of sixteen there shone forth a brilliantly gnarled sun on whose rays were impaled a number of flowers. A kid on a skateboard had pre-Raphaelite vines curling about his wrists. On close inspection everyone under the age of twenty seemed tattooed with a variety of mostly floral motifs with a psychedelic twist to them.

David confided to me that he had always wanted to shave his chest and to have a lawn mower tattooed there. I confessed that I wouldn't be adverse to having a Campbell's soup can, cream of asparagus, on my upper arm. I became quite convinced that we were the wedge of the future. The kids were bound to get tired of the conventional fantasies of MTV-style psychedelia soon enough. And then they would start being Americans, having Big Macs tattooed on their backs, slices of cherry pie engraved on their bottoms, candy bars and Coke cans everywhere else. Reaganism and Bushism had encouraged their current escapist fantasies. When this country was going to turn, as it inevitably would, back to its working-class and its suburban-class roots, we would see Americans illustrating themselves accordingly. Irony will return to the land, along with the products that make us free. And crazy. David and I saw the future. Andy Warhol was back.

July

July is when poets die. I can't believe it's been eight years since Ted Berrigan, my teacher of things American and one of this century's most purposefully alive people, passed away. And it was in July too that my friend Jeffrey Miller, who wrote poems that still make the young tremble, drove into that tree in Monte Rio, California, and left us here to our clunky prose. And now I read in the newspaper that they are rioting in Paris at the grave of Jim Morrison, another poet soul parted in July.

They had much in common, these three, namely an intimate acquaintance with something beyond this life that caused them all to love their lives most fiercely and to conduct them with an intensity that makes us stand in awe. Ted Berrigan's favorite phrases were taken from the store of things we say without thinking. He gave them meaning, and he caused dozens of people to speak them as meaningfully as he did. "All pictures would look instantly better," he used to say, "if you add to them a balloon that says, 'Hi, folks!' " And when he said, "Nice to see you!" he lit up the air with something electric because it was true, he was truly pleased.

Nice to See You is the name of a collection, a *Festschrift* in his honor published by Coffee House Press, whose editor, Allan Kornblum, was one of Ted's devotees. Here, one hears, in a variety of styles, Ted's inimitable voice speaking through the community Ted created with it in New York's Lower East Side in the late sixties, seventies, and early eighties, until the day he died, in fact. Jeffrey Miller, who also loved Ted but never met him, wrote a poem dedicated to Ted. It was called "Then She Hit Me and It Felt like a Kiss":

> *It's 8:30 and I'm not Ted Berrigan.*
> *He's sweet but I'm Jeff, deliciously*
> *hungover . . .*

And he was, much of the time, a hangover as personal as his poems and as impersonal as July. And when Jim Morrison sang "Riders on the Storm," we all knew exactly what storm he had in mind, and the storm came, in July.

Dog Days of July

The dog days of summer are in August for most people, but here in New Orleans they are in July. I don't know what dogs do elsewhere, but here they just lie down and melt in furry puddles that bite when you step on them. Even police dogs are out of commission right now, so the police are training pigs to do dogs' jobs. A narcotics-sniffing Vietnamese pot-bellied pig named Tootsie and her porcine partner, Baby Doll, were introduced by the New Orleans police to the press. At approximately the same time, a police surveillance team *sans* pig swooped down on two lovers smooching over a parking meter. When the lovers unclasped they clinked something fierce, and all the coins in the meter spilled. Apparently, the kiss-and-steal couple had been ripping off meters for years by kissing over them.

A parking meter as an aid to passion is not a bad idea, but now it turns out that passion itself plays second fiddle to something called nitric acid. Researchers at Hopkins isolated this chemical that causes erections in both males and females. The injected rats became passionate, the others just lay there. The next step, I suppose, is to try this acid on something larger like, let's say, narcotics-sniffing pigs. This would make press conferences in the dog days a lot more entertaining.

Meanwhile, local farmers are pinning all their hopes on ostriches, large, broomlike creatures that weigh as much as a pig and can be turned into earrings, nose rings, and emu-burgers. They lay eggs like crazy and they taste like beef, which puts an end, I suppose, to the fact that all weird things until now tasted like chicken. Ostriches, whose necks look like major erections, have no idea that they are the next other white meat. But that's evolution. Pigs get jobs sniffing drugs. Rats get passionate. Cops get their meters out of lovers' arms. Americans pin their hopes on ostriches. Dogs just wanna lie there and die. Dog days of summer. And there are more of them ahead.

Workaholism

Once upon a time there was a man who liked to do nothing. He would get up whenever he pleased, put on whatever clothes he pleased, and then, after a brief stroll through the verdant groves outside his perch, he would come to his favorite café. He would sip his pensive coffee there, glancing now and then at the fresh newspaper neatly folded before him. Much of the morning passed in pleasant reverie out of which there rose now and then a sharply delicious half thought that would become full when he committed it to paper, something he rarely bothered to do. He was content to just sip at several cups of coffee until it was time for lunch at the house of one or the other of his many friends, who were also in the business of doing nothing. During lunch, he would test the thoughts he'd had during breakfast, and was gratified to get several new angles on them. In the afternoon, he would climb onto a grassy knoll and nap, having a number of notable dreams in the process, that would then add themselves to the thoughts born in the A.M. and grown in the P.M.

By evening he was brimming with energy and enthusiasm, and he would go to the bar, where the powerful thoughts he contained would spill forth in explosive abundance between more affluent but less imaginative people. No question about it, doing nothing was what suited him best, although he never had any money to pay either for his coffee or for his beer. But one day, someone bought one of his do-nothing ideas, and asked him for another. After a few weeks, he started to do nothing on purpose, that is, he did nothing deliberately in order to get one of his great (and profitable) do-nothing ideas. He now had enough money to stop doing nothing. His walk to the café became brisker, less noticing of the verdant brilliance. The coffee was indifferent, and he started actually *reading* the newspaper he had merely enjoyed for its smell before. Even his friends, instead of conversation companions, became sounding boards. And his dreams got grim and apocalyptic. At the bar, he got into fights. And that's the story of how this man became a workaholic. Instead of doing nothing he was always doing something. If you are like this man, my friend, if you like doing nothing, beware of those who'd pay you for it.

Death

Every few years I have a powerful dream about death. In this one, I died in a burst of gunfire from someone I liked a lot. I asked him why he killed me. "Because you're famous," he said. That seemed reasonable enough, and, after I died, I continued to ponder the question of reasonableness. Being dead was the same as being alive, only I didn't have a body and people didn't see me. Nevertheless, I continued to influence them through a channel called "the crystal passage." Things were so ordinary that I even read my obituaries in the newspapers and noted that they made excessive use of the phrase "full of life." I had been full of life. But now I was dead. And felt just the same.

My last dream on the subject had been ecstatic and colorful. Dying was a liberating experience, and although briefly interested in human affairs shortly after croaking, I took no more notice of them after a while and dissolved instead into a shimmering fabric of sheer joy. I even noted the fact that death was "negative copying" while birth was "positive copying," a sort of Xeroxing process that reproduced DNA in two opposite directions.

Ten years have passed between one dream and the other, and the difference seems to be that the world has gained greater weight in me. I mean, it would have never occurred to me to read my obituaries ten years ago. I was in too great a hurry to get to the fun stuff, the cosmic light show. Ten years ago I thought nothing of abruptly leaving the human dialogue unfinished, in midsentence, and going off to play with something else. Now, it seems, I'd like to keep talking as if there was somewhere to get to that way.

Nonetheless, it was a liberating dream. There is an Indian legend where Satan makes a body and tricks an angel into momentarily inhabiting it. The angel does, and then Satan won't let him out. But after living in this body for a few years, the angel discovers that a powerful god also lives in there with him. It is Death, and she can let him out anytime he wants to. It's a nice discovery. It comes in dreams.

Who Do You Belong To?

I like to think that I don't belong to anybody. I think I have a constitutional right to that effect, but times being what they are, it isn't easy. Everything and everybody gives off this plaintive wail: Belong! Belong! Be a member of our guild, our gun club, our 10-billion-strong credit-card family; be a member of our family, our generation, our nation, our world—and pay those dues, dammit! In truth, there are certain things you can't help being part of either because you were born into them or you got yourself in too deep. You can't help being an earthling, for instance, and if you're in the Mafia or the CIA it isn't so easy to get out.

Other things you can presumably help. I belong to only three organizations. In order of importance: the Reptile Defense Fund, which fights snake killers and frog dissecters; the Jewish-Romany Association, which takes stands against persecutions of Gypsies; and the Modern Language Association, or the MLA, which is the professional outfit of literature teachers. The Reptile Defense Fund holds its annual conventions in Texas at the snake roundups. Its proceedings consist of overturning snake baskets and tearing snakeskin boots and belts off gun-toting cowboys. It's a lot of fun, and we always have a party at the hospital afterwards. The Jewish-Romany Association, which is run by Toby Sonneman from her wilderness cabin in Cashmere, Washington, holds conventions in front of the embassies of countries, like Romania and Germany, who persecute Gypsies. The Modern Language Association is a little more formal in this regard, but its reasons for choosing the places where it meets are a lot more puzzling than those of the others. In 1988, the MLA, 88,000 strong, met in New Orleans. This year, it served notice to the city that it wouldn't meet here again as long as sodomy was illegal in the state of Louisiana. It seems perverse, if you ask me. If you want to save snakes, you go to where the snakes are. If you want to help Gypsies, you go to where they are hurting them. If you care about literature, you go to where they need some. I think the MLA has mistaken its mission for its procedures. Its mission is to promote literature, the way it functions is, well, illegal in this state.

The Check Is in the Mail

I've come to live with the post office. For years, I would rage at the post office. They used to keep my mail, especially my checks; they threw it in thistle fields, they handed it to dogs to chew. The mailmen all used to work for a variety of secret services, and I would catch them dozing behind a hedge with a spyglass glued to my fascinating communications. I lived in places hard to get to, roads that got muddy, streets only recently mapped or that had their names changed. Mailmen never bothered. And, of course, they never came enough times. Once a day, no mail on Sundays. That's not enough for a young writer who needs mail like plane-crash victims need water—lots of it, all the time—mail filled with love, acceptance, but mostly cash. For two years there in the wilds of northern California I was utterly dependent on the $250 per month the publisher of my autobiography doled out begrudgingly and not at all monthly. The mortgage on the shack was $200, the $50 was for food—you can imagine the grand-scale gourmandise we practiced. The sum would never show on time; I blamed the mailman. I wrote furious stories in my spare time—I had lots of it in those days—about the postmistress, the agent of mysterious powers who read all the town's mail and knew everyone's secrets, an evil woman who made me suffer.

It's centuries later now, and while I still await the mailman with feigned eagerness in memory of my youth, I kind of dread him, too. Too many nothing letters demanding rapt attention to the young, eager, talented, underappreciated, hungry, and mail-poor. I *was* surprised, though, when I got a call—not a letter—from the new Postal Museum in Washington, D.C., asking whether I'd contribute a few words in praise of the P.O., words to be blown up and put on a billboard for all to see. My pay for the job: $1,000, American cash, four times the monthly mortgage and food in 1974, but then this is the nineties. So I wracked my brains for goodwill and came out with the thought that the U.S. P.O.

is good because it still costs less than FedEx and fax. Good going, and who am I to sneer at one grand?

That was in September.

The check's still in the mail.

They set me up. The seventies, the eighties, the nineties—it's all the same. Money shrinks, time flows, the P.O. stays the same. In a changing world, it's good to see steadfastness, slow though it might be.

Culture Vultures
and Casserole Widows

A friend of mine was complaining recently that her seventy-five-year-old mother just got married again and was making love four times a day in the room next to hers and, frankly, she couldn't stand it. Well, why shouldn't she? I said. You don't know the half of it, replied my distraught friend . . . the things that go on with old folks! Have you ever heard of casserole widows? I hadn't. It appears that no sooner does a wife die in her neighborhood than single women swoop down on the bereaved husband with a consoling casserole, and before you know it they're in bed doing it four times in the room next to hers.

Now, I didn't want to impute any untoward paranoia to my friend who is, after all, a well-balanced young adult, but swooping down on people isn't limited to casserole widows. How about academics who wrest permission from dying relatives for exclusive biographies, minutes before they pass away? I know two such people, one successful and one unsuccessful, who flew thousands of miles to be at the bedside of the heir of a famous person with a contract ready to sign. You might say that there is a whole swooping class out there, just waiting for a hole to open in the fabric. At its worst, this class has some despicable members in it, like the thieves who read obituaries and then rob the house while the family's at the funeral. At its best, however, as in the case of the casserole widows, the swooping class performs the service of relieving loneliness. The academics fall, I suppose, right in between. There is a new theory now that says that the earth's oceans were formed by a constant bombardment of snowballs from outer space, and it's going on even as we speak. The earth's atmosphere is riddled through and through by these constantly falling snowballs swooping in on us from the great cosmos. It's true that we can't hear them in the room next door, but aren't they intruding nonetheless?

Why not take a lesson from the universe, I told my friend, and let humans behave at least as actively as planets. Let them make love while the snowballs come down. Tomorrow might be too quiet to object.

My Israeli Relatives

Great issues wash over us like clouds in the upper atmosphere. Until something brings them down and suddenly the roof caves in. The truth is that unless things hit us where it matters, in the heart or in the pocketbook, we have little real feeling for them. It was thus between my loved ones and me last week.

My Israeli relatives have lived in Israel as long as I've lived in America, about twenty years, and though we still communicate in the language of our childhood—Romanian—there are differences. My cousin and I are roughly about the same age. I used to spend summers with her at my grandmother's house. I remember long, lazy, hot afternoons when we were happy just to lie next to each other on some patch of grass, without speaking. What was there to talk about? The sky was blue and we were children. The political world of Romania where we lived was far from us. Much water has since flowed down the rivers of the world.

My cousin's two Israeli children speak Ivrit, her husband speaks Ivrit, Lithuanian, and English, and my aunt speaks Ivrit, Romanian, German, and Hungarian. My children speak English. But languages are the least of it. We get along in bits and pieces of them. Other things are more trenchant. Her children have seen a lot of real machine guns but she won't let them play with toy ones, while I have two American tots who've worn out arsenals of toy Uzis. Her husband flies fighter planes for the Israeli air force, and her brother, my other cousin, saw action in two wars. That's the same kid I used to carry piggyback across the living room rug. My aunt is a sweet old lady but she too has some firm political ideas. Everybody in Israel does, apparently, and they aren't shy about expressing them. They are Israeli, and I am an American. And we aren't children anymore.

We managed to avoid arguing about Israel the whole first three days of their visit, but on the fourth and last all hell broke loose. The argument started when my cousin said that everything you hear or see about Israel in the American media is lies. "Some of it may be slanted," I said, but she didn't let me finish. "They want us dead!" my cousin shouted, "or they would tell the truth about the Arabs, which is that every one of them gets paid to throw rocks, a dollar for every rock!"

I laughed, which was a mistake, because it was downhill from there. You're either for Israel or you're against it, and laughing doesn't figure in it. Nor did it help when I said that at that price I wouldn't mind throwing rocks myself, you can make a hundred bucks an hour. I've always been a devil's advocate.

My aunt was hardly more reasonable: "God will do something about it!" she said. "God may do something," I replied, "but maybe he shouldn't because he's already done too much. I think we should make the whole Middle East a 'desanctified zone' patrolled by anticlerical UN forces, as suggested by Reverend Ray in an obscure pamphlet I just read. Without God, people might get more specific."

"You know the first thing I saw when I came off the plane in Israel?" said my cousin, "An eighteen-year old mother with an Uzi on one shoulder, nursing a baby on the other! You don't show *that* on your TV, do you?"

She was saying, I believe, that war is a fact of life in Israel, while in America we live in some kind of dream. I was at a distinct disadvantage: how could I explain to her that television is a land all its own, and that, like everything else here in America, there are two of everything, Israel included—one in the Middle East and one on NBC? In the one in the Middle East they have trouble. In the one on TV they have pictures. We sometimes confuse the two, but mostly we can tell the difference. Or so I hope.

While we argued thus, the children played video war games in the other room, whence issued eerie pings. They'd been getting along peacefully during the above, but when we fell silent, they began to fight. It seems that somewhere in the video war points of order had been raised. My kids were outshouting in English the Ivrit-speaking tots. Forgetting our grown-up differences for a moment, all of us, big people, Israelis and Americans, rushed in to break it up. We gave the kids hell.

That was one way to take care of the problem. And maybe things weren't all that peaceful when my cousin and I were kids. Maybe we'd been fighting in the grass. When we weren't being quiet.

The Golden Bird

I've seen Brâncuşi's *Golden Bird* or *Magic Bird* in countless pictures, and I once had a dream about it. I dreamed that I was hiding the Golden Bird in a secret room. Two policemen came and dug up the whole garden in search of it. They found nothing, and I was amused to think that policemen should be so stupid as to look for a bird in the ground. The whole time they were digging the bird was there in the room, but they couldn't see it because it had become "the invisible bird." Looking at this bird, poised radiantly at the beginning of the twentieth century, Mina Loy, the great poet, wrote in 1922:

> *The toy*
> *become the esthetic archetype . . . This gong*
> *of polished hyperaesthesia shrills with brass*
> *as the aggressive light*
> *strikes*
> *its significance.*

This poem appeared in the *Dial* in the same issue as T. S. Eliot's "Wasteland."

Brâncuşi, the Romanian-born peasant who carted his sculptures to Paris in a wheelbarrow, created in the bird an enduring antidote of light to the coming darkness of police states and war. Another Romanian, the poet Lucian Blaga, said of the bird:

> *Are you a bird*
> *a travelling bell*
> *Or a creature, an earless jug perhaps?*
> *A golden song spinning*
> *above our fear of dead riddles?*

For seven decades Brâncuşi's hopelessly utopian bird in flight soared through the dimming lights of our century, looking terribly naive during the two world wars, only to charm us again when our souls were at rest. As I followed the recent events in Eastern Europe, I kept seeing the Magic Bird, now rising, now eclipsed, now rising again. This bird is more than a sculpture, it is, like Mina Loy said, something "archetypal," something we always had inside of us that simply took its place in our consciousness when Brâncuşi made it.

A few days ago I saw the real thing. In a back room at the Chicago Art Institute, the great bird was being readied for exhibition. Having grown to mythic proportions in my mind, I hadn't realized its quite modest dimensions. But that was, in fact, its secret. Rising there at an angle from its two pedestals, a wooden and a stone one, it elongated my hands and my face in its reflections, pulling me up with it. We soared together. Gravity be damned, it's okay to fly.

Confessions
of a Video Vigilante

Part II

Video News

I'm a channel surfer and a video vigilante. It's the only thing to be. With world-event shows popping up all over the place and the programming wars out there, the only way to keep up is with your finger on the remote. Like when, let's say, this tele-revolution was beamed out of Romania at the same time that we gave a tele-war in Panama. The only way to keep up was to be on your electronic surfboard every half hour catching the waves between Bucharest and Panama City.

Now, you can certainly OD on tele-news, so you've got to figure in the start of sitcoms when they tell the whole story in the first two minutes, and then you can surf past commercials to a few preachers and pick up their best phrases and maybe catch a real bargain on the shopping channel and one or two wisps of culture and/or nature off PBS and Discovery.

You can spend your life channel-surfing, of course, but it's not good for your figure, so you should alternate surfing with video vigilantism. Take out your video camera, you never know what you might find. Cops beating up somebody. A couple doing it in their bathroom. A baby-sitter slapping a baby. It's a bit of a lottery, but if you keep in mind that an illegal act occurs in the United States every half second you stand a pretty good chance of catching *something* on video. A kid smoking dope. A Pee-Wee type in an adult theater. Fellatio in a forest. Cunnilingus in a dorm. There is little out of bounds for the vigilant video vigilante. I don't mind telling you that I think the channel-surfing video vigilante is a new kind of human being, a better, gentler American who's going to bring this country law and order and better consumer values. If you can surf fast and well, the manufacturers of programs and products will have to make faster, zippier, and newer p&ps all the time. And if you can video-catch even one criminal a day, you'll make this country a lot safer for channel-surfing. So it's a deal with yourself: watch 'n' surf, watch 'n' catch, surf 'n' catch. Nice to be living right now, isn't it?

Sex Mania Replacing Real Sex

I talked to a woman in Santa Fe who was kidnapped by aliens who performed a long medical procedure on her. She now wakes quite often in the middle of the night and sees "many beings standing in her bedroom." She was most earnest about her experience, looking at me with sincere though flat eyes that exuded objectivity and resignation. She reminded me most forcefully of Anita Hill testifying solemnly about her defilement by sexual innuendo.

Judging by the current hysteria about sex raging through the country today, I think that all of us have been kidnapped by aliens who have taken the sex out of us and are now standing in all our bedrooms babbling about it through the mouths of TV, radio, and other unidentified sources. Real sex is but a memory these days, when discoursing about and mostly against sex has become the national addiction. The net result is a society that wants to castrate its leaders, substitute genetic engineering for natural attraction, take sex out of the body, and put it on television or in the telephone.

Who are these aliens and what do they want? Well, some of them are religious people like the Reverends Swaggart and Bakker, who think sex is filthy and the work of the Devil, who leads them to twenty-dollar hookers and seedy motels. Some of them are gossip-hungry trash mongers who see the fast buck to be made from the low mental level of Americans reduced to idiocy by television. Some of them are feminists who think that sexual pleasure should be approved by a correctness board armed with razor blades. But most of them are just plain, frustrated, right-wing ideologues who would like the poor to stop having sex and babies. And the rest are techno-whizzes who cash in on the paranoia produced by the others to sell us fake sex on the phone and the TV at a rate directly proportional to the decrease in real sex. As the nation's libido shrinks, so does our sanity at a time when it's most needed, with the world going crazy all around us. "What do these aliens want?" I asked the woman in Santa Fe. "To use our genetic material to strengthen their weakened strain." That makes sense. The weak and the sexless prey on the timid and the hopeful.

Having a Life

Lately, this business of "having a life" has been getting in the way of just living it. Everywhere you look, the famous are telling their life stories, in print or on TV. Very few of these Lee Iacocca/Donald Trump types have written anything longer than a memo to their slaves. Yet here they are, telling the world what they've been through. At the American Booksellers' Association meeting last year, every book being pushed was an autobiography by someone who wasn't a writer. Writers, in other words, if they wanted to live in the same world as the Iacoccas, had to hide their lives in novels.

Autobiography has become a form for the rich and famous, as if the rest of us have no lives at all. I have a theory about this. I think that time is flowing backwards now. When Andy Warhol said that in the future everyone will be famous for fifteen minutes, it sounded funny because time was still flowing forward. Then fifteen minutes became five minutes, then nanoseconds, and now we can safely say that everyone *was* famous for fifteen minutes, at one time or another. Time flows back from the future now, already full of the velocity of a superfluous past, which is being divided by several Iacoccas. We can only long nostalgically now for being part of a picture we've already been put out of by these Iacoccas. The future of autobiography is bright like a TV set for the very wealthy, but dim for the rest of us. The wealthy dead can even have video displays installed in their tombstones now. Push this button, ye stranger going by, and see a life-size Iacocca appear on screen telling all about his life. A coin-operated contraption, this video display can spew anywhere from fifteen minutes to five hours of life, depending on whether you want the distilled essence or every single detail on what it took to bury such a great man.

The rest of us, however, will spend our lives in the video glare of wealthy men's gravestones. Or, if you don't want to drive that far, you can just turn on your TV set and meet your real family, the Channings from "Falcon Crest." They're so much more alive than the shapeless couch potatoes next to you.

Master of the Universe

Every day the gap between our newsweeklies and the tabloids narrows. I defy anyone to tell the real difference between *Newsweek*'s "Master of the Universe" story on British physicist Stephen Hawking and the *Enquirer*'s "Daredevil Risks Life Sitting in Exploding Car." Actually, "Master of the Universe" is more like "Child Tells of Trip to Heaven" from the *Weekly World News*. "Stephen Hawking," *Newsweek* tells us, "the heir to Newton and Einstein, is racing against the ravages of disease as he takes the measure of the cosmos from a wheelchair." Hawking, furthermore, "is trying to read the mind of God." Wow! Granted, Hawking is a brilliant scientist and a courageous man. Reading the mind of God from a wheelchair through the use of mathematics is a daunting task. Kind of leaves the rest of us gasping for breath.

I had a friend who without particularly intending to read the mind of God, did so one day, and now he is spending quiet hours at Bellevue in New York City. Reading the mind of God is possible even without creating a unified theory that explains equally quantum physics and relativity, as Hawking is trying to do. The poet Jack Anderson, for example, believes that

> Everyone has a turn at being God: that is God's plan and helps explain why God's ways are mysterious . . .
>
> Your mother was God once, so were your father and your dentist and your grocer.

That's a sensible, ununified, though democratic way to look at it, and it explains why God's mind is so hard to read. The day God was a grocer the universe looked peculiarly like a shelf of dry goods.

Without slighting Hawking, who is obviously a serious man, one has to wonder where *Newsweek* comes by such a golly-gee attitude about science. It's as if thousands of years of private and public religious, direct, unmediated experience of the universe means nothing without a mathematical theory. It's not the mind of God that awes *Newsweek*, but the abracadabra of science. All the shabby thinking science has done for us, plus the deadly technology it has spawned, mean nothing to *Newsweek*'s simpleminded optimism and mystical awe of its powers. Who needs the Inquisition to test the peasants' faith when we have *Newsweek* enshrining the cult of scientific progress? In the end, I'd rather read *The National Enquirer*: the same wide-eyed stupidity reigns there but there are fewer fact-checkers interfering with the fairy tale.

Pentagon Relic Worlds

A few years ago I was putting all my hope for world peace in the Pentagon and in Hollywood; in the first for its well-known ability to create large death machines that didn't work, and in the second for smashing so many of them in the movies. The trick, of course, was to smash enough of them before we got too broke to go to the movies. Since then, they've had the Gulf War, which proved that some of the machines actually work and that the Pentagon doesn't really get rid of the ones that don't, but keeps making and *storing* them. Storing useless machines testifies to the linearity of the military mind. In that mind, tomorrow will be just like today, only more of it.

It turns out the Pentagon has been preparing for a better tomorrow since its inception. They have billions of dollars' worth of things, like: 150,000 tons of tannin used for cavalry saddles, enough, an official said, "to refight the Civil War"; 1.5 million pounds of quartz crystals, used for antique radios; 3.3 million ounces of quinine, which is no longer used to fight malaria; 22 million pounds of mica, good once for camp stoves and radio vacuum tubes. There are also 16.3 million carats in sapphires and rubies and 47 million carats in natural industrial diamonds. Those, I imagine, are to be used as accessories to parade uniforms. The bigger and better wars the Pentagon foresaw didn't take place. Smaller, deadlier, and costlier things came into vogue, things such as leaky nukes, which, in their turn, will be carefully stored in quantities that boggle the mind. I mean, the mind that needs to keep saddle grease from World War I won't give up one megamicrogram of anything else.

Which leaves only Hollywood on the side of peace. We must prompt Hollywood to dream up epics that will use up all the Pentagon surplus. Everybody, to the movies!

Rethinking Techne

I have often sided with the detractors of technology, aware all the while of a certain hollowness in the argument, namely that technology was here to stay no matter how I felt about it.

Now I believe that there is an alternative. I recently saw the work of Mark Pauline and John Reiss of the SRL (Science Research Laboratories) in San Francisco, work that seems to me to define very clearly both the possibilities and situation of art today and a potential answer to the technological question. SRL researches, designs, and creates fantastic machines, and then puts on big spectacles involving these machines. The machines themselves are useless in the conventional sense of that term, since they exist solely to dance, hiss, crash, self-destruct, catch fire, and act out their whimsical designs. The SRL spectacles often have a polemical edge that provokes the audience to think and to participate. In Amsterdam, one of the machines was an insane windmill that attacked itself, while in Copenhagen a giant cow filled with sour milk was busted open by a mechanical worm straight out of *Dune*.

We have arrived at a certain stage of technological sophistication where we are much too good at what we do in relation to the ends to which we put our machines. How many perfect F-15s and other fancy killing machinery can we produce? The uses to which we put our machines are medieval, ideas that make sense no longer. Combat, the way it was once understood, is no longer noble. Yoking everyone to the insane production-consumption cycle of an endlessly greedy and increasingly faster capitalism makes no sense either. The machines originally meant to give us more "leisure time" have in fact done the exact opposite. We are on a treadmill.

And yet, there is no doubt that, as a species, and as a nation, we very much enjoy inventing and creating machines. Americans have a mechanical genius that is wonderful. What better use, then, for this spirit than the creation and invention of machines for play? If all hints of usefulness and martial assembly-line production were removed from these machines we could have our cake and eat it too. We could make sophisticated machines for play and storytelling.

The SRL solution to the technological problem is to reprogram our machines to play instead of working us to death or killing us. It's a good way out.

In Praise of Heloise

The morning paper is such a sea of tormented tidings, you look in vain for comfort. The agitated globe rages on the front page but even beyond it there is little ease. This morning there are rapists in Ann Landers' column, warnings about making-money-at-home schemes, bad news for the TV networks (though actually this may be good news for the rest of us), dire astrological possibilities (one must, for instance, "avoid" one's "usual haunts" for fear one's "social life" may collapse), and even the usually mindless Cathy is unusually deep in her despair over her hair—sorry for the rhyme but it fits the theme. There is no calm anywhere until one stumbles upon it. An island. Surprisingly still there after all these years. Comforting. Sturdy. Like milk. Like mother. Like "Dear Heloise."

Like an ancient and gentle dinosaur that has somehow survived ages of ice, fire, and crisis fabrication, Heloise floats serenely there, a placid lily on the black pond of time, another time, a time when people still fixed things instead of throwing them away, when simple solutions brought inordinate joys. Should one rent a flute instead of buying one? To this question there are a myriad of answers but it is sensible, we discover, to rent one with an option to buy. "Check out the difference," Heloise reasons, "of buying outright compared to the total amount it would cost to buy a rented flute." And furthermore, "if possible, take someone along who knows how to play the instrument." Notice the gentle wisdom of "if possible." There is no imperative, no aggression in Heloise's world. There is tolerance, instead, an acceptance of the possible. Nor is Heloise really out of touch. We find, for instance, the solution to the vexing problem of gardening while carrying one's cordless phone: "I made an apron for it with a large pocket on the side that's just the right size to hold the phone.

Not only does it keep it safe, it stays clean since it's away from the dirt and dust." So right.

I don't meditate or float in wombs of salt water. No time. I read Heloise instead. I rest briefly on the island of Heloise. It's peaceful here.

Barbie's Lawyer

After hearing me talk for an hour, Alan Berg said, "Enough already, namedrops keep falling on my head. . . . Maybe you know famous poets but I had dinner with Barbie's lawyer!" I wasn't aware that Barbie was in court, but that's just where she is. She went to court over a new doll called Miss America, which is fashioned after Miss America. Arthur J. Levine, Barbie's lawyer, claims Miss America ripped off Barbie's head. Mattel, Barbie's manufacturer, says they copyrighted Barbie's—quote—look of compliant joy—unquote. Miss America's head has that on it, too. The bodies are not on trial, just the heads, even though the bodies are even more alike than the heads. Miss America claims their dolls were modeled after the real Miss America, not Barbie. Of course, the real Miss America modeled herself after Barbie, which is what millions of women model themselves after, so perhaps Barbie should sue her human clones. Barbie's lawyer, whom my friend had dinner with, argues that Barbie "is a stylized doll which does not look like any known human being." Miss America's lawyer, whom nobody I know ever had dinner with, says that "the concept of fashion dolls is to look like human fashion models."

Now, who's right? How many of the 600 million girls who've been buying Barbies since 1958 have become "stylized dolls who do not look like any human beings" by now? Hard to say. It's a chicken-and-egg question. All we know is that in the beginning there was Barbie. After that came Miss America, both the human and the doll. Furthermore, Barbie is made in the USA. Miss America's made in China. There is global politics here. The Chinese have also been exporting the live organs of executed political prisoners. That's bad enough, although Mr. Bush still thinks it's okay to trade with China. But now they are making our Miss Americas. That just can't be. There is no room in the New World Order for that.

End of the Nuclear Family

I get my hair cut at Whodunit, a mystery bookstore–barbershop. Charles, the barber, cuts my hair while his son sells mysteries to people waiting in line. Across the street from Whodunit is Reginelli's, an eating gallery that serves food and displays art. You're handed two menus when you sit down: one for art, one for food. *Pasta con funghi*, $9.50; *Sunset at the Dump*: $4,750. Most people take the pasta. A few streets over is the DMZ Laundromat-bar, where single people with small loads of laundry drink while blue jeans spin. On the same corner is Suntan Clean, a dry cleaner and suntan parlor where both you and your clothes get the same treatment.

The couples I see in these places are as oddly matched as shampoo and Chandler. As the nuclear threat recedes, so does the nuclear family. I talked to a nostalgic conservative at Whodunit who told me he felt proud of all things nuclear but that his own household had never been nuclear, consisting as it did of his libertarian boyfriend, five members of both their bankrupt farm families, and several foreign students from good Latin American families. I suppose the corresponding liberal family, on the other hand, would consist of adopted children with a sprinkling of homeless and a hard-to-disentangle gaggle of ex-spouses. Apolitical, misanthropic types will just add multiple personalities when they feel the need for company. "You'll need a computer to know for sure who everybody at dinner is." Charles grinned while snipping a healthy segment of my flowing mane. Well, why not? Complexity without hostility is my motto, and the more complex people get, the more interesting will be the services that will cater to them. I mean, where does someone with twenty-eight personalities go to get their hair cut? Whodunit is a start: at least one of them can read mysteries. The other twenty-six have to wait for the future. State communism's dead, long live the new communalism!

Shoes, Now and Then

After the movie premiere of *sex, lies, and videotape* there was a party at a chi-chi disco called City Lights, so I ambled up over there to see if anyone was going to recognize me. There was a long line outside, young folks wearing the upturned faces of the ever hopeful. I shoved my VIP person right through the mob and came face-to-face with the square-shouldered Cerberus toward whom the young faces were upturned. "With the movie in one way or another!" I grumbled. "I have bad news for you," intoned the disco St. Peter, "you can't come in with shoes like that!" As I stood there, feeling a wave of forgotten humiliation and tonic rage course through me like a river of yore, I looked at my shoes and demanded in all innocence, "Whatever might you mean?" He snorted briefly in the well-rehearsed manner of a seasoned trough-master and said the single word: "High-tops!"

Years ago, when I was but a mere trout and not the premiere-going celebrity that I am now, I had had many dramatic encounters caused by my shoes. Thrown out of a coffeehouse in Laguna Beach for wearing no shoes, I fashioned some from napkins and Scotch tape, and then argued for an hour with the owner of the joint as to what exactly constitutes a shoe. Is it mere footwear for the protection of customers from the shocking sight of toes, or is it a social must stamped by shoe manufacturers? My own mother, one day long ago, had burst into tears upon beholding a pair of fringed moccasins on my feet. There was nothing I could do to assuage her despair short of divesting myself of my mocs, and this I was not willing to do. We didn't speak for three years. These and other incidents convinced me that shoes were a crucial part of the American way of life, so much so that I named my second autobiography *In America's Shoes*. And now, here I was, the author of *In America's Shoes*, published by the world-famous company City Lights, being refused admittance to a nightclub called City Lights because of my shoes. Of such splendid ironies is life made. Muttering savagely in Romanian, my head held high over the derisory razzing of the crowd, I backed my way from the front door of America in the late eighties and swore to avenge myself. "I will come back wearing big boots" is what I said.

Why Whales Beach Themselves

Why do whales beach themselves? The mystery has eluded scientists, who do not believe in despair they cannot measure. It's been said that pollution might be responsible. A Japanese scientist claimed that nuclear submarines may be at fault because they refuse to respond to the good-natured entreaties of the large beasts, who then kill themselves because they feel unloved. That's too much sensitivity per pound, if you ask me, and let's not forget that the Japanese have killed more whales than have ever committed suicide. Guilt translates into scientific theory better than any other sentiment.

Anyway, it appears that at long last the mystery's been solved, not by a scientist but by a poet, Mr. Jim Nisbet of San Francisco, California. Mr. Nisbet has found that the places where whales beach themselves all have heavy concentrations of AM radio. It appears that whales are able to tune in AM, and become extremely depressed, particularly during commercials. "Some of the promotions," says Mr. Nisbet:

> *with*
> *just the right copy, jingle and hook*
> *they find intolerable.*
> *If the irritation continues long enough*
> *it will as in an oyster form a pearl*
> *in the whale's head.*
> *This pearl is death.*
> *The only way to turn it off.*

Next to jingles, what irritates the whales most is the Rush Limbaugh show.

Mr. Nisbet has proposed a large-scale project involving the silencing of AM airwaves for brief periods. Thousands of whales would be saved this way. The government could conceivably reimburse the advertisers for lost revenues with some sort of "whale credits." If this isn't done quickly, the beaches will be choked this summer with whales murdered by Limbaugh & Company. What's worse, there are indications that humans are also beginning to acquire the ability to tune in AM without the need for a radio. It's pouring in through ozone-burned skin and tooth fillings. Don't be surprised if large masses of humans drown themselves in the ocean this summer while passing the whales heading the opposite way.

The Well: How I Fell In

Well, well, well . . . that's only part lament. The Well is the name of a computer network of the Whole Earth Catalogue people, and a few days ago I fell in. Or was pushed, depending which way you look at it. If I fell in of my own will it's because I'm one of those curious types who feel personally slighted by things they don't know. If I was pushed, I'm nothing less than an Aztec princess. I've been sacrificed for the tribe so I'm now waiting for the dragon of info to come and eat me.

I know you don't know what I'm talking about. Let me try again. You get into the Well with your computer modem. Once you're in there, you find thousands of people writing to each other on subjects ranging from African bees to Mongolian word processors. You can go visit any number of "conferences," as these powwows are called. Some of them have been going for five years so it's like dropping into the living room of a strange family. They have nicknames for each other, and speak in foreshortened mutual grunts. Other "conferences" are more like anarchist conventions for simultaneous monologuists.

Who are all these people? It's an info conspiracy, for sure, but it could be more than that, a kind of superhuman nervous system, let's say. My first shock after I logged in was to find that I was no longer alone with my computer screen. It's hard to find privacy these days, and what goes on between me and my screen is one of the few privileged islands of it. But as soon as I plunged down the well, I found that there was mail for me, and while I was reading this mail someone said to me, *Let me know if you need help*. This someone, Mr. Len Coleman, to be precise, was there live somewhere, in California, offering me a typing hand. I stand poised now, between another plunge into the electric earth and my favorite thing, which is—doing nothing. It's either the bar or the Well. I know for a fact that you can get a well drink at the bar. I'm not sure it works the other way.

World Between Quotes

It seems to me that the older I get the more I see public events as occurring between quotation marks. Especially televised ones. I always knew that official pageantry was fake but I had no idea—until Romania in 1989 and the Gulf War—that revolutions and wars can be, too. I remember watching May Day parades in Romania when I was a child and thinking that everything I saw, the marching bands, the embalmed officials on the rostrum, the shouted slogans, were fake. The real thing, the one outside quotes, was our picnic on the lake that followed the official display.

After seeing the riots in Moscow on May Day I realized what the quotation marks were for: to contain the disorder that was always present outside. Everything that is carefully arranged within a framework, ideological, aesthetic, or typographical, is bound to explode and bleed into the unruly real world. As we approach the end of the millennium, more and more of our ceremonies, rituals, and beliefs will leave the safety of their quotation marks and wreak unpredictable havoc.

Millennial bumper stickers on cars proclaim that IN CASE OF RAPTURE, THIS VEHICLE WILL BE UNMANNED. The "rapture" is, for certain religious fundamentalists, the moment when they will be sucked up into heaven by Jesus in advance of his second coming. The rapture is also that obscure feeling that a great many ways by which we keep ourselves bound will burst and we'll be outside without warning. My generation lived for forty years under the atomic umbrella, but that's shredded now, and the unpredictable skies are visible once more. The change from a relatively produced world to one that will look like a syntactically uncanny sentence by Dada master Tristan Tzara will be cataclysmic and sudden. Unless it will be framed by fireworks and greeted by bands. Many people must already be occupied in producing the pageantry of the millennium. New, fancy quotation marks may be ready in the bowels of circuitry to frame our millennial anxieties. It's possible. The only thing still unpredictable is the weather. Big winds can't be quoted.

Demise of the Progno Biz

The future is an abstract dog who comes when you whistle. That is, if you are a candidate for office, high or low. For the rest of us, the future is a real dog, that bites you when you least expect it. The future, candidates tell us, is when things will be better if you elect them. If you do not, the future is when things will be worse. Facts are dragged into their crystal balls like frogs into a high school lab, and there dissected and made to behave accordingly. But facts, unlike frogs, are a fickle breed: some are old facts, like death and taxes, while others are new facts, like inflation and toxic waste. Facts, like President Reagan said at the Republican National Convention in 1988, are "stupid things," when they are not "stubborn," that is. Incidentally, the phrase "facts are stubborn," comes from one of Mark Twain's *Letters from the Earth*, where Twain castigates the stupidity of religion, a sentiment I'm not sure the ex-president subscribes to.

Be that as it may, the future, while subject to both old and new facts, has another, wholly consistent feature: it is unpredictable. You can pile up your facts in any shape you please and you won't explain World War I, or why the Dodgers beat the A's in the World Series. Astrology, and its facts, does just as well as economics and sociology when it comes to the future, which is why Nancy Reagan continued to believe while the world laughed. Last Sunday I bought the *Houston Post* and read my horoscope in there. "Try to keep yourself on course," it said, "not pulled off on a fruitless tangent." I could buy that. I tried writing this very piece but it meandered fruitlessly like a drunk in Salt Lake City after midnight. Next day, I looked in my copy of the *Times-Picayune*, and there it was, my horoscope: "Try to keep yourself on course," it said, "not pulled off on a fruitless tangent." I could hardly believe my eyes. Still? I put the two papers side-by-side: sure enough, Sunday's *Houston Post* horoscope was the same as the *Picayune*'s Monday horoscope. New Orleans and Houston are only one hour away from each other, but they clearly have different futures. Now if I'd been your run-of-the-mill reasonable person I would have laughed and considered this further proof of the silliness of astrology. But I looked instead at the matter at hand, this piece, which, try as I might to keep on track, still wandered off like a Muscovite in search of shoes. And it was still true. The fruitless tangents are everywhere. But then, so is the future. The less you talk about it, the better your chances for being right. As for the candidates: the future has surprises for them. It will disregard their facts like the wind outside disregards the plants on the porch. They didn't know about this wind last night on the news.

Café Types in the Prophecy Biz

The following prophecies were spoken aloud by my wife in a deep, dark corner of the Napoleon House, last table on the right: "A powerful dictator dominates the Middle East; a meteor strikes the earth; Muslim unification in North Africa; the fall of Israel to the Arabs; an earthquake shakes Greece and Turkey; a military alliance between the United States and Russia; China launches a surprise nuclear attack; the destruction of Monaco; liberation of Israel; Western attack on Iraq; death of the Arab commander-in-chief; World War III ends in Iran."

"She's really good," said a guy from another table. She is, only this time these weren't her own prophecies. She was reading aloud to our eleven-year-old son from a book entitled *The True Centuries*, written in verse by Michel de Nostre-Dame (Nostradamus) in the year 1555, just bought from a street vendor for one dollar. It all seemed pretty reasonable to the patrons of the Napoleon House, which is set up for prophecy, poetry, babble, and even delirium tremens.

This is how Nostri himself puts it, re the powerful dictator of the Middle East:

One who is Ugly, wicked and infamous will come to power
And tyrannise all Mesopotamia.
The Prince of the Arabs, when Mars, the Sun and Venus are in Leo
Will make the rule of the Church suffer at sea
Towards Iran nearly a million men will march.
The true serpent will also invade Turkey and Egypt.

Pretty straightforward, eh? My son took out his star map and his calculator to try to figure out when Mars, the Sun, and Venus go into Leo. I ordered another shot of the thing that makes the Napoleon House famous. A guy from the next table said, "What's with Monaco? What did Monaco ever do?" "Maybe he meant Texaco," offered another patron. "Maybe he got Mobil and Texaco mixed up and came out with Monaco." That made sense to me. Five hundred years into the future is a long way to see, even with star map and calculator. Hell, even a second's too much— five minutes ago I couldn't have predicted us sittin' here prophesyzing the end of the world. We'd just gone out to buy the paper.

Fax Your Prayers

You can fax your prayers to the Wailing Wall now, which proves what I've been suspecting for years, namely that there are no more people. All there is now is God and technology, which may be one and the same thing. I mean, if you take away the journey, which has to be undertaken by a real physical being in a body, and that body's physical experience of place, all you have left is the ideas. There is the idea of "prayer," and the idea that you can send it off to God. All you need is a fax and a god, two things that most people seem to have these days. The merging of high tech and higher purpose has been going on for a while now.

People, or whatever you call those plugged-in entities on the couch, have, for a while now, been sending their money long distance to televangelists to pass messages on to God. Drive-in churches are the coming thing, and telephone confessions are a growing business. Of course, the gods have always been remote entities, reachable only in certain places like churches or sacred groves. Those places served, in effect, as primitive fax machines or telephones. You traveled to Mecca, Rome, the Wailing Wall, the Sacred Cave, or Mount Athos, and poured forth your wishes, dreams, and hopes, certain that God had some kind of terminal connected to these places where he'd receive them. Back in those days, you had to be there in person, in a body. The physical fact of body meeting place gave the operation a certain quality one might call *human*. It was experience, not the idea of experience.

Now we've dispensed with the body, leaving only the message and its terminals. Arguably, the prayer's still an individual thing, and turning on the fax is an almost physical thing. But just as arguably, prayer is pretty generic *(Dear God, fill in need, wish, and address)* and the fax can be turned on by the cat. Fax me outta here!

Vanna vs. Samsung Electronics

My favorite Dada artist, Vanna White, sued Samsung Electronics for airing a commercial depicting a Vanna-like robot next to a "Wheel of Fortune"–like wheel with the caption LONGEST-RUNNING GAME SHOW, 2012 A.D. Vanna did not, apparently, relish being replaced by a robot in the year 2012, so she accused Samsung of "appropriating" her "identity." The court ruled in her favor, with a strong dissent articulated by Judge Alex Kozinski, the only sane voice in Los Angeles. Judge Kozinski wrote that

> future Vanna Whites might not get the chance to create their personae, because their employers may fear some celebrity will claim the persona is too similar to her own. The public will be robbed of parodies of celebrities and our culture will be deprived of the valuable safety valve that parody and mockery create. . . . The last thing we need, the last thing the First Amendment will tolerate, is a law that lets public figures keep people from mocking them, or from "evoking" their images in the mind of the public.

Right on. In defense of "future Vanna Whites," the judge does not even mention the hundreds of foreign Vanna Whites already turning over letters in languages like Chinese and Russian. Should they stop turning? And what of the rest of us who like to dress like Vanna and have "Wheel" parties before our TV sets? Or the rest of the rest of us who have a Vanna within our souls, going through life guessing the letters that lead, conceivably, to some sense-making phrase?

Furthermore, Vanna herself is not really Vanna, but the projection of an archetype, an optimistic anti-postmodern god who promises us meaning in the form of things, phrases, and foreign expressions. Should this archetype sue his emanation, Vanna? And is Vanna, this projection, Vanna all the time, or does she have non-Vanna moments when she refuses to make sense? How much Vanna there is in Vanna White has to be weighed against how much Vanna there is in everybody. An archetype cannot be copyrighted. Lose a turn, Vanna.

New Moon Ready for Launch

Imagine this. You are lying on your favorite mossy bank by the river, watching the first stars in the evening sky. Your heart is full of that sweet longing for those faraway worlds that were once your ancient home. The moon rises full over the river, filling you to the bones with her familiar radiance. And just as you abandon yourself to the sky and begin to float among its mysteries, another moon appears suddenly, blotting out your cosmic ocean. This new moon has a picture of a soda can on it and big, bright letters that announce: UH, OH, BABY, ITS THE RIGHT ONE! End of cosmos as we knew it.

This bad dream is moments away. An advertising agency, Space Marketing, Inc., of Roswell, Georgia, is planning to hijack the sky. They will launch a mile-long billboard into space that can be seen from anywhere on earth. It will be as big as the moon. It will fittingly close the twentieth century, too, by putting an end to all the unproductive stargazing that took such a bite out of the economy. We weren't put on this planet to escape it by dreaming. This is a prison planet. The new moon makes the penal colony escape-proof. Space Marketing CEO, Mike Lawson, said that "we could fly a corporate logo such as McDonald's Golden Arches into space." Welcome to the new gateway to heaven! Will there be much protest? Probably not. Only people living in the Amazon who have never had a Big Mac will kill themselves in terror when they see the Golden Arches. The rest of us will get in our cars to go and get one. The inconvenient old moon doesn't have much longer, either. Space marketing, of one kind or another, will eventually blow it up because its unsettling tides interfere too often with shopping. At best, it could be used for projecting public-service messages on it, since it won't be seen much anyway, what with all the other moons up there, agency moons, network moons, ABC, NBC, PBS, the Ross Perot moon, electoral campaign moons, BUY U.S. BONDS moons. Eventually, the night sky will be available by subscription only. Anyone caught looking up without paying will have his eyeballs impounded. We still have a few seconds before they shut down the night sky. I say, let's get together with the Amazonians and go to war for the moon. Space Marketing, look out. You mess with da sky and we breaka your face.

McDonald's Saw That It Was Good

Jesus came back and he went to McDonald's. "I've analyzed the data," Jesus said, "and saw that of all the corporations on earth you are the one that reaches more people more places than anyone else, including Federal Express. Therefore, I have decided to begin spreading my message through you."

"What's the message?" the public-relations director asked, eyeing suspiciously the besandaled dude with the beatnik beret.

"The same old one," said Jesus. "Love."

"And how do you propose going about this, mister?" the PR head hissed, suspecting that a vegetarian might be hiding under Jesus' slightly unsanitary appearance.

"Well, it's true," Jesus said, reading his mind, "that I personally don't scarf down scoops of cow, not even two for two bucks, but distribution's distribution and this is the best means to convey my message of love, especially to teenagers, who seem to congregate here far more than in churches. What I propose is that we give away a condom in every burger."

The PR man considered briefly the difficulties involved in buying all the American rubber companies back from the Japanese. It wasn't cost efficient. "I don't think so," he said.

"Maybe you don't understand my message," said the Savior. "I didn't mean putting a condom *in* every burger, but *next* to it, in the box."

"I know," PR said, "now get outta here. Try Burger King."

"Okay." Jesus sighed. "I see that things haven't changed much in two thousand years. People are more selfish than ever. Can I at least take a picture of this place to take back to the Heavenly Father to show him what the new places of worship look like?"

"Now, that's a definite no-no!" PR said. "We have a firm policy about that. No pictures in McDonald's."

Sadly, Jesus put the Polaroid back in his knapsack. He'd hoped to make the Second Coming a gentler affair. Now he'd have to go by the Book. Bring on the Apocalypse.

The Things I Am When I Buy

When I wear my sneakers I am James Dean. I get a scowl on my face. Life is bitter and there is a rage in me that finds no release. I am going to run fast and die young, become a poster on teen walls from Dubuque to Moscow, and I will father two, maybe three, generations of young rebels that will flame from the spark of my rage. I throw the camera over my shoulder and go out into the shapeless world to click away at its loveless face.

When I take its picture with my camera I am Albert Einstein. Through my viewer I see not only the bland photographic face of the arrangement of lines and shadows they call "reality," but also the flows of energy and the laws of matter behind phenomena. I see the curve of space and feel the shrinking of time. People go on around me immersed in the electronic world of their TVs, oblivious to either my madness or my genius. But then, I watch TV also, and I am not gone to the world when I do. I hurl the ball of my thoughts way out of the normal range of human passivity.

When I watch TV I'm Babe Ruth. When I don't drive fast, watch TV, or picture the universe, I go shopping and feel immensely voluptuous. When I shop I'm Marilyn Monroe. And sometimes when I have a headache I take a pill. At those times I'm Sigmund Freud.

A few years ago, I wasn't so many people. I was maybe George Washington on his birthday, or Lincoln on his, and now and then, at Halloween and Mardi Gras, I was Dracula or Frankenstein. But lately, the dead have been coming among us more regularly to sell things. They are being brought back by advertisers who find the dead pretty game. The dead get a whole new lease on life and I get a whole new set of identities. What's wrong with that? The other day, I was taking my kid's picture. Why are you taking so long? he said. Time is relative, I told him, Einstein said that. Einstein? my kid said, isn't he the guy sells cameras on TV? Yeah, I said, among other things. I didn't tell him that I was Einstein. He bounced impatiently on his sneakers. James Dean, I said, you're a regular Dean. And he was—stalked right out.

Bible No Longer the Book

The Bible is no longer the Book. And it's not because there are other books. Or because another Book has appeared to take the place of the Book. Or because Gorbachev and the pope got together and decided that henceforth the Bible and *Das Kapital* are both the Book and therefore there is no longer one Book but rather a Co-Book. No, it's not any of those. The Bible is no longer the Book because now we have the Franklin Computer Bible. The Franklin Computer Bible is, and I quote, a light-weight, handheld electronic King James Edition. Its comprehensive index puts any chapter or verse at your fingertips, and it includes four AA batteries and carrying case. In the Beginning there was no longer the Word but the Chip.

And now we can see what God intended when he said "Let there be light!" He intended the four-line Liquid Display Screen, which Lights Up on command. And when the Spirit moved upon the face of the waters the Liquid Display Screen is also what was meant. No longer will the faithful swear on the Book, but they will, rather, lay hands on the Franklin Computer Holy Bible to take their solemn vows. Men of the cloth need no longer memorize long passages to awe their flocks. They will, instead, keep a nimble hand inside their pocket, punching the required numbers. And speaking of numbers, there might now be a way to make sense of all those numbers in the Book of Revelations. The numerical pad is better suited for quick access to the four horses of the Apocalypse, and to the number 666 on the forehead of the Beast. There will be those who will say that the Franklin Computer Holy Bible is itself the Beast, with its permanent 666 imbedded in its chips. But those people will be on their way out, as will other sorts of fiery preachers who used to physically threaten folk with the book. Book-shaking evangelists and pulpit-pounding preachers will disappear now. You cannot pound on the Franklin Computer Holy Bible because its menus will shift and it will lose its memory. And as for shaking it, forget it. It's light as a feather, and it's not a book. Or The Book. It's a machine come not to deliver the Word, but to Display the Chip.

The Difference

There is a new Burger King going up down the street and nobody cares. In a couple of days when it's finished everyone will think it's been there forever. It bugs me for six reasons. Number one, they kill cows; number two, the cows they kill graze on the sites of murdered forests; number three, the cows they kill that killed the forests are full of hormones; number four, the hormone-filled cows they kill that killed the forests are full of bad-for-your-heart fat; number five, the bad-for-your-heart-hormone-filled-forest-killing-dead-cows are wrapped in bad-for-the-earth-plastic; and number six, what the hell's a Burger King, anyhow? A burger is, literally, and originally, a tradesman who lives in a city, while a king is an aristocrat. Burgers and kings were traditional enemies. Hence, the phrase is absurd. I know *burger* is short for *hamburger*, and *king* means nothing in America. Still, it bugs me that bad-for-your-heart-hormone-filled-forest-killing-dead-cows-wrapped-in-bad-for-the-earth-plastic are also linguistically unpalatable. Maybe you can live with that. I can't.

A friend of mine imagined a prison without bars where you go in skinny and then they feed you so many burgers you can't go out the same door. Who needs bars? We've got Burger King. I saw a dog the other day, eating a leftover burger in a parking lot behind another Burger King. Did he know he was eating a cow? Did he know he was eating something ten times bigger than he was? I asked him, and he said he knew all that but he ate it nonetheless because it was free.

I then asked a human coming out why he ate at Burger King, and he said that it was cheap. And then I heard someone say that the reason we treat animals so badly is because they don't have any money. We treat children badly for the same reason, though we don't eat them.

Perhaps the time has come for animals to get paid for what they do. Perhaps the time has come for us to eat our children.

Or maybe we should just tear down the Burger Kings.

Clones

My son went to see Led Zeppelin in concert. Only they weren't really Led Zeppelin, they were a local band called Stairway to Heaven. "They look and sound exactly like Led Zeppelin!" he enthused, "they even have groupies." Now groupies, as everyone knows, are the surest proof of authenticity. You may be a clone, but a groupie's real. "All they do is Zeppelin songs?" I asked him. "They did Hendrix, too," said my son. "Hendrix?" "Yeah, there was a black guy too, looks and sounds like Hendrix!"

None of this surprised me too much, to tell you the truth, because I've known about Elvis clones for years, and I once saw a whole crowd of wanna-bes with about fifteen Madonnas and nine Princes in it. I've seen remakes of every movie ever made, and I even heard someone pretending to be me. All this happened to me in my lifetime, and there was also an episode on "Star Trek" that covered the whole thing.

What did surprise me is that my son, who loves the records, would compromise the original anthems in this way. I still get livid when I hear them using the anthems of my youth to sell dog food. I heard the Doors' "Light my Fire" used in a TV show called "The Wonder Years" to highlight a first kiss between two insufferable little preteen brats. I still haven't gotten used to thinking of "The Rhapsody in Blue" as an accompaniment to airline commercials. Certain songs—especially the anthems of one's youth—should have their numbers retired, like baseball players', and be used in nothing but the original. The trouble with clones, and they had that real good in that "Star Trek" episode, is that the strains weaken over time, or almost immediately, until what you have is a clone emotion to go with the clone, which makes you a kind of clone—of yourself. Luckily, my memory's full of songs that never got popular and that I can barely remember. In fact, I prefer forgetting them to having them revived by cloning.

Cloning is the stairway to hell.

Seven Embryos for Seven Lawyers

The Tennessee divorce battle over seven frozen embryos is rife with implications. The husband, Junior Lewis Davis, wants the fertilized eggs disposed of. The wife, Mary Sue Davis, is infertile and wants the eggs to hatch. The husband's lawyer calls the eggs "a group of undifferentiated cells," while the wife's attorney has labeled them "preborn children." Between those two definitions lies the entire range of current propositions as to when exactly a human being does become one. Here in Louisiana, life begins at conception, but the law's unclear whether what goes on in a petri dish can possibly be called conception. Other laws envision a human as beginning either from the minute it loses its flippers or from the time it does its first uterine somersault. Other opinions maintain that there are no human beings until they complete a scouting program, or even pass an SAT test.

I've heard an advocate for the proposition that human beings aren't human beings until they prove it themselves in a court of law. Clearly, there are seven lawyers for seven embryos in every case. The seven frozen embryos in the Tennessee case could be used as tests for the various laws. One embryo could be a group of undifferentiated cells: that one would be thawed. Another could testify to the validity of petri-dish conception. That one could stay. Another could be raised into a fine Boy Scout and sent out to fight drugs for the president. That one can prove it's a human being in a White House ceremony. One shouldn't look at these embryos merely as frozen lumps contending for definition: they are seeds of the very laws they might spawn. Mr. and Mrs. Davis should not fight for these eggs as if they were a private matter between themselves and their petri dish. They are sitting on the very basis of our future definition of human beings. Their divorce mirrors the divorce of the diverse philosophies at work here. They should work out a custody arrangement for these eggs that requires a constitutional lawyer to baby-sit.

We need new laws that defend human beings against technology, that tell us exactly where the human ends and the machine begins. That's easier said than done in a world where people and cars, for instance, make a single organism. If you take an American out of his/her car you get only a half a creature, a handicapped something called a "walking driver" that can't find its way home. Observant Martians have long concluded that a human being without a car is like a "snail that lost its shell." (*Martian Chronicles*, vol. 8.) Likewise, what is a human without a watch? Something so indescribably lost we'd better leave it unimagined. The law has problems even with this kind of crude mechanical symbiosis. If a driverless car kills a person, the car is rarely destroyed. If a person commits a crime in a car, the car is never punished. If a man is late because his watch doesn't work, his watch isn't taken out and shot (after being fired). We have an outmoded concept of guilt and responsibility that puts the entire burden on the shoulders of human beings. And now we don't even know when human beings start being human beings. Is a human being without a watch a human being? What's an American without a car? Is a frozen egg without a car a human being?

There is a Native American tribe that calls its members "the human beings." Everything else is—others. Our society too is divided into "human beings" and "others." I am quite certain that we Americans define a human being as a "creature with a car and a watch possibly born from a frozen egg or a rented womb." If that's true, the rest of the creatures on this planet simply aren't human beings. So far, technology has helped us to see why we are not fish, or cows, or others. But we have come to a point where either we give ourselves up entirely to the gadgets that serve us for organs, limbs, and definition, or we stop the process with laws that say no to Dr. Caligari's cabinet where Dr. Faustus has his lab.

I'm of two minds about it. One of them says, Let's get rid *completely* of the old-fashioned way of making human beings. If you crave pleasure, you can always spend time in an Orgasmotron. (Be sure you have enough quarters.) If we raised genetically tested supercreatures in artificial wombs we'll have a fine, rational planet without any heavy metal or tattoos. The other mind says, Get rid of all the gadgets and have only those babies that can be conceived in the soft grass on a midsummer's night by lusty creatures in love. Is there a middle ground? I guess that's what the law's for.

Nazi Jew

The recent miniseries "Twist of Fate" on NBC has to be the most offensive single thing yet spewed by Central Control. It concerns a Nazi forced by circumstances to have a face-lift to become a Jew. He then loses his pursuers by hiding in a concentration camp. Later, he helps found Israel and marries Veronica Hamel. Now, this isn't just any Nazi, this is Super-Nazi, the last in a long tradition: Superman, the Hulk, the Six-Million-Dollar Man.

TV's always been a fountain of racism, but this goes deep.

Until now we only had the Jews' word that the death camps were hell. Now we have proof: if a Nazi says so, it must be true. And if TV says so, it must be real.

Now, there is no reason why this miniseries should stop here. In the next episodes, the same Nazi, now a white Ku Klux Klaner, should have himself made black and forced to live in the projects. He could then tell us what that's like. After that, he could change gender and become a pregnant teenage mother on welfare. Wherever there is oppression, this versatile Nazi could go, suffer, and then tell the truth. The oppressed everywhere are clamoring for the repentant oppressor to articulate their plight.

Will we, the viewers, identify with Super-Nazi? It's hard to say. Unlike most past superheroes who transformed themselves from pathetic schmoes into muscled miracles, Super-Nazi goes backwards, from Aryan wonder to suffering Jew. It's an unlikely direction for the fantasy of your basic couch potato. On the other hand, he triumphs over his misfortune by becoming Super-Jew, a twist that saves the day. In the pantheon of superheroes, Super-Nazi falls somewhere between Superman and the Hulk: like Superman he gets power from righteousness, but like the Hulk he gets uglier when he serves justice. His basic split personality confirms something that we TV addicts deeply feel, mainly that we too, in reality, are well-muscled Nazis who have temporarily become ugly in order to experience the world. We really live on TV and are only visitors here on earth, television Nazis with Jewish faces fighting our way back to the light.

Of course, the image factory needs no help. Real Nazis don't watch TV.

My Head Is a Sequel

Mr. Smith called from St. Louis to tell me that I was inside his head. "Sequels?" he said. "Pardon me?" "Sequels," he reiterated, "my friends and I were discussing sequels at my house when I heard your voice discussing sequels—so I'm calling you up to say to you that you ought to do something on sequels." "Lemme get this straight," I said. "You heard my voice in your head discussing sequels and now you call me to ask me to repeat what the voice in your head said. You want me to imitate the me in your head. Write a sequel, as it were." "Something like that."

After Mr. Smith hung up I considered the fact that Mr. Smith isn't alone in hearing me inside his head. My friend Susan has dreams with a commentator. That commentator is me, and he comments while the dream's still going on. She has often asked me to comment on her dreams to see if I'll say the same things as the me in her head. I don't: the me in her head is much smarter than I am. The sequel to Mr. Smith's sequel story will no doubt be disappointing to Mr. Smith. The original using my voice in his head is no doubt more to Mr. Smith's liking than anything I have to say. What intrigues me is all these "me"s floating in peoples' heads: are they attached to me with invisible fibers, or are they simply blossoms of sounds that pop open in receptive heads? If they are attached to me then there is two-way communication no doubt, and all these people using me in their heads can yank the strings and make me go ouch, which is often exactly what they do, by picking up the phone and calling. On the other hand, all our heads may be filled with the disembodied voices of the media ghosts haunting us. It may well be that several media yakkers reside in everyone's head and when a person becomes tired one of them floats up and starts commentating. Walter Kronkite never retired: there are millions of people out there in whom he continues to speak. That's one kind of sequel. And this is another.

Mr. Smith, can you hear me?

The Lone Pundit

I was entertaining some notion the other day of becoming a syndicated pundit whose words would be spread far and wide over the Wonder bread whiteness of the nation's newspapers, resulting in a mountaintop château–cum–hot tub in Colorado. To this end, I studied one of George Will's columns in search of that elusive something that might turn a Transylvanian wit into a media mogul. "Daddy, Who Was Kerouac?" was the name of this particular square of fish wrapper. In it, Mr. Will commented on the dedication of a monument to Jack Kerouac in his native town of Lowell, Massachusetts, and came to the surprising conclusion that—quote—Respectability is the cruel fate of yesterday's radicals, especially in the eighties—unquote. In order to get there, he said that the sixties were a negligible time in American history. He much preferred the fifties, which, far from being boring, had exhibited such intellectual giants as T. S. Eliot, Robert Frost, and Lionel Trilling.

In the face of such assertions, one can but stand astounded, hoping that some kind of natural phenomenon, lightning perhaps, would take up the rebuttal. Lacking lightning, one would simply like to comment that the death of history equals the murder of facts by punditry, if that wouldn't be so flattering to the pundit. Simply put, what kills the truth of an age is cliché, not faulty memory. Obviously, George Will has an ideologically vested interest in wishing that the sixties and the changes they wrought never happened, even though or perhaps *because* he is a man of the sixties. But when this wish is supported by something as inane as the glory of the fifties, another territory opens, a truly postmodern one in which all things, words, and signs are equal, as long as they take up the whole square of print. The job of the pundit, then, is to erect a barricade of clichés between history and opinion, and to fire various placebos from behind it. I am perfectly capable of polemic, but I am floored by such self-loathing. I said good-bye to my hot tub in Colorado and picked up a copy of *On the Road*.

Escape from Politics

Among the things I never want to be when I grow up is a politician, and right after that comes TV commentator. I was immersed in some epic biblical sense in the world of both during the Republican National Convention. It's the Kingdom of the Overambitious. I have not felt such longing to escape since I was a teenager behind the Iron Curtain. After two days of being but a human mote in a sea of suits I had the mad desire to join the bums on Skid Row to drink Mad Dog 20/20 until all resemblance between me and politicians would become entirely coincidental.

Let me count the reasons: first, they shake your hand as if you were a tree and they were trying to make the fruits of your mind come loose and rain down. Or, to put it another way, they shake it as if you were upside down and everything in your pockets will fall at their feet. Secondly, they wear smiles made out of Teflon polyester enamel that slice like half-moons through your soul. They aren't smiling at you or even at anything in particular: their smile is a stamp, a brand that burns into your forehead to program you to vote for them. Thirdly, and most pointedly, politicians hate children and foreigners, which is why all of them are going to great lengths to pretend otherwise. Left to themselves, politicians bite babies, kick dogs, and call ethnics names, but in public they do the opposite. The absolutely nauseating spectacle of lovey-dovey families, wives, and children is another sham. "I would fall on a grenade for him," said Mrs. Bush of her husband. Oh, my. Why so violent? Why a grenade? Why the overkill? Nobody truly tender would invoke grenades. Loyalty and grenades is a highly anxious mixture. Which brings me to the other thing I never want to be. The anxious TV commentator who, it has been my unhappy lot to observe, runs off at a mouth clearly disconnected from any brain. Says the same thing over and over with all the enthusiasm of a provincial thespian on amphetamines. Inane smiles and disconnected gab rule both politicos and teleyakkers. In fact, both professions exist to create anxiety in sane people. The antidote: Mad Dog 20/20 and the crazy but real talk of those with nothing at stake.

Trust me, ambition is hell.

Honesty Rated

A recent Gallup poll confirms what I've been suspecting for a while: nobody's been thinking since 1988. In 1988 so many things began to happen in the world that people simply stopped thinking. The poll finds that Americans' overall opinion of the honesty and ethical standards of twenty-five leading professions has not changed since 1988. Most honest, at the top are druggists, clergy, funeral directors, bankers, and TV reporters. At the bottom are advertisers and car salesmen. I have no quarrel with the bottom, but the top?

Let's take druggists: most of their business is in antidepressants and cigarettes. We trust them because they make us feel good.

And who could disagree with the honesty of the clergy? I certainly trust anyone who says that if I don't give him $10 million in the next five minutes God is going to detonate him. The clergy's been selling the greatest product in the world since time began: something you can't see, taste, smell, or imagine. We can certainly trust them; their merchandise has been consistently unavailable.

The next trustworthy profession, closely allied to the clergy, is funeral directors. We trust them because they make us look better than we ever looked when we were alive. In exchange, they tenderly relieve us of our life's savings. We trust them also because they make the evidence disappear in any number of fanciful ways.

And how can you not trust bankers? Go into any savings and loan and find out how safe your money is. Bankers are not only honest but they are gentle: they rob you with a pen instead of a gun, as the folk song goes, and they own your house, your car, and your paycheck. You *have* to trust *them*, I guess.

And, finally, we rate TV reporters very highly on honesty. I agree with this unreservedly. TV reporters generally read things exactly the way they are written on the TelePrompTers. That's honest. They strain their contact lenses to be accurate while they read, and we appreciate that.

Personally, I think car salesmen are getting a bad rap.

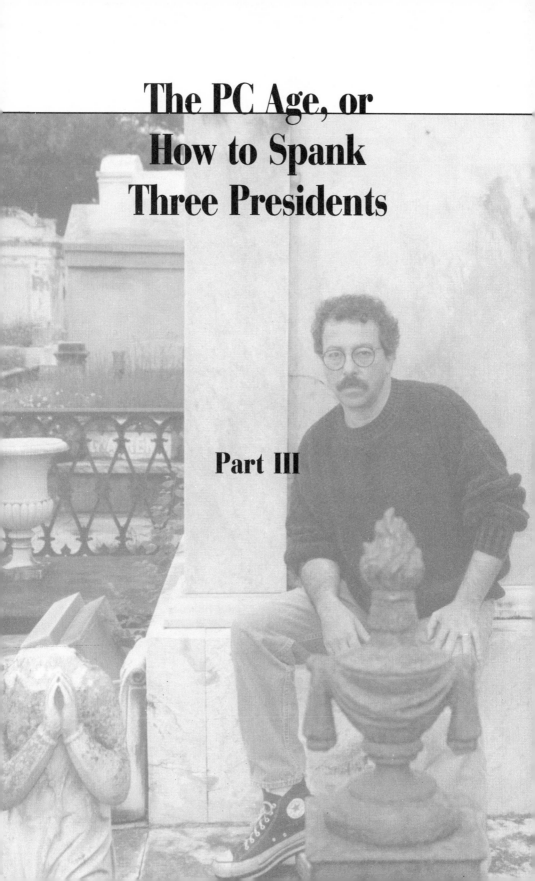

The PC Age, or
How to Spank
Three Presidents

Part III

The Politically Correct Thing, Oh Boy!

If you teach blacks black history, whites are being done wrong. If you let women tell their stories, men might have to shut up. If gays complain, straights are being abused. This is the currently raging logic of the plantation owners who have declared war on what they call the "politically correct."

Politically correct, *personal computer*, and *political commentator* have the same initials. *Politically incorrect*, *post-ideological*, and *power incentive*, or p.i., also share initials. It's been causing some confusion among conservative PCs writing in the newspapers about p.c. on their PCs. The conservative PCs say that blacks, feminists, and professors are trying to make us all p.c. thereby oppressing the p.i. majority, which would rather follow such p.i. models as the S&L banker and the microchip soldier, which have been brought to us by the p.i. likes of Mr. Reagan and Mr. Bush.

Not to wax the alphabet too heavily, but there is some deliberate dyslexia here. The conservative PCs are scrambling their *p*s and *c*s on purpose so that we won't notice that in fact they are talking about the CP. Yes, CP, the Communist party which, by disappearing in communist countries, left them bereft of an enemy and made it necessary to recreate a domestic version called p.c. Today's p.c. is yesterday's CP. Thanks to everyone's office PC, it takes but one keystroke to transform yesterday's newspaper columns railing at the CP into today's fish wrapper against p.c. The new commies, the p.c. feminists, blacks, and professors, are trying to foist their wymmin, texts, preadults, personholes, and multicultures on the p.i. majority, which always consisted and will always consist of geeks, nerds, stiffs, squares, and frat boys. It's been a hard and uphill fight for the p.i. to restore the tie, the gun, the American flag, and the ethnic joke to their rightful places at the center of the American home on top of the TV set. It took years of retrenchment, a decade of oblivion, two hologram presidents, two wars, the end of communism, and a ton of programming to get us back into the shopping malls where we belong, and there is, by golly, no way we'll let some wimpy academic CPs, er, PCs, take us back to where the buffalo roam. So get thee back to your PC, CP profs, and write your MCs (*mea culpas*) before the p.i. (formerly the SM, or silent majority) hoists you on your own CPs (commie petards).

Who's Afraid of Walt Whitman?

Why are people still afraid of Walt Whitman? According to Sam Abrams, the editor of *The Neglected Walt Whitman*, published by Four Walls/Eight Windows, they are afraid enough to hide some of his best poems. The Library of America's *Complete Poetry and Collected Prose*, for instance, fails to reproduce one of the poet's most subversive works, "Respondez!" a poem that reveals a whole different Whitman, far different from the optimistic trumpeteer of American democracy known to generations of schoolchildren.

> *Stifled, O days! O lands! in every public and private corruption!*
> *Smother'd in thievery, impotence, shamelessness, mountain-high;*
> *Brazen effrontery, scheming, rolling like ocean's waves around and*
> *upon you, O my days! O my lands! For not even those*
> *thunderstorms, nor fiercest lightning of the war, have purified*
> *the atmosphere!; . . . Let the eminence of meanness, treachery,*
> *sarcasm, hate, greed, indecency, impotency, lust, be taken for*
> *granted above all! let writers, judges, governments, households,*
> *religions, philosophies, take such for granted above all!*
> *Let the priest still play at immortality! Let death be inaugurated.*

This angry, "unsafe Whitman," as Abrams calls him, has unsettled academic critics since the very beginning. After gaining the approval of Ralph Waldo Emerson in 1855, Whitman was willfully repudiated and neglected by the American cultural establishment, even as his fame grew abroad, gaining the love of poets from Europe to Latin America. When it became impossible to ignore him, a sanitized version was carefully carved out of his work. Whitman's angry poems, as well as his homoerotic songs to sexual love, were carefully obscured and excised from most editions. Despite the neglect of the academics, Whitman became genuinely loved by those who really matter, the lovers of poetry. The "neglected poems" printed here by Sam Abrams should go a long way toward restoring to us the bard of whom D. H. Lawrence said, "The Americans are not worthy of their Whitman."

Peyote

Dry peyote buttons are bitter, hard, and wrinkled. They have the texture of flesh and taste so vile your whole creature recoils when you bite into them. The white fluff under the button is poisonous and must be carefully removed before ingestion. People have ground them, mixed them with honey, and boiled them in order to make them palatable. Even then the bitterness was overwhelming and it was a heroic act to keep them down. In the end, if you were lucky, you saw yourself, a trembling creature in a fiercely alive universe, connected to plants, animals, and light. If you were a hippie you called this "finding yourself." But if you were a Native American, belonging to the Native American church, peyote was your sacrament, and your self was what you had to find in order to belong to your community. The unique self uncovered by your vision quest strengthened and affirmed the people.

These days, finding oneself isn't much in vogue among white Americans. Hippies are a thing of the past, and selling oneself is the going thing. Native Americans, however, are still here, and their sacrament is about to be outlawed. It is hard not to see in this another chapter in the long history of brutality against native peoples and their community. Hippies and the drug culture first appropriated peyote for their own uses, television and movies trivialized it, and now, at last, it is time to eliminate it. Tobacco, let's not forget, was also a sacramental plant, used by Native Americans as a peace offering. It too would have been outlawed if there hadn't been money to be made from it. Now that it's killing everybody and it has lost all sacramental uses, we wouldn't dream of banning it. It has become a white drug in a way that peyote never could because it is too bitter. Native American church members use peyote in the sweat lodge to purify themselves for their vision quest. They can achieve the same result fasting for several days, and surely no one can ban that. Or can they? In the end, it may well be that it isn't peyote that is being banned here, but the quest for self in the age of Sell.

They force-feed people, don't they?

The Theater of Operations: Dispatches from the Front

As the war on drugs enters its second month, the theater of operations is widening. In downtown Los Angeles the other day, I was approached by a street person. "Got a cigarette?" he said, "or a joint? Or some other stuff?" I handed him my pack. He took it in his hand, breezed through it briefly, and said, "Don't ever hand your pack to anyone like this. They're bound to find the joint hidden in there." Clearly, the territory around downtown L.A. is still in the hands of the enemy.

In other parts of the country, however, stunning successes are being reported. In Depew, New York, an eight-year-old boy turned in his mother for allegedly smoking marijuana two days after he listened to President Bush's speech urging children to help people with drug problems. Back when I was growing up behind the iron curtain, one of my second-grade classmates turned in his mother for listening to Radio Free Europe. This was during the Stalinist war on radio. She went to jail and the boy went to an orphans' home. He is now an alcoholic ham-radio operator in a remote village who relays distress signals from lost sailors who want to get back home. The eight-year-old in Depew is in the custody of his father, while his little brother has been turned over to the child-welfare authorities. In Tres Orejas, New Mexico, a small community is being terrorized by enormous helicopters belonging to the National Guard, which hover over houses scattering children, chickens, and livestock. They are looking for the marijuana sure to be found on the rooftops.

These signs of success must be very heartening to an administration originally worried about giving a war nobody came to. They were so worried, in fact, that they staged it at first. The bag of crack that President Bush held up dramatically during his first war speech turns out to have been bought by his own people, who set up the buy as close as they could to the White House. Well, things like this may have been necessary at first, but now that children are getting the message, things are okay. When that eight-year-old in Depew grows up he can reminisce with the other veterans about the early sacrifices.

Translator for the Police

A friend of mine in New Orleans was talking on the telephone to a friend of his in Romania. They could have talked in Romanian because they are both Romanian, but they chose instead to talk in English in order to give the secret police a bit of work. Secret policemen have been getting lazy. They still listen in to everything, but they would rather not have to translate, or otherwise exert themselves. The police would love it if everybody started talking Esperanto. Their job would be a piece of cake. Having to translate is the only thing that stands between the police and happiness.

Police translators are not very good, for one thing. No matter how hard they try, they can't render the hidden meanings. Perhaps because hidden meanings are precisely what they are after, and if they can't find any they have to fabricate them. But they can't be just any hidden meanings: they have to be criminal hidden meanings. In totalitarian countries, the police get around this thorny problem by considering all hidden meanings criminal.

In our country, things aren't so clear-cut. Police translators have to come up with translations good enough to prove something before the law. Not so long ago, a Russian sailor who tried to defect was sent back to his ship, and the immigration officer claimed that all of it was a problem of translation. The translator said that what the sailor said and what the officer heard was not what she translated. In this case, the meaning was what hid from translation. But it is in the world of everyday crime that a crisis of translation is brewing. As crime gets worse and criminals more foreign, the police will need more and more translators. Police translation will become a major profession. Foreign-language training will intensify not just in order to produce more translators, but also to produce bilingual criminals who can translate themselves. This would be much easier on everybody, failing universal institution of Esperanto. Another solution is to punish some bilingual criminals by making them translate for the police instead of going to jail.

The future looks foreign to me, but then I hear voices.

History in Trouble

People don't have a very good opinion of history. This is why when lovers fight, or someone's about to shoot somebody, they say, "You're history!" Now, it turns out, the American Federation of Teachers has analyzed high school history books and it has found that they depict history as "colorless, without point of interest," in short, boring. In an effort to balance things out, the writers of textbooks are "passionless" and "neutral."

Well, that's no news to my students, who consistently confuse World War II with World War I and are not sure if the Crusades took place before or between those wars. If it wasn't for the movies and the cartoons, they would know even less. Those fortunate enough to have parents and grandparents probably know the most because they have to fight the older folks for the remote control when history comes up on TV.

It is possible too, that in families where people still talk, the older folk actually tell stories. But it's a remote possibility: there is no talking button on the remote control. The only people interested in history are people who feel that they've been done wrong by the way it's being told. Thus, feminists are sick of his story, and are passionate about her story. Indians find little to cheer in the optimistic version of the white man's successes. Nature, if it had a say in it, would be most distressed by the recitation of civilization's industrial progress.

History's been nothing but trouble to most people on earth, who'd rather forget about it if it didn't have the nasty habit of repeating itself. High school history should be taught by guests with differing views of events, while the books should be telephone directories containing the numbers of other parties passionate about the retelling of it. A tree teaching the history of paper would be ideal, for instance. Without such measures, history itself will be history, and then either we'll start again from scratch, or pay for the same movie twice.

The Poetry of Destruction

My son said the other day, "There was lots of forests in the world before God made my dad a poet."

Which poses the question, exactly. Why, for all the forests I consume with my conflagrations of words, am I incapable of describing lyrically and powerfully the destruction of the environment? It is our single most burning problem, even as the great forests of Brazil burn, and yet I am unable to make it live. And I am not alone.

The other day, an environmental group arrived from California to perform a lovely ritual at the Mississippi. They brought with them fresh water from the source of the Mississippi and from some of its tributaries and, after chanting appropriately, they emptied them into the filthy mouth of the once mighty river that is now our greatest sewer. Let the healing begin from the end, they proclaimed, and why not? Anything will help now, when even the most hopeful activists secretly suspect that it's too late. A ritual act needs press to impress, but the local newspaper wouldn't cover the event. Why? The abortion protesters were also in town and the paper covers no more than one group of outside agitators a week. That would be funny if it wasn't so true, but the reason is not some dark and mysterious plot but a kind of weariness.

We all know by now that nearly everything we eat, drink, stare at, touch, or breathe in is capable of killing us. The enemy is abstract and has abstract names, sometimes no more than initials, PCB, DDT, polyvinyl chloride, carbon monoxide, etc.

It is very hard to become indignant at the faceless things that kill you. One of the pleasures of anger is the ability to see what the object of your anger looks like. The brighter the uniform the better. It is hard to imagine going to war against a toxin. We need the equivalent of that smell they put in gas to identify the killers, and only artists can create that sensual equivalent.

What means of expression do we possess capable of giving sensual form to the new enemy?

Only our children, I think, who are not weary, and stand most directly before the burning world.

"There was lots of forests in the world before God made my dad a poet." Indeed. And then there was hope.

Once Upon a Word

I was leafing through *The Vegetarian Epicure* by Anna Thomas, published in 1972, in search of either my youth or something healthy to eat, when I came upon the author's biography. "Anna Thomas," it said, "is strongly committed to the women's liberation movement and has been involved in its activities." Now here was a phrase we don't much hear lately. *Women's liberation*, like the other L-word, has fallen into disuse. Current replacements include *feminism* and *women's movement*, more muted phrases that carry neither the charge nor the challenge of *liberation*. What's more, *women's liberation*, in the form of "women's lib" has become a mostly derogatory term, used by enemies of the ERA, and those who like to say "I told you so" when Geraldine Ferraro's name comes up.

The word *liberation*, much in vogue in the early seventies, was the obligatory qualifier of most radical activity. We had "liberation fronts," in the Third World, on campuses, and in ghettos. The experimental goal of every socially rebellious group was "liberation," a utopian state that was largely assumed to be worth dying for. On a less dramatic scale one took LSD to "liberate" oneself, and "liberated" things from capitalists who had too many of them. Although *liberation* and *liberty* share the same linguistic crib, they were ideological enemies, the first being on the far left, the second on the far right, as in the "Liberty Lobby," for instance. There must have been a certain point, about the middle of Ronald Reagan's first term, when "liberation" suddenly lost its appeal. Women became interested in sharing the unliberated world of labor, a substantial shift from the dangerous business of "liberation." In the Third World, "liberation fronts" became "national movements," while on campuses and in ghettos they just evaporated under pressure. Not only did *liberation* vanish suddenly, but it dragged in its wake other linguistic kin, such as *liberal*, and *liberalism*, whose funerals were given much media play. It must feel strange to have once been associated idealistically with an obsolete term. On the other hand, it was only a word. The impulse hasn't gone away.

Family Values

Before Reagan and Bush you could still get "family value" at certain discount stores. But no more. Everything is so expensive. So I don't really know why the Republicans are talking about "family values" when families can't get good value on anything anymore. Of course, the Republicans don't live on the same planet where most families live. They live on Planet TV. On that planet, there is a war going on between the Waltons and the Simpsons. It's one of those wars that always goes on on TV. It's a war between new shows and reruns. The Republicans are for reruns. Their great hero, Ronald Reagan, is in reruns all over the world. The Waltons were this family during the Depression who lived about twelve to a room and starved and saved to send John Boy to college because there weren't any college loans. That's how Mr. Bush would like us to be. Great vision!

Another of the Republican battlefields, Murphy Brown, is going to have a baby in the future. The Republicans want to run the film backwards so she won't have any baby. They say that they are against "abortion" but they have no qualms about aborting Murphy Brown's baby. Running film backwards is what Republicans promise the country if they win. That, and a lot of reruns. Many of them regret the demise of the handy red bugaboo, communism. But if they win, no problem. They'll run the tape back to the fifties where young Joe McCarthy and fresh-faced Richard Nixon whip America strong.

The only problem Republicans have at the moment is that their opponents don't want to fight the battle exclusively on TV. They are leaving the tiny world where reruns work forever on the hypnotized couch potatoes and are pointing out the general disaster around the house where the TV sits. The disappearing neighborhood. The vanishing road. The absence of any "family value" whatsoever in the stores. It's enough to make even the Waltons lose their cool. The Nielsens say people preferred watching reruns of "Roseanne" to the Republican Convention. I guess people have already chosen their rerun family. It wasn't the Waltons. It wasn't the Bushes. Stalin used to tell people on all occasions, "Family is the basis of society." Or how about, "The family is the smallest but most valuable unit in the complete structure of the state." Hitler said that. The rhetoric and demagoguery of "family values" is in reruns, too.

The Stars and I

I've been saying for years that Ronald Reagan was a hippie but nobody believed me. Now we have proof. Not only do the Reagans run the country by astrological signs, they probably also chant mantras and try to levitate off their horses at the ranch. A gypsy with an oversize tarot deck lives in a closet just off the presidential bedroom. A shadowy adviser to the White House kitchen mixes herbs in the brew while chanting things. The forthcoming memoir of the White House cook, entitled *The Cauldron and the Power*, will throw light on this and other matters.

Ronald Reagan was California governor in the hippie years and it rubbed off. At least one of the Reagan children argued with mom and dad about smoking pot, lesbians, love, peace, astrology, and sex. This New Age business, even if you're against it, has a way of getting inside. Take the Reagans' belief in the end of the world: the hippies all believed it. I sat through five imminent ends of the world in Golden Gate Park. They didn't come, but nobody stopped believing in it. Before the Christian fundamentalists made such a big deal out of it, the End of the World used to be property of the hippies, who thought that they were early Christians anyway.

And how about that linchpin of conservative gospel: Less Government? Just like the Reagans, hippies thought Big Government was evil and the less of it the better. Dismantling the bureaucracy was the fond dream of most people living on welfare in the late sixties. Ronald Reagan simply picked up those vibes and put them in his platform. "Vibes," like astrology, are also greatly in vogue at the White House. According to Donald Regan, people were in or out depending on the vibes Nancy got off of them.

The hippie dream as I remember it was a spread in the country where you could do your own thing. The Reagans run to their ranch every time they feel like doing their own thing, which is often. There, under the blue sky, atop a horse, with the sun rising before you, it is possible to commune with Creation. And that's a big job, let me tell you.

And take the hippie attitude toward work. They were against it. Nobody can accuse Ronald Reagan of being for it.

And how about the hippies' avowed distaste for conflict and their horror of decisions? We hear that the president likes to waffle and deliver himself of general philosophical pronouncements rather than nail down the specifics. That too is but an old hippie trait. Ronald Reagan once said, "Welfare mothers are ruining this country." That's but a modification of the hippie adage, "The mothers are wrecking the world." The ability to generalize while skipping over the particulars is most characteristic.

Are we getting closer? This isn't all: Nancy Reagan's famous "Say No to Drugs" is but a less euphonic version of the hippie "Just Say No!" which is itself a shortening of "Hell no, we won't go!"

And then there is love, which is Ronald Reagan's greatest political problem. He loves his aides so much he just won't let them go, no matter what they did. The hippies were forgiving, too: their slogan was "We'll straighten it out right here! No cops!"

Given these things, why would anyone be surprised that the White House consults astrologers? One shouldn't disregard the specific kind of hippies the Reagans are. Southern California hippies are quite different from ones in Oregon. The White House likes the Beach Boys, not the Grateful Dead. The Reagans are from Hollywood, and the star system is what that's all about. As the poet Frank O'Hara said, "Even the heavens run on the star system."

Pass the miso.

The Grammar Lesson

There are certain acts that *trans*cend—notice the prefix *trans*—ordinary human measure. Take President Bush's display of paternal love: starting a war to get his son out of the news. That's megalove—notice the prefix *mega*—and the fact that it didn't work doesn't make it any less *extra*—notice prefix—ordinary. People have been writing to Ann Landers about their wristwatches lately to say that something in their bodies wrecks their watches. Some say it's the pulse, others blame biorhythms, while others simply attribute the phenomena to *meta*—are you prefix-careful?—physics. Metaphysics, metalanguages, metamorphosis, and metaphor, all of them formed with the prefix *meta*, were popular things in the sixties.

Then came *tele*—are you paying attention?—vangelists and *trans*formers. Metaphysics became telephysics, metalanguages teletalk, metamorphosis telemorphosis, which is when someone sitting on a couch is teleported and transformed into a shade inside the *hyper*—are you there?—space of TV, and metaphor became telephor, which is the process whereby everything we encounter is transformed into something we saw on TV. For example: the desert sand was the color of Captain Picard's head.

The *meta-tele* prefix switch has been marked by instability of the prefixes *trans* and *mega*, which could mutate into *hyper* and *ultra* any day now. For example: The transcendent nature of President Bush's megalove for his son Neal caused him to start an ultraconflict in hyperspace to get him out of teletalk. One man wrote to Ann Landers that the way to start one's watch going again after the biorhythms broke it was to rub a fresh clove of garlic on it every day. That's an ultrasolution to a metachronological problem. It might also solve the extraordinary problem of telereality messing with Chronos, the metaentity that lives in my watch under a desert sky the color of Milk of Magnesia commercials.

The Bush Generation

Is there a Bush generation? Looking over the equally blameless faces of the new crop in Creative Writing 101, it's hard to tell. The same un-mapped look of excessive health, touched here and there by pop fashion, beams out of them. The six-dollar Supercut special vies with mall-bought tie-dye.

I ask them to tell a story, any story, to the class. This way I can tell how they talk, how they tell a story, and what they think a story is, all useful gauges on the long and painful road to graphobia or mania.

The first to stand is a clean-cut, athletic young man who lopes determinedly to the blackboard. "I was in the Coast Guard for two years," he says, "because I wanted to fight this war on drugs every day out there in south Florida . . . and that's where I went . . . I wanted to show my father that you can do something right away . . . My father is a West Point colonel but I rejected him and his way . . ." He lets this sink in, then makes a slow rotating motion on his left temple, "Of course," he admits, "there was quite a bit of 'Miami Vice' in there. . . ."

Next to rise is a young woman tightly accoutred in frayed short shorts. She is barefoot. Around her left ankle there is a gold chain. She too lopes forward and takes several steps right and left before she tells the story of a young woman who threw up for thirty days. She describes in vivid green and orange flaky detail the interface of toilet bowl and contents. She then writes something in her diary. Her mother appears. Her mother takes her diary out of her hands. At this point, the story changes from the third person to the first person. "So my mother grabs the diary from my hand . . . I mean her hand . . . and she screams at me: 'Why do you want to kill yourself? Everything you write is so depressing!' So I say, 'Mother, killing yourself is so *passé!*' And then I go back to the bathroom and vomit for another thirty days. I look in the mirror and think, Mother, don't you know?" That was the end of the story, and the cheerful-looking child sat down, pleased with herself. I was baffled. Her mother didn't know, and I didn't have a clue, but everybody else in class knew. A minute later it hit me. Of course. Bulimia. More fashionable than suicide.

Is there a Bush generation? Yes. They are just like the Reagan kids, only much more extreme. The clean-cut man on my right—as it happened—was more clean-cut and more on my right. And the cheerful bulimic on my left—also as it happened—was more intent on the edge. Life and death are both a little closer now and a little more *present*.

The New Age

There was free beer for everybody the night the Republicans kept the White House. The fraternity house down the street shook fearfully every time a state went for Bush. At some point, shortly after the victory speech, I looked out the window and saw a dozen or so young men lined up facing a wall and resting their foreheads on it. Perhaps these are Dukakis supporters waiting to be executed, I thought, but then I realized that the odd formation was due entirely to a state of beer-induced beatitude.

Next day, walking to school, I beheld an immense flag flying from atop the university flagpole. It was bigger than any flag I had ever seen, including the one over the used-car lot in Metairie, Louisiana. Was the university going into the used-car business?

In front of the student union a crowd had gathered about a jet fighter, which had appeared there miraculously overnight. Two military types were assisting eager young men and women into the cockpit. "I had one just like this when I was a kid," said one of the cheery young'uns. That's when I remembered where I'd seen that jet before: at the toy store, considerably smaller. I ordered my coffee, which seemed no different from the coffee I'd had the day before, and opened the student newspaper in search of clues. There were three letters to the editor. One of them recommended a new policy, called Minimum Tolerance, toward feminists and homosexuals. Another demanded an end to minority scholarships and grants. The third one was a delicate reminder to all that the elderly were robbing us blind with their Social Security checks.

I leaned back in my temporary chair and considered the signs. The "kinder, gentler America" of George Bush had certainly begun.

My Invitation to the Inner Circle

I got a letter from Vice President Quayle. It said, "Dear Friend: It gives me great pleasure to inform you that at the last meeting of the membership committee of the Republican Senatorial Inner Circle, your name was placed in nomination by Senator Phil Gramm and you were accepted for membership . . ." for demonstrating, the vice president said, "a solid commitment to our nation's ideals and principles."

Wow! I knew that my commitment to the nation's ideals was indeed solid, but I wasn't too thrilled with their recent application by the Republican party. I, for instance, didn't think much of the patriotic breast-beating over the Gulf War. I didn't think much of Jesse Helms or of flag-waving. Nonetheless, the VP knew all this, and still . . . "Senator Bob Dole," he continued, "will be sending you your formal invitation in a few days. . . ."

Sure enough. Two days later, a large envelope from Senator Dole arrived. "On behalf of my colleagues in the United States Senate," said Senator Dole, "it is my privilege to invite you to accept membership . . ."

Man, now they were begging me! In addition to this plea, the envelope contained a beautifully engraved card with my name on it and a nomination-acceptance form that said, "I hereby accept. Enclosed please find my check in the amount of $1,000 for my annual Inner Circle membership . . . $2,000 for my spouse/additional member . . ." Aha! If for some reason I couldn't join the Republican Senatorial Inner Circle just then I could enclose a special contribution of $500, $250, or $100.

So I wrote back:

> Dear Vice President Quayle, Senators Dole and Gramm:
>   Thank you for the honor. On pondering the $1,000-per-person fee, however, I must sadly decline. Walt Whitman, my favorite poet, would have never been invited to your circle

because he never had $1,000 all at once. And my guides to politics, Mark Twain and H. L. Mencken, would have been downright rude about the pitch. Happily, I'm neither a Democrat nor a Republican, though if it came right down to it I'd probably belong to the party that lets people hear their leaders for less than 1,000 bucks. *One* dollar, let's say.

Sincerely, Andrei Codrescu.

I do feel better now, thank you.

Marxist Dialectics Replaced by Republican Dyslexics!

There are no more Marxist dialectics; they've been replaced by a new ideology, Republican dyslexics. Attorney General William Barr said that "crime is causing poverty in the inner cities." Is there something wrong with this picture? How about "poverty is causing crime"? Just in case we might misunderstand him, the attorney general goes on to explain that the riots in L.A. were the premeditated work of gangs, not the result of outrage at the Rodney King verdict. In other words, the riots came first, the Rodney King verdict later. Not to be outdone, Vice President Quayle blames the riots on Murphy Brown, which goes beyond reading history backwards, to the very root of the Republican project: replacing facts with fiction.

Ever since Ronald Reagan, the actor, the Republicans have been at war with reality. Reagan was so good at it he got poor people to believe that if the rich got richer they would be better off. He got workers to blame the unions for their plight, he convinced the middle class that the poor were the enemy, he showed us that peace can be won by increased military spending, that self-reliance can be obtained by borrowing more, that crime was caused by movies and paintings, and that everything that didn't fit into this scheme of things was the work of the Devil and it ought not to be shown on television. But George Bush is no Ronald Reagan. The seamless fairy tale is coming apart. Murphy Brown and the L.A. gangs cannot be blamed for a policy that approves multibillion-dollar Stealth bombers while rejecting a less-than-two-billion-dollar aid program to the cities. Are we going to use Stealths against children locked out of closed playgrounds? "Lax values," as VP Quayle calls them, are the problem all right, but they are the "lax values" of the folks who gave us the S&Ls, the Gulf War miniseries, Willie Horton, and Rodney King. They also tried to prove that all pollution comes from trees, and that the ozone hole doesn't exist. In fact, the ozone hole of the Reagan-Bush fiction is getting bigger, and they are all about to fall through it.

Riots

I was in Detroit in 1967. We were driving down John Lodge Expressway and listening to Jose Feliciano sing "C'mon Baby, Light My Fire!" At that moment, downtown Detroit went up in flames. The first day was like a festival or a block party. Neighborhood people, black and white, old and young, walked out of stores with brand-new TV sets and stereos, and some of them met for the first time. When army tanks from the 101st and Eighty-second airborne divisions started rumbling up Woodward Avenue, the mood changed. If anybody stuck their head out of the window after curfew the soldiers riddled the building with machine-gun fire. I was new to this country, and the astonishing experience of finding myself in a war zone did not fit very well with the image of the America where "the sidewalks are paved with gold," or, as my grandmother used to say, "dogs walk around with pretzels on their tails."

I learned very quickly that some people's dogs were indeed covered with gold while other people's sidewalks were covered with dog pretzels, and not the edible kind. It's different now in 1992. The people with the gold have more of it and the others are living more of a dog's life than they had then. The riot in L.A. looked just like the riot in Detroit, but the angry young blacks on the streets don't have anyone explaining the world to them. No Black Panthers, no SNCC, no radical left, not even liberal white agendas. Gangs have stepped into the vacuum left by the suppression of radical politics.

My son, who is thirteen, is playing Jem in "To Kill a Mockingbird." The show opened on the night of the L.A. riot. Set in the 1930s, the play is about the unfair trial of a black man accused of rape in a small southern town. Everyone in the audience was painfully aware that things hadn't changed that much. My son wasn't even born in 1967, but he already feels some of the anger of that time. He wears tie-dyed shirts and listens to the protest music of the sixties. Black kids his age are also looking back to that time: they are quoting Malcolm X and wearing big, angry Xs on their shirts.

I'm not a new American anymore. I know where both the gold and the pretzels are. Detroit has not yet recovered from the devastation of 1967. Los Angeles will take a long time to come back, if it ever does. But if somebody doesn't listen to our children, things will be a lot nastier ten years from now.

Capitalist Ideals

While Eastern Europe waits with bated breath for capitalist guidance, we are working hard indeed to provide them with inspirational examples. In Texas recently a mother was convicted of attempting to murder the mother of her daughter's rival to the cheerleading team. That shows several capitalist virtues: a mother's love making use of the free-enterprise system; a daughter's determination to achieve one of American girls' highest goals, the cheerleading squad; and the working of our justice system.

The mother appears to have been put up to it by her ex-husband's brother, who was hoping to become rich by selling the details to the movies when the plot was revealed. This also shows several things: that the free-enterprise system can be counted on to reward a clever idea; that movies are the goal of anyone who can't make it to the cheerleading squad, such as a man; and that family is important. The ex-husband himself wanted only custody of his daughters, including the would-be cheerleader, and as such, he too, gives us an example of how divorce works under capitalism.

So far, it isn't clear if the daughter achieved her goal, but we know that at least twenty film companies have approached the ex-brother-in-law for his story. We can also see here the influence of pop psychology, via TV, on the mother, who did not want her daughter's *rival* murdered but rather her mother, in order to distress the daughter from her cheerleading tests. This was between mothers, you might say, a clear example of the code of the West, which is still functioning in Texas. Of course, such ambitions, insights, and movie plots are not obtained in a day or even in a decade: they take years of dreaming of winning beauty contests beginning with Miss Baby America contests in early age, years of patient TV watching, years of normal family life with backyard barbecues at which the brother-in-law was always present, and years of healthy competitive attitudes about what matters. Pay attention, Lithuania!

Soothsayers off the Wall

A while ago, while the whole country was biting its nails in nervous anticipation of the elections, I went to see a famous astrologer in New Mexico. This guy predicts the future in detail for movie stars and politicians and now and then for mortals like me if they have the cash. Naturally, I asked him who was going to win the election. "George Bush," he answered without hesitation. "However," he whispered significantly, "he won't live out his whole term. Dan Quayle will become president." I was so dismayed by this news that I barely heard the personal part of the reading, which said, I think, that the stars were not too keen on my own affairs, either. Convinced that both the country and I were in trouble, I immediately consulted a channeler for confirmation. The channeler was more cagey than the astrologer, but the 10,000-year-old entity that spoke in a gravelly voice, which sounded like it had just smoked 10,000 cigarettes, said essentially the same thing. George Bush will be reelected.

Predicting the future is risky business, but it's rarely been riskier than it is now. History's gotten too fast for prophecy. It happens before you think about it. Neither psychics nor statistic-armed think-tankers predicted the collapse of communism, for instance. In fact no one has even yet predicted the rise of fascism from the ruins of communism, which has already happened. Soothsaying's come to a bad pass if it can't even foresee what's already taken place.

Personally, this confirms my belief that what happens is precisely what is not predicted. On TV this time of the year, there are as many ads for fortune-tellers as there are for SaladShooters and Veg-O-Matics. The less predictable things are, the more people want to know the future. Perversely, the more mistaken the soothsayers, the more business they get. Prophecy's like gambling: the more you miss the more you hope for a strike. I'll make one sure bet, though: this year, like the last, they will all be wrong.

The Clinton Age: How Old Are You?

I am the same age as the president of the United States. This is very weird. I don't feel grown-up enough to be president. I don't even think I'm old enough to be an office manager at Kinko's. In fact, I don't think I'm old enough to be *any* kind of authority figure. This may be personal, but it's also generational. I don't have any problem seeing people much *younger* than myself being in charge. I always thought that the generation just after ours, the kids of the seventies, were prematurely old. My own philosophy was that you should let your parents take care of you until your kids are old enough to. I know, that's so *irresponsible. . . .*

Ah well, I'm an extremist, and it didn't work out that way, anyway. But the main virtue of my postwar generation was that we were Young with a capital Y. And the main feature of capital-Y Youth is Energy. As William Blake said, "Energy is Eternal Delight." We deployed our energy mainly to the purpose of seceding from old age. We grew up thinking that all authority figures were despicable old men who waged war. We were done with war—period—and we were going to stay young forever, and long after everyone else.

The generation just before us had its youthful energy stolen by fascist and communist ideologies. Those who survived the war, men like Reagan and Bush, never stopped fighting the war that killed their youth. The generation that came after us, the Reagan-Bush kids, had *their* youthful energy stolen by these anxious old men. So there we were, forever young, right between the old men of the past and the old men of the future. When Bill Clinton said that time had come to stop using "us" versus "them," because we've nearly "them'd" ourselves to death, he was referring as much to an internal tension in himself as to the country at large. To our generation, which thought itself younger than any other, presidents were always and forever automatically older. They were "them"s. It's weird to watch "us" become "them"s. It's scary, too. The easiest way to keep that fear at bay is to say the "them"s ought not to exist anymore. It's only "us" now. Of course, the *really* young kids don't believe it for a second. To them, we are just old "them"s with some odd scruples about it.

We Have a Right to Gloat

The election's been over for a while, but I'm still high. Americans went to the polls and voted for the separation of church and state. Thank God. Hallelujah. This is still a great country. For several years now I've had the growing suspicion that we were turning into Iran with mullahs Falwell, Robertson, Swaggart, Bakker, et al., ready to start telling us all how to live and killing us if we didn't listen. The mullahs had spread their evil wings over almost everything that makes life worthwhile. They started invading our homes and telling us what to do in bed. They insinuated themselves into the private thoughts of women to dictate to them what they should do with their bodies. They tried to tell us what not to listen to on our own music boxes. To control what we read in our schools. They tried to banish and punish the artists of this nation for what they painted, wrote, or said.

They didn't always say it in plain words, but they worked relentlessly to divide us by our beliefs, our comportment, our sexuality, our thoughts. They created the atmosphere for the appearance of David Duke and Pat Buchanan. Racist churches, Jesus-worshiping Nazi enclaves, Christian Aryan brotherhoods, and other Lord-approved hate mongers sprouted like poisonous mushrooms after a good acid rain in the land of Bush, Helms, and the mullahs. While they tried to dismantle the Bill of Rights and make us fearful and guilty, they lavishly wallowed in the sins they castigated. One after another, the mullahs went down in sex scandals, money scandals, betrayals too numerous to list, and plain disregard for decent people. They preached so-called morality while robbing, cheating, and lying every time they opened their mouths. I know it's not nice to kick people when they are down. But I can't help it. I've earned the right to gloat for a while, and so have most Americans. Besides, the mullahs aren't out of the picture. They are growing new heads in their holes as I speak.

Advice to the New Chief:
Inauguration Day, 1993

My advice to the new chief is as follows:

Be sure to carry a tool kit with you at all times. In the next years everything is going to fall apart. The Japanese televisions that have so successfully sold you will fizz out within weeks of the inauguration. The Japanese cars carrying everyone to work they don't want to do will quit in the middle of colossal traffic jams that will take a major miracle to untangle. The Hong Kong–made music boxes and CD players that keep our youth from rioting will quit, and there will be a deadly silence in which—for the first time in their consumers' lives—our children will hear the horrifying but tonic emptiness of reality. Next, the toasters and blenders will go, leaving America truly defenseless in the suburban morning. After that, the mechanical birds that populate trees and answering-machine tapes will go out with a screech. Digital watches, disturbed by the magnetic pulse created by the other thingamajigs conking out, will sputter and go blank at once. If the surge of anxiety created by the sudden disappearance of time is not immediately checked, many of us will turn to stone wherever we are, in supermarkets and stock markets. Only the homeless in the inner city, wearing discard spring-operated timepieces, will know the time, though it will be of no use to them.

But the self-destruction of objects will be as nothing compared to the self-destruction of the delicate mechanisms of federation that now hold many so-called countries together. The Soviet Union, Yugoslavia, and India will break into a whole lot of pieces. China, Spain, Italy, Romania, Iraq, Turkey, and Britain will break into two or three big but unfriendly chunks. Here in the United States there will be outbreaks of sudden bioregionalism, which will cause wide east-west, south-north splits along natural boundaries that will completely disregard the intricate artifice of motor-caused infrastructure. The only thing holding the world together, toxins and commerce, will experience serious disruptions. And finally, people themselves will crack, because the things and places that glued them will be broken.

It is going to take a big tool kit, Mr. President. I, for one, am going completely manual.

The Dearth of Enemies

Everywhere I turn I hear that we've run out of enemies. The Pentagon worries about its big nukes, and says that dope dealers are the new enemy, but you can't use nukes against twin-engine Cessnas. Scholars who made careers out of reading between Russian lines wander befuddled about the ivy halls. Spy novelists are committing suicide. Exiled writers who trafficked in despair can go home again. Censored writers behind the old iron curtain can't think of anything to write about now that censorship's gone. It's all very sad, until you realize that we've only run out of *familiar* enemies, the enemies we knew so well they defined us. Let's face it, we were fond of our enemies, we felt for them the affection you feel for anything you've been living with for a long time. It's hard to feel the same passionate hatred for pesticides that you used to feel for Ceausescu. It would be nice to be able to turn one's full hostility toward such things as pollution, hunger, disease, and corruption, but they don't seem quite as *big* as communism, censorship, and the Gulag, if you know what I mean. They also aren't as simple as those old things. They are strangely connected; it's hard to know who the "us"es and the "them"s are. The age of clear heroes and unambiguous good and evil is gone.

The Third World must be mightily worried about seeing the big boys being chummy now, and confused. They know that the lions haven't really lain down with the lambs, they've only lain down with other lions. The lambs of the world are still scared. They would like us to adopt *their* enemies, to make us feel as they do about disease, poverty, and illiteracy. But how can they make them unambiguous enough for us so that we could feel like cowboy heroes riding in mean and getting out clean? The entertainment value of Third World suffering just isn't that great. Neither is the military threat. "Libya," a Pentagon spokesman said, "has more tanks than France and Britain." Wow! That certainly justifies a new arms race.

Perhaps, just perhaps, instead of looking for new enemies, we ought to look at how best to make new friends. Once we become familiar with them, we might begin to feel rightly that their enemies are our enemies as well. At the moment, the main enemy is right beside us: it's racism, our oldest family pet.

The Soldier of the Future

There is a picture in *Time* of the soldier of the future. This high-tech
creature resembling an early Wells Martian is accoutred in the latest
Pentagon fashions. He sports a helmet of high-impact-resistant Kevlar
with a short-range radio phone in it; a polarized visor to protect against
laser beams, equipped with toxic chemicals-and-gas detectors; night
goggles with infrared lenses for seeing in the dark; ID tags that are really
microchips imbedded in the molars that can be read by "scanners" for
complete medical and personal history; a gun that fires darts more effec-
tive than bullets, which open in midair; shirt and trousers that change
colors like a chameleon; and boots with inflatable aircushions in the
soles, real fighting Reeboks.

That's as complete and as expensive a soldier as you're likely to get.
The only problem is, he's all wrong for the wars of the future, or even
the wars of the present. Both the war on drugs and the war on art require
a different kind of fighting man. The war-on-drugs soldier, for instance,
would be wearing a disco ball on his head, equipped with biofeedback
helmet for sobriety control, a microchip imbedded in the tongue for
protection against gruel-lacing, clothes that *flash* colors, and a weapon
that laughs like a ventriloquist hyena while firing lit cigarettes and
bourbon sprays. The war-on-art soldier is a different creature yet. He
would be clothed entirely in swirling tobacco leaves, while wearing a
Jesse Helms face mask with monoblinders, padded sensor gloves
equipped with sex-organ hollows for palpating canvas and marble, ID
tags imbedded in the brain for detection of unapproved ideological contents, shoes trained to smell flag desecration, and an old-fashioned
grenade launcher to take care immediately of unauthorized art. It is
highly advisable for the war-on-art soldier to patrol bohemia together
with the war-on-drugs soldiers, since the enemy is often one and the
same. These soldiers should be better educated than today's fighting

men, because in addition to combat duty, they will be called upon to raid drug- and sex-influenced art from the past, such as Keats and Coleridge poetry and Michelangelo statues and church ceilings. When raiding the past, they will use National-Endowment-for-the-Arts-Jesse-Helms-issue-memory-blanket shooters.

So forget the Russians, Pentagon, and get with the program!

Trouble at the
Cultural Cantina

Part IV

Art, the Enemy

Listen to Pat Buchanan, presidential candidate, describe artists: they are the ones who set out to "injure, wound, offend, and insult Americans of traditional values, Christians and conservatives. . . . I don't care what they do in their garrets with their precious bodily fluids and their bullwhips, but I tell you when I'm president we won't be paying for it with American tax dollars."

That's as fine a volley as any Know-Nothing has ever loosed against the enemy. Let's take a closer look. Artists live in "garrets," those anti-social, syphilis- and TB-infected French dwellings of the nineteenth century where Mr. Buchanan's imagination last envisioned them. The choice of the word *garret* isn't incidental: it's related to garroting and the guillotine, which is what Pat would like to use on the critters, and to the French, which are one more ethnic group—in addition to Jews and Japs—which can come in handy should the xenophobia get thin or repetitive. But repetition is Mr. Buchanan's least worry. He updates these diseased French, syphilitic, antisocial garret-dwellers by giving them bullwhips and precious body fluids with which to make art. After all, why give them money for paint when they'll end up cutting up their wrists and using blood anyway? Good thinking, Mr. Buchanan. One doesn't need to wonder where Pat Buchanan's ideas of art and artists come from. They come fully clipped from that mental giant of pundit lit, Mr. James Kilpatrick, who has just conceded that as to controversial art "those of us in the media never have been able adequately to describe some of this stuff."

Jay Leno said on the "Tonight Show" that there is some controversy as to what to do with Hitler's bunker in Berlin. Some want it destroyed. Some want it kept as a historical reminder. Pat Buchanan wants it for campaign headquarters. I recommend the latter, where sayings like the one about the "garret" should feel right at home.

The Arts and the Public

What makes a pundit like James Kilpatrick go absolutely bazongas when it comes to art? So outraged is he by certain art performances and works that he would have this great nation of ours offer no public support for the arts whatsoever. He calls for the abolishing of the National Endowment for the Arts. He wants artists to go out like business gladiators into the marketplace where all good Americans are, tearing each others' heads off over shoes, razor blades, and soft drinks. Let artists, if they are any good, fight like Coke and Pepsi.

Mr. Kilpatrick, and his guru Jesse Helms, whose wisdom he is channeling, would have us taxpayers spared from art. Never mind the sad fact that the entirety of tax money our government spends on art is half that of the city of Berlin, or one-eighth that of France. But then, of course, we wouldn't want to be Berliners: decadent or, God forbid, sophisticated, or like the French, by gosh, who don't wear underpants. No, sir. Our tax money ought to go where it belongs: to meganukes and missiles, *tobaki*, and our friends Egypt, Israel, and Pakistan.

But the issue isn't really money. It's morality, the last-resort battleground of the panicked right. It's flags being insulted, lovemaking being pictured, genitals being exposed. In Romania last December, they cut a hole in the flag, people probably made love on top of tanks, and they showed bare breasts on television. That was a revolution, and if we know what's good for us, we don't want one of those happening right here. No, sir. We want people to go to sleep after the eleven-o'clock news, and we want them to die for the flag. Art is something that often takes place after dark, making people both immoral and sleepless, and dying for the flag is sublime, even though most Americans die of boredom. Mr. Kilpatrick and Senator Helms may hate art for yet another reason: they don't understand it. They fail to see why anything more challenging than a wall sampler that says HOME SWEET HOME or a good repro of Remington has to exist at all. They know that most people feel condescended to by art, insulted by what they can't understand, and mad as hell about naked people that make them feel fat and ugly. People love their TV, and this kind of art just isn't on it. The pundit and the senator are making a stand for the public, all right.

Obscenity in Search of Art

I got thrown off the Greyhound bus by a scab driver for pointing out that it's illegal to have old people standing crammed in the aisles while you drive ten miles over the speed limit. And not just old people, come to think of it, you can break all the bones of the young ones too if you have to brake suddenly. "It's obscene!" I said, and the driver braked suddenly and shouted, "Get off my bus!" I could hear bones cracking everywhere. So I got off the bus because I had called the situation obscene, which is one word that will get you in trouble everywhere today. Televangelist Pat Robertson, whose faithful ride the Greyhound in droves, found an obscene puppet show in Atlanta. The puppets were allegedly having oral sex while being funded by the NEA. Now how do puppets have oral sex? Only your televangelist knows for sure: he's pulled the string on more puppets than Greyhound breaks bones. At the Last Judgment all these sex-puppets will be standing in the aisles of hell waiting to have their funding cut.

Speaking of the Last Judgment, Michelangelo's, it turned out that, upon restoration, the picture was "even dirtier than the ceiling," according to the art critics. The nudity of Michelangelo's figures shocked church officials, and in 1564 Pope Pius IV ordered artist Daniele da Volterra—under penalty of withdrawing his grant—to paint over the offending private parts with veils and loincloths. The offending scene, of course, was *The Expulsion from the Garden of Eden*, the only authorized version of which is now in North Carolina. It's called *Expulsion from the Tobacco Garden*, and it shows two horny teenagers being expelled by Senator Helms for eating figs instead of smoking Marlboros. They had a public survey in North Carolina, where they asked people if Michelangelo was: a) a painter, b) a turtle. Most people said turtle, which means Senator Helms will be reelected. These same voters also believe that the practices of the Greyhound company are not obscene, that puppets have oral sex while on grants, and that televangelists should be tax-exempt. Verily, it's a wondrous world out there.

Americans and the Arts

A recent Harris poll on Americans and the arts is full of bad news. Since 1974 Americans have lost 37 percent of their leisure time. Attendance for six of nine surveyed arts activities has declined sharply. Only art museums, movies, and records have gained. Classical music, ballet, theater, pop concerts, and opera are losing audiences. Alarming as these facts sound, I can't bring myself to mourn. Most of these surveyed arts are the traditional mainstays of so-called high culture, which has been in crisis for a long time now. Not surveyed are the new and popular forms of art: poetry readings, experimental theater, art-gallery attendance, art/political happenings, folk festivals, summer gatherings. The years of the Reagan era have seen a return to privacy, a closure of private life from public life, new, sharp distinctions between social classes, and consequently a resurfacing of the old divisions between "highbrow" and "lowbrow" art. It is no wonder that the popularity of highbrow arts is declining: people are shying away from the entertainments of the rich. At the same time the vitality of the underground arts—which are truly popular—remains undiminished. There is also a large disaffected audience that simply doesn't know where to find living art. The decline measured by the Harris poll has less to do with the loss of leisure time than with the quality of the times, and the suppression of experiment in favor of nineteenth-century art forms that please ignorant rich patrons. The audiences of 1973 lived in an outdoor theater because life after Vietnam and during Watergate had become a public performance. The audience of 1988 lives in a hothouse. But there is life outside the glass walls. The only problem is finding it.

In July I attended a little-known event at the Jack Kerouac Poetry School of the Naropa Institute in Boulder, Colorado. Poets and scholars came from far places to discuss Dada and Surrealism, two literary and artistic movements that took the world by storm in the first three decades of our century, before World War II. Surrealism and Dada were not simple aesthetic revolutions. Their practitioners proposed no less than the overthrow of the stranglehold of scientific reason over the mind of the West, that mind which has given us World Wars I and II and still has us paralyzed in the grip of a permanent frozen war. The Surrealists proposed to do this through the use of dreams and the unconscious, through spontaneity and laughter, and through the formation of human communities based on these personal human facts. But their most radical proposal was the abolition of labor, a goal they shared with other utopian projects. "Eroticize the proletariat!" cried Gherasim Luca, the author of the Surrealists' "Erotic Manifesto." Today, much of the violent imagery of Surrealism has been incorporated by advertising and TV. MTV can deliver more Surrealism in one minute than André Breton did in ten poems. But the Surrealism of the media has no more revolutionary content than Cornflakes, which are another movement altogether: Cerealism.

If anything, the radical spirit of the Surrealist revolt is even more urgent today, when we live in a state of permanent extortion by the military powers of the world. More than two-thirds of our labor goes into the war machine. While the American people have lost 37 percent of their leisure time, the competition for this leisure has grown hundredfold. The liberation of human beings from work has not come to pass. But we need it more than ever, just as, more than ever, we must begin listening to our dreams and trusting our own reality, surreal though it may be, instead of the one handed to us by the state.

"God gave people language so that they could make Surrealist use of it." The French poet André Breton wrote those words in 1924 in "The First Surrealist Manifesto," the document that launched the Surrealist revolution in Europe and should have changed forever the way we look at our world. But sixty-four years after André Breton wrote those words, things are much worse. At the same time that our leisure time goes to the dogs, other studies estimate that the average person spends five years of his or her life waiting in lines, six months staring at traffic lights, one year looking for lost objects, six years eating, eight months opening junk mail, four years doing housework, and two years trying to return telephone calls to people who never seem to be in. And if that wasn't enough, most Americans are not happy with their bodies: women want more muscles, men want more hair on their chests.

The art of life is in worse shape than the life of the arts. The solution however, *is* art. And the understanding that no "entertainment" could ever replace the rich inner life of humans who crave more than cornflakes for their minds.

Culture Stamps

I talked to this French guy who couldn't understand food stamps. I explained to him that they give people food stamps instead of money so that people would actually buy food instead of movie tickets or art. "I see," he said, "and you have culture stamps for movies or art?" he asked.

"No," I said, "but it's a brilliant idea." Just think of it. All that wrangling over the National Endowment for the Arts would be over if there was a culture stamp program. Every citizen who could demonstrate a need for art could get culture stamps. They could use these to go to events sponsored by nonprofit corporations: independent movies, experimental plays, poetry readings, art shows, dance recitals, concerts. The artists would get all the profits from the culture stamps. The government wouldn't have to decide what art to fund: it would be up to the people to spend their culture stamps on anything they liked. Popular but noncommercial artists would make some money, maybe even a living. Others would still have to do whatever they do now. The art bureaucracies would disappear, the panels of grant-dispensing experts would vanish, and art would become truly popular. And how, you might ask, would one go about demonstrating a need for art? Simple. If you don't make enough money to see, hear, or watch at least four events a week you're below the cultural standard. And just like food stamps, which do not allow you to purchase liquor or cigarettes, you cannot use your culture stamps on Hollywood, Broadway, or TV entertainment. I'm willing to bet here that culture stamps would revive the arts, the cities, and the minds of the public. And best of all, this program would shut up James Kilpatrick and Patrick Buchanan, who've been beating the dead horse of the National Endowment for the Arts into a truly tedious pulp.

Should this idea fly, we'll have a Frenchman to thank for it. They always did have good ideas for Americans.

Art for Bums' Sake

My people, who sleep on the benches at the Greyhound station, had a hell of a time trying to get their rest the other night. There was loud music, screamin', dancin', and hollerin' into the wee hours, way past even the time when the last bus bound for Laredo pulled out. My people, the bench denizens, did appreciate that the music was blues-jazz of the highest quality, and truly they had nothing against drifting to sleep on the rich, dark waves of Ms. Marva Wright's songs, but they *were* bothered by the presence of so many well-to-do, well-dressed, would-be art lovers, philanthropes, and investors in their midst. They weren't bothered because the hoi polloi were there, in their bedroom, but because they were *separated* from each other, believe it or not, by a curtain.

This curtain made it impossible for my people to see all that elegance, appreciate the dancin' glamour, and bum a little spare change. Spare change, of the kind called "funds," was in fact at stake here because the party was thrown by a city arts group to raise those particular funds for themselves in order to get themselves a new building. The arts outfit was, in other words, homeless. Only they called it "quarterless." Now, my people on the benches have also made an art of the difficult job of living homeless. They travel hundreds of weary miles looking for work, collecting bottles and bags, standing in line for a charity lunch, and defending their benches at the Greyhound terminal. They also have one or more philosophies that go with that art, and they gladly tell them to the Laredo-bound folk in exchange for a quarter or a cigarette. In other words, my people of the benches do everything artists do except for the language they speak. My people say, "Spare some change?" while the arts people say, "Raise my funds." Now it would seem a small matter, but that's how it is today in America. If you're a homeless person you get to stay up all night listening to the rich dance for a homeless institution. But if you call it by name, they'll run from you. And just so they make sure you don't do it, they put a curtain up so you disappear. They're taking down the Iron Curtain in Europe, but the art curtain's going up as we speak.

Doozy Time for Symbols

Hey, I said to my friend, it's almost midnight and it's still light outside. Yeah, he said, and the city's more polluted than usual. When we took a closer look we saw little clumps of people everywhere, at café tables and at street corners, gathered around ashtrays and trash cans burning American flags. Which explained it. Yeah, it's a bad time for symbols, said my friend. Just the other day in Dhaka, Bangladesh, 300 people armed with sticks damaged shops owned by a Canadian shoe manufacturer because he was selling shoes with Arabic script on the soles. Arabic script is holy and should not be taken in vain. The government promptly announced that it confiscated all "blasphemous shoes in retail outlets across the country." My friend and I promptly burned our shoes. That added considerably to the smoke and confusion.

Symbols are funny things: whenever one of them is upset all the other ones go crazy, too, as if they were connected by nerves across the world. In Pasadena, Texas, school officials banned the peace sign because it looks like an upside-down broken cross signifying the defeat of Christianity. A twelve-year-old in danger of having his T-shirt disallowed said, "If they ban peace symbols, they'll have to ban basic geometry because of all its lines and circles." And he's right: symbols are everywhere. Nature, as Baudelaire said, is a temple full of symbols. This world's but a veil. Words are symbols for things. Things, even the most humble, are symbols for forces. Forks and spoons symbolize civilization, for instance, while the human body itself is but a collection of symbols pointing to the basics of life. Nazis thought Jews stood for evil so they started burning them. Once you start, it's hard to stop. Nothing is what it seems. It's insidious. If you let people burn flags, next thing they'll do is burn even more potent symbols: the Coca-Cola logo, or McDonald's arches, or the MGM lion. And after that, they'll go for the whole symbolic shebang: words, people, kitchen utensils. Everything was pretty quiet until recently, but it all started again with Procter & Gamble, if you want my honest opinion, said my friend. Their satanic symbol got into everyone's skin via soap and now people have gone symbol crazy.

That could be, I said. These damn shoes are hard to burn!

A Different Air

Postmodernism is definitely over. My friend Philip buried it at Graceland, where he stopped on his way to New Orleans. Expecting to be amused, he found himself embarrassed instead. The floor-to-ceiling-shag-carpeted playroom where the King frolicked failed to amuse him. Nor was he particularly thrilled when the tour guide proudly proclaimed that the King had picked out the grotesque neo-Tahiti *meubles* all by himself in less than half an hour. Elvis is really dead, says Philip. Before you hasten to dismiss my friend as just another incipient grown-up losing his sense of humor, please note that Philip is one with the culture of his time. The day he turned eighteen he came back sick from Mexico and threw up in a water fountain at O'Hare Airport. The newspaper reported that very same day that Syd Vicious, the leader of the English punks, had inaugurated his American tour by throwing up in the water fountain at San Francisco International Airport. If Philip is losing his sense of humor, so is the world. There are a few of us out here who are perfectly synchronized. Momentous events find us at crucial moments. Philip saw the postmodern age from *initio* to *finis*.

What happens now that the saving Sneer is gone? Well, for one thing, reality is coming back. It's not the same reality, mind you, that was sent into exile by television and fashion for ten years or so. It's a much sicker specimen, pale from living in the frigid basements of the image police, weak from doing hard labor in the lower reaches of the collective unconscious. For one thing, it's not coming back looking real, in that TV sense where a horse looks just like a horse. No, it's coming back looking awkward and absurd like a horse drawn by a palsied hand. The day after Graceland, Philip reports seeing a man walking on a stretch of interstate highway with three huge cabbages on each arm, two other cabbages speared on the end of two knives, and four smaller cabbages in a sack tied to his waist. Philip slowed down just enough to hear the man say in a voice gruff with the return of the real, "Today we have cabbages!"

Indeed. Until something better comes along, today we have cabbages.

Enter This Contest

The land is rife these days with art and writing contests. A major part of the American dream is now given over to winning fame for creative endeavors, and its practitioners are as relentless in its pursuit as their forefathers were in pursuit of land, cows, cash, and suburban digs. In those days, the arts were a crazy luxury, but they were cheap. Even a decade ago you could be a writer if you had a cold-water flat, a Bic pen, and a paper bag. It was dearer to be a painter, but you could always mix your own until you became addicted to the fumes and evanesced like Van Gogh into the Japanese future. That future is here now and it ain't cheap. A single, smallish painting now costs about $100 to make, that cold-water flat is about $1,000 a month, and if you want to enter a contest you have to pay a fee. These fees are for judges to look at your expensive slides and photocopied, word-processed writing, and they've been going up. From five to ten to twenty to thirty dollars.

The judges are rarely famous. They are generally artists and writers who are making a living judging other artists and writers for a fee. If you win, they put your painting in a group show or your writing in an obscure magazine and that's your fame. The only people who'll see or read you are the people for whom you buy the magazine or whom you invite to the opening. In other words, you make the thing, you pay the fee, you get the crowd, and then you feel famous. It is easier, methinks, to take the thousand or so bucks that you spend doing all this and paying ten strangers off the street never to forget you. That's pure fame, unattached to an object, and it's good forever. At the rate contest fees are rising, the $1,000 ante couldn't be far in the future. If you are poor and talented, go into engineering. You can't afford to make art because it's too expensive to be poor nowadays. And if you still crave fame, there are always the real contests: the ones on cereal boxes. Or you can live vicariously by putting up your children for Cutest Baby Picture.

From Euphoria to Depression in Three Years, or From the Suicide of Communism to the Rebirth of Fascism

Part V

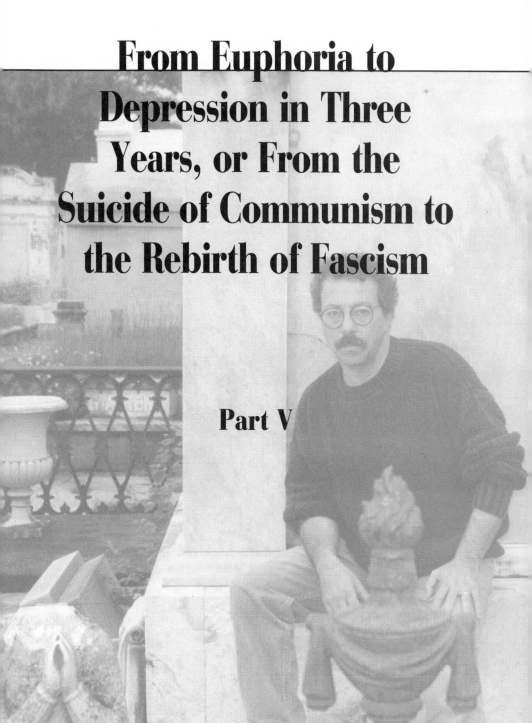

Freedom Is Home Cooking

I've been dancing since six o'clock this morning, when the phone first started ringing. Ceausescu's bloody regime is gone—I still can't believe it! The old proverb is true: dawn comes even after the longest night. Last night—December 21, 1989—was the longest night of the year, and it looked for a while that on the blood-spattered streets of Romania dawn was never going to come again. But it did come this morning, and the Romanian people have given themselves the greatest present in a quarter of a century of unhappy history: freedom. For me, personally, it's even more than a Christmas gift because yesterday was my birthday, and nobody ever gave me a gift this wonderful.

I was born in 1946, the year communism came to Romania on the turrets of Russian tanks. My mother named me Andrei so that the Russians wouldn't harm us. The Russians didn't, but the misery of life under two consecutive hard-line Stalinist regimes did, and in 1966 we were forced to leave our homeland. There is an untranslatable Romanian word that expresses with great precision the kind of unbearable longing and nostalgia that grips one's heart when thinking of home. The word is *dor*. Nostalgia for the beautiful medieval town of Sibiu in Transylvania where I grew up, longing for certain golden autumn afternoons at an outdoor café, drinking new wine with friends, all of us young, intoxicated with poetry and song. I miss the smells of flowering linden trees, the blue reflections of deep mountain snow in the evenings, the old peasant villages that Ceausescu's insanity almost wiped off the face of the earth.

I heard someone say today on Romanian television that the word *comrade* was dead in Romania. It's about time. Like all the other Orwellian speech of the soon-to-be-dust tyrants of the world, *comrade* has meant exactly its opposite for forty-five years. Few things are certain in this life, but good things are even less certain than the few that are. The next months will be critical for the Romanian people. They need the goodwill and support of the world. Personally, I have my bag packed.

I've had it packed for twenty years.

Who Are the Elect-ED?

I tried to call a friend in Romania for about three weeks before the election. Every time, I heard anywhere from two to four clicks and then a series of melodious pings followed by a recorded message informing me that the country of my "choice" was "not available." Well, a country isn't like an item on a menu, so I got the creeps. I imagined a big hole where the available country might have been. I called at high noon and in the dead of night. My country was unavailable. I got the idea somehow that Romania may just not be available until after the election.

Two hours after the polls closed, and I heard the projections on CNN that Iliescu and the National Salvation Front won big, my call went right through. My friend on the other end was all excited. "How were the elections?" I asked him. "Nobody knows the results yet!" he shouted, though I could hear him fairly well. "Yes, they do," I said, "Exit polls say that Iliescu got about seventy-eight percent, and the Front got sixty-five percent of the vote!" My friend was silent, pondering, no doubt, the strangeness of my telling him what the results were from many thousands of miles away. After I hung up, the strangeness of it seized me as well. In the largely unavailable country that he lives in, phone calls and news still travel at the pace decreed by whoever controls the ancient technologies of communication. Now that Mr. Iliescu and the Salvation Front are firmly in power, are they ready to speed things up? Do they want to make their country available? For forty-five years Romania was an untrustworthy member of the international community, a place where phones were tapped, news suppressed, communications monitored. For those forty-five years Romania's foreign policy consisted of putting on a good face, stealing industrial secrets, and selling anything to anyone who cared to buy. That will all have to change if the phones start working. If all that changes, it will be unnecessary to keep on a good face. Instead of a hole in the map or a gap in the menu, Romania will be there, warts and all.

The King of Romania

Salvador Dali once said that he loved kings because they were surrealist. He also said that they were divine, and that monarchies will surely return to Europe in the near future. Soon after the Surrealist painter announced his approval of kings, Juan Carlos took back the throne in Spain. There is yet no Bourbon king in France, but a score of deposed monarchs have risen from their coffins to call for their thrones. King Michael of Romania, a Swiss businessman from the Hohenzollern family, is ready to take a campaign swing through the fiefdom his family used to plunder. He was told to wait until after the election, which is only right because kings shouldn't be elected, they should be chosen.

Michael's family took the throne of Romania in the nineteenth century after the three Romanian principalities couldn't agree on a native king. They imported an impoverished German Hohenzollern, who promptly proceeded to get rich. The subsequent rulers wrote poetry and drove fast cars. Queen Marie was a glamorous creature of the 1920s who had a museum dedicated to her in the United States by a lumber baron who fell madly in love with her. King Carol, her son, fell in love with a red-haired Jewish beauty named Magda Lupescu, and briefly had to abdicate his throne to follow Magda to Paris, where they stayed up late and had lots of champagne. During this episode he installed his fourteen-year-old nephew Michael on the Romanian throne. When things went awry between him and Magda, he took back the throne. But the fascists had come to power by then and he didn't get to be much of a king. Michael also didn't get to be much of a king, because the communists came soon after and sent him packing. He had very large Swiss suitcases, incidentally! That would seem to be the end of the story, but everywhere I go these days, people ask me about the king. "What are his chances?" said a reasonable-looking someone after a talk. A few weeks ago, I would have said, "About the same as mine or yours?" But I'm not so sure. Radu Florescu, the man who wrote the Dracula books, told me that if elections were held today King Michael would get 16 percent of the vote in Romania. Maybe Dali was right. Surrealism is the new realism.

Romanian Money

I'm going to tell you a deep, dark secret. When I was about ten years old I went to a Pioneer summer camp in the Carpathian Mountains. Pioneers were communist Boy Scouts—we wore little red kerchiefs around our necks and did stuff in the woods.

My father came to visit one weekend. It was the first time I'd seen him in about a year, so I was quite thrilled. We did some father-son stuff like kick a ball for five minutes, and then I watched him smoke. When he finished his cigarettes, he gave me 200 leis and left. Two hundred leis was a lot of money in Romania in those days. An engineer made almost 1,000 leis a month, and engineers made more money than anyone.

The camp had these scary outhouses deep in the woods. After my father left, I had to run to the bathroom. Once there, I realized to my horror that there wasn't any toilet paper. There I was, a young Pioneer in the scary Carpathian night with 200 leis in my pocket and no way to clean myself. I was faced with a terrible dilemma: use either my father's money or the red kerchief around my neck, which represented everything communists held most sacred, for toilet paper. It was a confrontation between family and state. It was also a clash between capitalism and communism, the cold war in a nutshell. Father-state, who was every-where, and father-father, who was nowhere, faced each other suddenly under my distressed bottom.

In the end I chose to use my father's money. There *was* a practical reason: the worn-out, threadbare bills were better suited for the purpose than the red kerchief. But, in the end, it was a fateful choice. It explains how I feel about many things, money and fathers among them. And now that communism's gone and history has used our red Pioneers' kerchiefs to wipe its problematic self, I get the news from Romania that the government is "recycling the national currency as toilet paper." "Every week," the report says, "five to six tons of shredded banknotes are sent to a toilet-paper factory in Bucharest."

Everything that happens happens because a young boy on a scary toilet seat somewhere makes a critical decision.

Communists and Shrimp

I was peeling shrimp for the gumbo and the thought occurred to me that peeling shrimp is about the hardest job in the world except maybe for being a hard-line communist these days. The first few dozen are not so hard, but around the 140th shrimp your fingers start to chap and you get sick of pulling and yanking. Likewise it must have looked to old-line communists that the aberrations brought on by reformers would soon stop and things would get back to normal. But around the 140th reform, especially in Hungary, they must have felt like their sides had burst and the waters of ideology were gushing out to drain on the ground.

I know what you're thinking: you can't push this analogy between communists and shrimp this far. It's absurd. Maybe. But a shrimp always looked to me like a hard-line communist, even when I was a kid: all stretched out and buglike when in power, all curled up and pink and scared of lemon juice when out of favor. The best evidence I've yet had for this seemingly incongruous pairing of commie and shrimp comes from my friend Sandie Castle's play *What the Shadow Knows*. In it, this old-style radical is trying to reform a young working-class girl by bringing her Marxist books to read. But all she wants, like most sensible people, is a TV. But he keeps bringing her books and begging her to tell him filthy stories from her less-than-bourgeois past. It's the only way, you see, that he can have sex.

Something like that is happening in the communist countries now. The old Party hard-liners keep bringing out their well-thumbed Lenins and Marxes but all the young ones want is TVs. Also, the only thing that would please the old ones would be mass confessions of guilt (or "self-criticism" sessions, as they used to be called), but no one is cooperating. This leads to a shrimplike shriveling of the hard-liners. You see? There is nothing in the world that can keep prawns and Marxists apart. I, for one, am overjoyed to have the shrimp safely in the gumbo already, where they belong, and the old-time hard-liners retired in their shells, where they too belong. Eventually, everything becomes food.

Soviet Maps:
Reality and Its Next of Kin

For fifty years the Soviet Union has deliberately falsified all public maps of the country, misplacing rivers and streets, distorting boundaries, and omitting geographical features, on orders from the secret police. In other words, for fifty years, most Russians had no idea where they were really living. They had no idea why the river they always knew as flowing north flowed officially south or why the streets they were living on were either missing or misnamed. Hello, George Orwell, wherever you are!

Maps, of course, are symbolic representations of the real world, but these Soviet maps are symbols of something entirely different. Instead of representing the features of the geographical world, these maps represent the features of the police mind. The Soviet Union, thus, seems to have existed on two simultaneous planes: the hidden real one and the official fake one. These maps symbolize Soviet life more accurately than anything else I can think of. For several generations, Soviet citizens were asked to believe in the image of a phantom ideological reality over their own experience. For fifty years, relatively sober people pretended to agree with things all of them knew to be untrue. Symbolism enforced by the police eventually congealed into a kind of mass delusion that Gorbachev had a hard time dislodging. Correcting the geographical maps was a relatively simple task compared to the fantastic job of surveying and removing the falsehoods, delusions, and detours of the many historical, psychological, sociological, and economic maps that covered every aspect of Soviet life. History alone will have to be rewritten from the beginning, a task of enormous complexity and tremendous consequences. The first timid attempts in this direction have already resulted in nationalist ferment in the Asian republics, new religious revivals in Russia, and such extraordinary revelations as Brezhnev's clinical death six years before he gave up power (and simultaneously, once again, the ghost).

Creating an enforceable reality took a long time. Soon after the triumph of the Russian Revolution, its leaders began mistaking symbols for reality. Geography was the obvious place to start. They changed the names of everything: Petrograd became Leningrad, the tsar-grads became commissar-grads, mountains and rivers took on new revolutionary monickers. The Bolshevik Revolution, like the French Revolution before it, tried to erase geography and history by manipulating language. The passage from idealism to terror did not take long. What began as poetic license soon became a license to kill. Reality is no great strain on language: from new names to false maps is but a pirouette of the pen. Real places, real human beings, all fall in the gaps between words. Between the analytical passion of Karl Marx and a Marxist society ruled by a dead man stretches a vast sea of words, remarkable for their indifference to truth and reality.

I was born and raised in Romania, a Soviet satellite where the cynicism of official language attained such heights that no one heard a single word uttered by officials, printed in the newspapers, or splattered on billboards. Our own reality as human beings had as little to do with that language as it had with the mumblings of fish in a distant sea.

I'm glad that glasnost has come to map-making in the Soviet world, but I fear that it is only one more symbolic gesture. After having been lied to for so long, people will have great difficulty knowing exactly where they are, no matter what the new maps tell them. They will not trust them. The habit of cynicism (a health measure under the circumstances) is more deeply ingrained than the hopeful pronouncements of their new ruler. It is easier to correct the maps than to gain the people's trust. Not having used maps in so long, they have learned to navigate by their stomachs: that's one infallible compass.

But let's not congratulate ourselves here in the heart of plenty. For entirely different reasons, Americans also don't know where they are. A poll commissioned for the 100th anniversary of *National Geographic* reveals that a full 50 percent of us can't find New York City on a map, one in four can't find the Pacific Ocean, and the rest don't know north from south, and think that most foreign countries are either in Canada or in Africa.

Now what's the use of correct maps if one can't navigate them? Paradoxically, the freedom to know becomes an overwhelming indifference to reality. The vast menu of consumer society has on it many infinitely more attractive options than mere truth and understanding of the real world. All of us, in the East and the West, are now negotiating the world with our stomachs. The Russians are magnetically attuned to food lines while our true north is the next shopping mall.

But the real world won't go away, whether hidden by the police or by ignorance. The most accurate maps will make but little difference if we do not have the ability to use them intelligently.

Overkill Metaphors

Occasionally, a bit of news is so overwhelmingly metaphorical, it cries for poetic attention. We hear from Moscow, for instance, that the flowers thrown by people mourning the violent demonstrations in Soviet Georgia have absorbed the poison gas used against protesters, and sixty cleanup workers were hospitalized picking them up. It's a fact all right, but the factualness of it is but the seed of its metaphor. Here are flowers, symbols of light and peace, filled with evil poison.

I remember demonstrators at the Pentagon during the Vietnam War putting flowers in the barrels of soldiers' rifles. It was as poignant and sappy an image as the times—and just as unforgettable. People also bring flowers to the dead to symbolize their belief in memory and the continuity of life: they are a fragile reminder of beauty against the terrible facts. When you have a grim fact you put a flower against it and for some reason you don't feel so bad anymore. That reason is metaphor: no matter how final and grim the fact, the fragility and beauty opposing it somehow change the finality and the grimness. But what does it mean when the flowers themselves fill up with the poison of the fact? It is then as if they'd switched sides: instead of serving the symbolic order of good they've gone over to evil. We feel symbolically bereft at that time, a situation more serious in some ways than the actual horror.

But there are farther complications. Government officials in Georgia have so far refused to identify the poison gas so doctors can treat the injured. They will reveal neither the toxic ingredients nor the name of the poison. I very much doubt that this is out of callousness or fear. No, this is denial, pure and simple, of the horror of having violated a symbol. The Soviets are symbol-worshiping people. They display their symbols prominently and proudly, from sickles and hammers to Picasso's peace dove—and they would much rather, I am sure, destroy a person than compromise a symbol. Russian poets are grandly sentimental as well, and something like this can set them—and their numerous readers—on fire for a hundred years. Facts can always be covered up, but messing with symbols can be devastating. This is one story that will one day ascend into myth.

Where We Live

The Soviet Union is no more. It's strange. For the whole of my life the Soviet Union was always there, part of my mental and emotional geography. When I was a schoolboy in Romania I loudly swore allegiance to it. Under our breath some of us cursed it but in a tone of resigned terror. Its eternal nature was not in dispute. We knew that empires had collapsed in the past but that had been long ago, in history.

The communist monolith did not go away when I came to America. *Au contraire*, the Soviet Union was our stodgy official enemy for most of the twentieth century. We based our foreign policy on it. We based our domestic policy in it. It was the springboard for political careers and the excuse for witch-hunts. It was our mirror. The United States, like the USSR, was also founded as a utopia, and the two utopias were mutually exclusive. For some, who found the promises of America disappointing, the USSR held the promise of a different way. They closed their eyes when the utopia's gritty idealism brushed them with its all too real wings. But no matter how we felt about it, one thing was indubitable: the Soviet Union was there, mind-scape, geographical giant straddling continents, locus of ponderous and heavy symbolism, generator of utopian propaganda and sentiment. Among the facts that comprised our picture of the world the Soviet Union was one of the essential ones, a kind of Archimedian support that lent coherence to the others. What, for instance, is one to think of the modern state now in the absence of an ideological enemy? Has it in fact withered (or sizzled) just like Marx predicted? Is there any reason now for the clumsy militarized mechanism of any state? The USSR, that clumsy acronym that was as familiar a part of our speech as WWI, DDT, UN, Ph.D., NATO, or, for that matter US of A, is no longer part of living language. Nor is the geographical entity part of our globe. "America, love it or leave it" and "Go back to Russia," once popular slogans, have become meaningless. If you leave it, where can you go now?

I do not miss the vast concentration camp and the ubiquitous lie that was the USSR. I miss only the certainties of yesteryear. Which were pretty horrific in their seeming coherence.

Missing the Russian Revolution

The 1917 Russian Revolution took ten days to shake the world. But the 1991 unrevolution took less than a week. It was this week, of all weeks, that I went to the woods and I was without a phone, a radio, a newspaper, or a TV. These woods were in the Adirondack Mountains in the very place where Rip Van Winkle slept for 100 years, during which time he missed only the Industrial Revolution. When I woke up, the world was changed just as profoundly. New countries had all but appeared on the map. The bloody utopia that ruled a large chunk of the planet for three quarters of a century was ended in my sleep. And this may be the proper way for a nightmare to end, a nightmare that began in my native Romania the year I was born. I woke to this life as Soviet tanks gave us communism. Now I'm awake again, and it's gone. It makes sense too that 100 Rip Van Winkle years are equal to seven Codrescu days: time's been speeding up, and whatever happens now happens fast.

When nightmares end, all the good dreams that couldn't be dreamed can be dreamed again. The end of communism may mean that socialism, for instance, can be dreamed of again. And so can all the ideas of community that were obscured by the *-ism*. Those new countries on the map can redefine their communities along any lines they choose. There is the danger, of course, inherent in any waking, of disorientation, crankiness, and anger. The desire for revenge, the easy lure of nationalism, the urge to break things may all surge through the escapees of the nightmare. My own urge, however, is to celebrate. During these last two years I have experienced violent, alternating states of hope and despair. The euphoria of the December 1989 revolution in Romania gave up to the bitterness of the stolen revolution of June 1990, the joy of finding my childhood followed by the grief of seeing it under the watch of the secret police, still. I am euphoric again, but I'm not innocent anymore. The sleeper is groggy and the nightmare is stubborn. And maybe I'm not really awake: maybe it's that time between sleep and waking when the monsters still have meat on their bones.

The Mystery of the Disappearance of Communist Ideology

The disappearance of communist ideology is producing more mysteries than explanations—in spite of the appearances. It *appears* to us that the Soviets are giving up communism for capitalism. In reality, the Soviet Communist party and its leaders did not defect to the capitalist camp, they committed ideological suicide. Suicide is not a defection. It's final. Gorbachev abolishing the Party is really Gorbachev abolishing himself *and* his ideological parents, a suicide and a patricide at the same time. Communist history is rife with literal suicide as well, from Vladimir Mayakovski, the poet of the Russian Revolution, who killed himself in disillusionment with Lenin's policies, to the recent suicides of the failed coup leaders.

Suicide, metaphorical and literal, is a measure of the seriousness of the faith that is being abandoned. It also leaves nothing behind. The denial of everything that made up their official existence from birth onward is an eerie moment for the peoples of the collapsed empire. Communism was all they knew, whether they believed in it or not. That it's suddenly gone is a great tear in the fabric of reason. There is a suspended moment occurring now that is not a transition from one thing to another but a gap, a hiatus, another reality. The peoples of Russia and Eastern Europe are living through a scary timelessness when they can see clearly that their world is dead and that nothing has yet come to replace the utopian promises of the suicided ideology, that, in fact, they have been abandoned to their own devices. "The people," who had never been more than a rhetorical figure anyway, are even less than that now. Which is why, in great panic, they are turning to their families and their tribes for reassurance, and not quite turning up to protest coups against Gorbachev. Who wants to clamor for the ghost of a dead utopia when reality itself is yet unborn?

Ukes with Nukes?

A nuclear Ukraine? Ukes with nukes? Give me a break! The Ukraine's desire to keep the Soviet nukes and raise an army makes my hair stand. I mean, what are they going to do with them? Convert Jews at nuke-point? Play nukes with next-door Russia? Finish what Chernobyl started? Chernobyl, you may recall, is Russian for the Evil Star mentioned in the Apocalypse. There might be some Ukrainian priests out there impatient with the pace of developments. Speed up that Apocalypse, will you?

I know it's only human to want to keep what you've got, but these toys are very, very bad. Especially in the hands of a new country with a few hundred years of hurt national pride. I mean, would you hand a baby a nuke after he's just been spanked? I'm convinced that the true insanity boiling in the new nationalist entities and subentities of the old Commie Empire hasn't even been tapped yet. And if the Ukes have nukes what's to stop all the others from wanting some? Why shouldn't the "hyphenated people," as Professor Balzer of Georgetown University calls them, have some too? The Moldavian-Gagauz, the Nagorno-Kharabakians, the Chechen-Enguish, the Yakut-Sacha? Personally, I'd trust Siberian shamans with nukes more than I'd trust Christians with them. Anybody who believes in the imminent destruction of the world for its sins should have his guns checked at the door.

What the Ukraine needs, frankly, is not nukes but psychiatrists. And not just the Ukraine. But everyone else too, including Romanians, many of whom I have personally observed being insane. All the people of the former Soviet Empire have had their reality seriously messed with. While some of them are keeping a grip on it and relearning how to speak sanely, many others are hallucinating. Everything from kitsch ancestors in a cartoon history to trees full of nylons, transistors, and ham.

Meanwhile, let's have a nuke buyback like the gun buyback in Illinois, and then let's take them apart nicely, okay? Easy does it.

What to Do About the Secret Police?

Only in a few countries of the former Red Empire are the secret police
still employed. In Romania they still run things, though it's more and
more on a freelance basis. Their clients range from politicians who
need extra muscle to nationalists who want to scare minorities. There is
competition, moreover, between various Securitate gangs, and the quality
of the service varies. But the market economy is operating already and
the sloppy find no work. They hang dejectedly in hotel lobbies striking
their idle palms with their unemployed blackjacks. Some of them have
metamorphosed into ecologists who advertise themselves as ready to
clean up the city, the country, and the planet, you just name the pollut-
ant. Students and intellectuals are prime candidates, and after that come
Jews, Hungarians, and Gypsies and now and then you get lucky and find
a Hungarian Gypsy Jew student intellectual and make a real example
out of it.

In the ex–Soviet Union the KGB is having an identity crisis. In
Albania the clouds have been assigned code numbers so the secret police
there are busy counting: for each cloud that drifts into Italy a hundred
shots are fired. Elsewhere, in Poland, Czechoslovakia, Hungary, and
Germany, vast masses of unemployed ex-policemen wander aimlessly
about without many marketable skills. Well, they do have some, but
retraining them is expensive. Their main skill, beating people up, could
be channeled into jobs in slaughterhouses and boxer-training but chances
are that demand will be low. But other of their talents, such as watching
people who do not want to be watched, could be of use in the writing of
fiction so some of them could go to writing programs in America to get
creative writing degrees. Skill in filming and taping people in their
houses, in hotel rooms, and in cars could also have artistic applications.
The only distress would come from the sudden swelling in the ranks of
already poor writers and artists, but society at large would be rid of the

menace. Meanwhile, countries without a secret police of their own—or only a rudimentary one—could get one ready-made. Even private citizens can now get themselves a private army. It's the postmodern world: some of the shadows are for sale.

Lifestyles of the KGB in China

It's no picnic being a spy these days. Look at what CIA chief Gates is going through: they are trying to make him tell the truth. That's organically impossible for a spy. *Contra naturam.* They train spies to fool lie detectors. If Gates says that he tells the truth it means that he's lying. Only if he's lying (which he won't tell us) might we assume that he's telling the truth. Cretans were liars. Therefore they were spies. Furthermore, spies talk in codes. They *are* codes. What do Watergate, Irangate, Contragate all have in common? They were all Gates, as the third-grader said. Frankly though, no matter how the CIA comes out of these Gates—not very smartly, I assume—its travail is nothing compared to that of the KGB.

The KGB has no more ideology. What in the world are its spies supposed to be dying for? If they are not spying for communism any longer, they could only spy for cash. Our side has more cash. Therefore, and henceforth, the KGB will be spying for us. Therefore, the KGB is the CIA. After the failed coup in the Soviet Union, thousands of KGB agents crossed the border into China. These were, one assumes, the believers, though after a few months in China they will doubtlessly change their minds. I will refrain from imagining the lifestyles of the Soviet KGB in China. Severe caviar rationing.

Under pressure from the truth and lack of ideology, many spies might just throw in the towel. Or pretend to. They might go into presumably legitimate business like the former KGB clones in Eastern Europe who are buying cruise lines, body shops, and corner bodegas wherever they can.

Like us, they will strive to take over the world overtly, not covertly, at night, on a road strewn with errors of judgment and faulty estimates. Of course, they may have already taken over and are just buying bodegas to make it look good. Ask them, they will all lie about it. Therefore, it must be true.

Cosmonauts Lost in Space

These days are filled with both pathos and silliness, tragedy and comedy, and nothing says it better than the two cosmonauts floating up there in space above their vanished country. There they float, in the borderless cosmos above our gridded planet, eating powders and chewing pills, while the Soviet Union has disappeared from under them, and with it, their *raison d'être.* The Soviet Union had sent them up there as representatives of the religion of hope that was the official faith for all its existence. The USSR was set up as a hope factory whose main product was the future, a future praised, sloganed, pushed, symbolized, and represented with all the available energy. The space program with its picture-book cosmonauts was the foremost expression of that future. Toward the end, though, the energy needed to run the propaganda of hope ran out, like everything else, and the cosmonauts remained stranded in the future. In the end, it turned out, nobody cared about the future. The present, with its urgent cries for potatoes and bones, extinguished the ether of utopia. And the cosmonauts, alone up there, have little reason to return to the present: their jobs are nearly gone, their salaries won't buy them solid food, the machinery of enthusiasm has been dismantled, and the reality whose symbols they were is no more. They will now join that vast store of symbols without reality which is the ex-USSR's greatest commodity: the heads of Lenin—billions of them—statues of workers and peasants, dusty sickles and hammers, pins, buttons, medals, and singing soldiers on dusty LPs.

The future, of course, was not the exclusive concern of the USSR. For reasons of synchronicity the United States also concocted a rosy future in space that is only nostalgic now. Speaking of that glorious future that is now past, John Glenn, the first American to orbit the earth, said, "When they get around to doing a geriatric study . . . I'd like to go up again."

Makes you wonder where all that future went.

The Last Bear

The first piece I ever wrote for "All Things Considered" was a lament about the fate of the bear. I mourned the passing of that great animal from the forests where he had once lived into the captivity of zoos and the pages of children's books. But I refused to believe that the end of the bear had truly, truly come. "Where could all that bearness go if not in *us* who so delight in it? It is possible that at any given time, in any gathering, a number of us are bears." That's what I wrote in the bittersweet optimism of a decade ago when, nasty as people seemed to be, there was still a hope that something natural and uncontaminated still lived in them.

But I believe it no longer! We have killed whatever redeeming bearness still attended us. Listen to the news: a bear, the last survivor in the Sarajevo zoo, died of starvation. He died after eating his mate, as did all the other animals, the eagles, the leopards, the lions, the tigers, and the pumas. They each ate those closest to them, their mates, the members of their own species, and then starved to death. The bear held on the longest, waiting, perhaps, for some bearness or at least some pure animal nausea to put an end to the shelling.

Of all the horrid news coming out from Bosnia these days, this seems to me most poignantly criminal. It brings home what the pictures of murdered children, raped women, and executed civilians have failed to. Namely, that nothing of the sense of fairness, justice, and, yes, compassion that prevails among animals exists in us any longer. There is no pure hate among bears. They do not kill each other because they do not like each other's way of eating, singing, or living. They do not destroy each other in the name of ideologies; there are no hate-mongering Nazis, nationalists, and communists among them. And no members of their species stand by watching the slaughter of their kin on television without lifting a finger. The last surviving bear of Sarajevo accuses Europe and the United States of what used to be called inhumanity but which is, I'm afraid, humanity at its barest.

On the Relationship Between Miracles and Catastrophes

I went to the St. Anthony of Padua Catholic Church in Lafitte, Louisiana, to listen to a woman named Dolores talk about her encounters with the Blessed Virgin at Medjugorje, Bosnia. (Lafitte is the place where the pirate by that name lived, an outlaw famous for hidden treasures and for helping Andrew Jackson fight the British at the Battle of New Orleans. His descendants go to church now.) Dolores had taken three journeys to see the Virgin, who calls herself the Queen of Peace, and has been speaking to the faithful since 1984 until recently. She may still be speaking, but the faithful are staying away from the shelling. The Virgin's messages these many years can be summarized as follows: "Unite with my prayers" (March 22, 1984); "Every family must pray family prayer and read the Bible" (slight Bosnian syntax here, February 14, 1985); "I beg you to pray" (March 27, 1986); "Pray without ceasing" (January 1, 1987); "Pray, little children" (May 25, 1988); "Therefore, little children, pray, pray, pray" (October 25, 1989); "Make a decision for prayer" (February 25, 1990); "Dear children! Pray, pray, pray!" (October 25, 1991).

Each time Dolores went to see the Virgin she received, in addition to the above messages, reassurances about peace. She was told not to worry about war because Jesus would take care of everything. Dolores also received the gift of healing, which she promptly exercised on the mountain by restoring breath to a woman who was gasping for air. She also received a picture from a stranger who spoke English, a picture that had the face of Jesus hidden in a cloud. When Dolores returned home her green enamel medallion turned to gold. Dolores pointed to her medallion, but I was too far away to see the color. The Virgin also caused Dolores to write a poem, which was instantly published. When she needed an artist to paint a picture to accompany the poem, Dolores received a miraculous invitation to an art opening, where she asked the artist to paint a picture of Jesus. The artist, reluctant at first, agreed.

Dolores mentioned the war in Bosnia obliquely once more when she quoted a churchman, saying that, "Medjugorje is now part of us. We take it wherever we go."

We left the sixties-style modern St. Anthony of Padua church and went to Boutte's, a lovely fishermen's diner where the waitress wanted to know if Mass was over so that they could start frying the shrimps and oysters for the crowd. I wondered what the relationship between miracles and catastrophes was. Bosnia was far away. But Hurricane Andrew came the next day.

The Tree of Life and Death

They found a tree in India called a neem tree, which is capable of producing an antifungal, antibacterial, and antiviral substance while simultaneously being an insect repeller and a powerful nonpolluting pesticide. In fact, the neem can do so many things it may be the ultimate cure.

We had a tree like that in Transylvania when I was growing up. It was called the Tree of Life and Death. If you ate its bark you were cured of ailments and got to live forever. The catch was that only Gypsies could pick its bark. And the truly strange thing was that the Gypsies could pick it, but it didn't do them any good. They had to hand it over to whoever wanted it, mainly because whoever wanted it was usually holding a sword over their heads.

It's still like that. Romania, where 2.5 million Gypsies live, is coming up before the U.S. Congress for renewal of its Most Favored Nation status. But after 500 years of slavery, and a few dozen years of quasi-slavery, the Gypsies are still being persecuted in Romania. Since the fall of Ceausescu's communists and the regime of Iliescu's neocommunists, Gypsy homes have been burned, their possessions destroyed, they have been chased out of villages, and, in certain areas, have not been allowed to return to their homes. Many have been killed. The so-called miners who beat up antigovernment protesters on several occasions spent much of their drunken enthusiasm on terrorizing and harming Gypsies. Helsinki Watch has issued a sobering report on the situation entitled "Destroying Ethnic Identity: the Persecution of Gypsies in Romania." We need to look closely here at the Romanian Tree of Life and Death before we start buying up the bark. It seems that the ancient tree still has its bark picked by people under the sword. Romania shouldn't be able to trade freely until it improves its human-rights record.

Where Have All the Jokes
in Eastern Europe Gone?

The editor of a Romanian humor magazine, Mr. Ioan Morar, came to visit me around Mardi Gras. I asked him what happened to all the jokes that people used to tell before the fall of communism. It seemed to me that there were no new political jokes, a worrisome development that indicated some deep spiritual malaise. Before 1989 people used to live on jokes. There wasn't anything else. At the joke contest back then, there were three prizes: third prize, 100 dollars; second prize, 50 dollars; first prize, 10 years at hard labor. You can write the history of communism in jokes: they had them for every phase. Now they don't even have a joke *contest* anymore. People scream, swear, weep over stupid nationalist songs and beat each other up. They don't tell jokes.

Mr. Morar said that it was true, jokes had disappeared, but that Romanians had other venues for political humor now: satirical-political magazines like his own, standup comics, and musical-comedic revues that played to sold-out crowds.

I pointed out that these things were okay, but that they were rather highbrow affairs, while jokes are for everyone. I kept thinking about this phenomenon later, while we watched a Mardi Gras parade. Mr. Morar enjoyed the carnival immensely: he jumped up and down like a kid when floats went by. But when the navy bands and the ROTC drill teams appeared, he drew back with a worried expression on his face. I reassured him that these military types were not out to harm us. Some of them, in fact, had beads and feathers on their rifles. I don't know if my explanation satisfied him, but I had an inkling about why there may be no more jokes in Eastern Europe. On the one hand, everybody still jumps up and down about being rid of tyrants. On the other, the uniforms keep marching by. At least, during the familiar misery of the past, the rifles were within constant view. But this odd alternation of clowns and rifles, exaltation and anxiety, this is too unsettling for jokes. Jokes need stability.

1993: In the Year That Was

In the year that was, the riddle of the elephant was finally solved. And we found out the name of the beast slouching toward Bethlehem. The whole elephant, only partially reconnoitered until now, is fascism. And that's also the name of the beast. Fifty years after it was buried, fascism has come out of the grave, healthy, rested, and bloodthirsty. In Bosnia, the Serbian fascists have been having a field day while the United States and Europe watch from the coliseum seats. In Russia, Hitler number two has garnered more votes and has better mass-destruction weapons than Hitler number one. In Croatia, dead Ustashi Nazis are honored with the names of schools and live ones are given ambassadorships. In Germany old and new Nazis firebomb foreigners and deport Gypsies. In the Slovak Republic the prime minister declares Gypsies a threat because they will soon outnumber white people. In Romania, they erect a statue to the war criminal Ion Antonescu, mass murderer of Jews. In Italy nearly a quarter of the people vote fascist and nearly elect a new Mussolini. In France, a fascist misnamed Le Pen—why not Le Sword?—sees his shock-troops grow. KKK hate-specialists from the United States travel to Germany to give lessons in modern PR and management. Holocaust revisionists take out ads in college newspapers.

The beast is back, no doubt about it, but our government is just waking up to it. Until recently, the State Department was content with the partial (and mistaken) descriptions of the elephant. Bosnia, it's just a local conflict. Germany, it's an immigration problem. Romania, it's the postcommunist aftershock. But it's clear now that the beast is one: it's fascism and it's back and it doesn't even bother to wear masks anymore.

The Grinning Skull for Zhirinovsky

Charlie Chaplin and Adolf Hitler were born four days apart like the joined faces of comedy and tragedy over the gaudy portals of Western civilization. Chaplin mocked the Führer in the *The Great Dictator*, which upset Hitler because Chaplin was his favorite Reichstag viewing. After watching Chaplin, Hitler delighted his intimates by imitating him. But when Chaplin imitated him, Hitler abruptly ceased imitating Chaplin. It might have been possible sometime between the time Hitler did Chaplin and just before Chaplin did Hitler for them to exchange places.

Ah, history, why aren't you as clever as cinema? Or at the very least as clever as art? Imagine the world if only someone had bought Hitler's watercolors! Looking at them, I see that Hitler had a feeling for buildings but was very bad at people. The architecture in these labored washes is rendered to the finest details, but the people are stick figures, stiff little scarecrows crushed by buildings. They look, in fact, like Chaplin caricatures blown helplessly about by mysterious winds.

Chaplin, on the other hand, knew how to do people down to the last detail, and when he was through with them, only stiff, scarecrow buildings remained, blown about aimlessly by those very same winds. Hitler's scarecrows were the product of incompetence, self-hatred, and disdain for humanity while Chaplin's were the result of compassion and art. Hitler's bad artistry managed to obscure the difference between life and art so radically that his little mustache covered the sun and plunged the world into the darkness of grotesque caricature. If he could have drawn people he might have found a way not to be Hitler. As it was, he had Albert Speer build him buildings that would stand for a thousand years and "look good in ruins." They stood for a few years and didn't look so good in ruins. Chaplin's buildings, on the other hand, called movie palaces, flourished and continued to grow until they conquered the world. People stayed out of Hitler's buildings and cried, but they flocked, and still flock, into Chaplin's to laugh. Today Chaplin's mustache is thoroughly superimposed over that of Hitler. Comedy is better than tragedy. If the world had laughed at Hitler right from the beginning, he might have been only a smaller Chaplin. Politics is a refuge for bad art, and we should be always leery of bad artists smuggling their frustration into the social arena. Particularly if they are overly fond of buildings.

Zombification

The world is undergoing zombification. It was gradual for a while, a few zombies here and there, mostly in high office, where being a corpse in a suit was *de rigueur*. There were also common zombies, couch potatoes who sat down and never got up, not even after the TV went off. Still, that weren't more zombies than I could take, but it's becoming massive now.

The other day in Colorado, 20,000 people showed up at a bake sale for Rush Limbaugh, calling themselves Ditto-Heads because they have no thoughts of their own, only a voice that says "Ditto" every time Rush speaks.

There are degrees of zombiedom, of course. The Ditto-Heads are benign compared to the legions of fascist corpses coming out of their graves in Europe and killing everyone who doesn't speak their language. Nobody has the slightest idea how to stop them.

There is an ex-zombie on the lecture circuit in Haiti who claims that he was a slave on a zombie farm supervised by a naked dwarf with a belt of twinkling bells. This dwarf was in charge of making sure the zombies, who were called "beef in the garden," toed the line. But the escaped ex-zombie has no more suggestions on how to fix the problem than François Mitterrand or Bill Clinton. And the dwarf goes on twinkling his bells.

Mass zombification isn't new: twice in this century, suicidal mobs of followers gave up every thought in their heads for the sake of slogans that led them directly to mass graves. They were called "cannon fodder," another way to say "beef in the garden." The worst part about zombies raging unchecked is the slow paralysis that they induce in people who aren't quite zombies yet. The rest of us un-zombies turn our heads, hoping the ghouls will just go away. They won't. It's time we sharpened those stakes and started swinging that garlic.

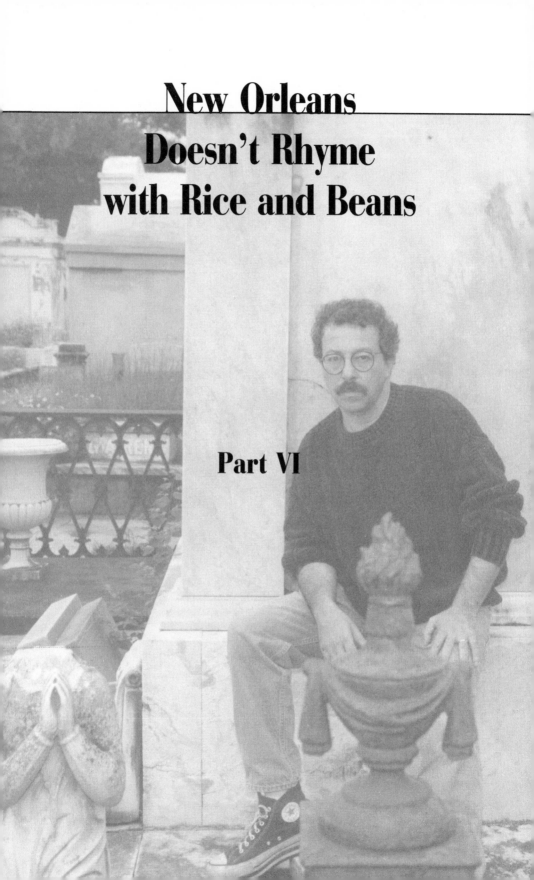

New Orleans
Doesn't Rhyme
with Rice and Beans

Part VI

New Lags

Forget jet lag. Try temperature lag. And money lag. I left the cozy steam bath of New Orleans for the fogs of San Francisco, and experienced both these new lags within a few hours.

In New Orleans I had just begun to lower my blood temperature and to slow down to the pace that is the prelude to the immemorial slowness of the swamp dream where all life comes from. I started to rise only in the evening to make the short trek to the terrace of my favorite café to watch the barely clad natives slither languorously past my perch lost in clouds of gardenia and jazz. A few days before, whatever chance Louisiana might have had to become part of the high-energy America we all know and love had evaporated when the few voters who had the energy to get up and vote turned down the governor's ambitious let's-get-out-of-the-hole tax package. The secret is that we like it in the hole: it's hot and steamy here, and the nights are long and romantic.

When I landed in San Francisco, I was slapped vigorously awake by a chilly breeze off the ocean and woke up with a start amid the din of booming money, growing skyscrapers, swinging briefcases, and two-dollar cups of coffee. A homeless person asked me for ten dollars. Everywhere I looked, people propelled by wind made loud deals in the hotels of lobbies, consumed ruddy portions of exotic Persian and Thai food—which they ate directly out of cartons using their gold American Express cards instead of silverware—slapped each other on the back with tennis paddles, and wiped energetic sweat from jogging foreheads. The editorial in the abandoned paper on the cold marble table in front of me bemoaned the terrible dilemma of the state's $2.5 billion budget surplus. I thought nostalgically about our miserable $750 million deficit and how easily it could be solved if California opened its windy coffers to us for a loan. I could take the cash back home myself on the next plane, and would even promise to pay it back before long. This kind of thinking was no doubt inspired by the fact that the brisk breeze off the ocean now chilled me to my sensitive bones, filling me with advancement and initiative. Before long, I was riding a wicked draft over Mount Diablo on my way to Sacramento. I succeeded faster than you can say "silicone chip," and next day early I was on my way home, with a suitcase full of cash. But when I stepped off the plane in New Orleans, the suitcase got very light, and I became very sleepy. A whoosh of wind escaped the battered Samsonite and I headed through the steam for a cold beer and an evening of joyful lizard gazing.

I'll take this dream state over the other one. And the heat.

How Hot Is It:
Summer Vacation in Louisiana

It's so hot in Louisiana now that if you met an alligator he wouldn't even lift up his head to scare you. I like to slowly drag myself sweating through the shimmer. Everything's slow and far off, which explains, at least in part, how the mind of the average Louisiana politician works. Stranded here in the swamp of unreality, we watch David Duke shimmying up a greased pole hoping to hang a Nazi flag in the U.S. Senate. It's an interesting show.

Not to be outdone, the other legislators just passed a law levying a $25 fine for beating up a flag-burner. That's the cheapest price in the whole country, and already there are people lining up at the courthouse to put $100 or $200 in escrow for the summer, hoping to beat up a whole passle of flag-burners. It's a little like buying a fishing license early, before everybody gets the idea. It's a good law, says my friend Chris Rose, because if you accidentally do something real bad, like run over a kid with your car, you can always plant a flag and a lighter by the body and you'd be all right. The thing is, says Chris, you should always carry a few spare flags and lighters in your car, just in case.

Besides Duke-watching and beating up flag-burners, there ain't much else to do hereabouts since the shrimpers stopped shooting feds over turtles. And there isn't much Vietnamese-Cajun conflict going on over shrimp these days. Everybody gets to spread their butterfly nets as wide as they go and scoop up as much as the sea holds plus some. That's good. That way there won't be anything squishy in there when we go for a dip. And we've just made abortion illegal so nobody's going over to the abortion clinics to beat up flag-burners anymore. Maybe the lottery bill will pass. I picked up a copy of *Bingo News*, and I can't for the

*It sure did. As did, later, casino gambling.

world of me figure out out how to do it. A lottery, now that would be just the right speed while watching Duke and stomping a flag-burner or two.

A Model for the World:
A Louisiana Fairy Tale

Here is a Louisiana fairy tale:

On the wake of all the horrible revelations about the Louisiana environment, the people took notice. Many of them stood in their hospital beds, where rare forms of environmental cancer kept them, and wrote letters to their representatives. Fishermen dropped momentarily their nets overflowing with cadmium-full oysters and poisoned fish and took up the pen. Even people whose houses had long ago floated out into the gulf because of oil company–induced coastal erosion grabbed their two-way radios and commenced to protest. Choking, gasping, puking, and reeling, the citizens of our state stood in the eerie light of toxic dumps and filled the gross air with appeals. And our representatives *listened*! It was a phenomenon unheard of in the most corrupt state in the Union, where for a long time it seemed that the only rays of hope came when chemical-company lobbyists opened their pockets to air the legislators firmly ensconced in there. A score of laws were passed calling for clean air and water, tough emission standards, toxic dump cleanup. The Department of Environmental Quality was charged with enforcing these new laws. The Environmental Protection Agency set about ordering priorities. Governor Roemer, elected partly for his tough campaign rhetoric on these issues, seemed to lead the charge. The entire state breathed a huge sigh of relief: the patients lay back on their beds, the poisoned fish were hauled ashore, the unmoored houses extinguished their lamps. And then came the Budget Battle. When it was over, most appropriations came through okay, with one big exception. The state cut *70 percent* of the budget of the Department for Environmental Quality, rendering its enforcement abilities completely useless. It was a beautiful piece of Louisiana politics: let them have what we won't give them. The rays of hope went out as chemical executives closed their pockets with the politicians still in them. Well, next time around, folks, when the fat cats reach for their cigars again! Meanwhile, the tumors grew bigger, the fish got sicker, the shore receded, and the dumps swelled.

Things were back to normal. Nobody lived happily ever after. In fact, they didn't live at all.

Letter Home

This is Andrei Codrescu, in hiding somewhere in Louisiana. It is still early in the David Duke era. The Nazi flag is flying over the major car dealership in Metairie. A gigantic pelican, our state bird, with a swastika painted on his chest has been erected at the Metairie Mall. With their shades drawn, some Louisianians are bemoaning Duke's election to out-of-state newspapers. "They would vote for the devil himself if he was a supporter of the homestead tax exemption," says one of them, apologetically.

Duke himself is a picture of calm. When somebody smashed in the window of his VW, El Duce didn't lose his temper. He merely deplored the act, instead of foaming at the mouth like a TV Nazi. The citizens of Metairie, like their Duke, are clean-cut Americans who voice their beliefs in tones as well behaved as their postage-stamp lawns. David Duke is a lawyer, a graduate of LSU, and a well-mannered gent. His childhood and adolescence have been gone over by amateur psychologists with a fine-toothed comb but few traumas were found. El Duce apparently came by his racism while on his high school debating team, where he once defended that unpopular point of view. So clever was he at it that he convinced himself. His constituents, the citizens of lily white Metairie, are likewise reasonable people for the most part. They have come by their racism when they moved away from New Orleans, where blacks roam free. Metairie is America, while New Orleans is God-knows-what. There is lots of neon and many Burger Kings in Metairie. The local sheriff, Harry Lee, who is not quite so reasonable seeming—perhaps because he is vaguely Chinese—once ordered all blacks driving cars in his parish to be stopped and searched. The order was officially rescinded under outside pressure, but it remains the status quo. The only thing Metairites say they want is for outsiders to lay off. Paradoxically, every outsider in the country, particularly Jews, outsiders par excellence, have turned to tiny Metairie to watch closely the growth of native fascism. But observe as they might, there is little to see. Everyone is clean, well mannered, white, reasonably educated, and above all, banal. Once more, as Hannah Arendt put it, evil is banality. Metairie is American banality at its purest. David Duke is the boring flower it puts forth in its little window boxes.

Nonetheless, I have decided to hide and to shine the rails on the old underground railroad. Things are *too* quiet.

Duke, Edwards, Swaggart

If I was a preacher, which thank God I'm not, I'd say that we are living through the final days and that three out of four horsemen of the Apocalypse are raging through Louisiana right now laying waste to an already wasted land. There is Duke, so slick a Nazi he's had plastic surgery to look just like George Bush. If we didn't know about his past and just listened to what he said, we'd swear he was Bush. His marching orders include law and order, an end to busing and quotas, and tax cuts. Of course they also include genetic selection of people with above-average IQs which, at this point, would eliminate most of his voters.

The opposing horseman, Edwin Edwards, promises only to deliver the state into the hands of polluters who are not yet happy with our high cancer rates, our filthy air, and our undrinkable water. They want to pump us so full of chemicals we'll shine like gas flames in the dark of the last years of the twentieth century. Between you and me, I think Louisianans were chosen to be the flambeaux in the millennial parade.

The leader of this hellish procession will have to be Jimmy Swaggart, the preacher with more lives than a cat, whose tear-swollen countenance hovers over his followers like that of a pudgy pseudo-Christ. Once more Swaggart has been caught in the wastelands of cheap sin, an almost harmless addiction compared to the major failings of his fellow horsemen Duke and Edwards, but one that smells of sulfur nonetheless. It won't matter to Jimmy, who's going to be governor. If it's Duke he can always find a constituency among the new compulsory Christians of white Christian Louisiana. If it's Edwards he'll make him the official drive-by preacher on Airline Highway, pastor to casinos, bordellos, and leaking backyard wells.

I wonder who the fourth horseman might be. The CEO of Marine Shale Processors? Of Exxon? Grand Gulf Nuclear?

If it weren't for the New Orleans Saints, we'd be screaming in our sleep.*

*Note (1993): We scream in our sleep.

Post-Duke Blues

I've got the post-Duke blues. I don't feel like being from Louisiana these days. When I go out of the state, people invariably ask me how David Duke got as far as he did. "*I* didn't vote for him!" I tell them, but it's a hollow excuse when 44 percent of the voters in this state did. That's the majority of white people in Louisiana. Well, I'm not white, and if I ever was I'm giving it up right now. Still, Duke's near miss is enough to give me the heebie-jeebies whenever two or more voters are present. It makes it kind of hard to stand there by the garbage can in the morning and make friendly chitchat with the guy with the spotted dog from next door. Who knows what *he* did in that voting booth? He's throwing out last night's Bud cans, and that's one dead giveaway. At Duke's big campaign rally in Grand Isle, Budweiser had a big balloon that said BUD FOR DUKE. I've been drinking Miller since because I already know who *Coors* is for.

I *know* the pharmacist on the corner voted for Duke because he had an ugly truck plastered with Duke and NRA stickers parked on the block and only *once* did he get a rotten egg on his windshield—I'm a terrible marksman. *He* might not be, though, and guys like that use bullets, not eggs. One of the side effects of Duke's near miss may just be an influx of guys who make points with bullets instead of rotten eggs. After all, it wasn't so long ago that a Baton Rouge gun store proudly displayed "the rifle that killed Kennedy." This is a fertile land for your homespun Nazi no matter what they say about Duke-like sentiments all over the country. It may be true that there are thousands of Dukes ready to sprout everywhere from the Republican-mulched soil of the last decade, but here in Louisiana we are in the avant-garde. While the whole country was weeping over the tragedy of the Civil War on PBS, we damn nearly elected a Nazi to the U.S. Congress.

I can either move or get plastic surgery.

Manners Part One: Mammie Dolls

Good manners. I approve of 'em. I think you should have 'em as long as you can keep 'em. Which is a real trial sometimes, here in the Kingdom of Manners—not to be confused with the Empire of Manners, which is Japan. Over there, if you lose your manners, you have to kill yourself. Here, you just have to move north.

Take Mammie dolls, for instance, an old local product for which sales are booming these days. Renamed "Black Heritage Products" by their manufacturers, they live unharmed in shop windows. There is a huge one, in fact, in front of the Old Town Praline Shop. The *Times-Picayune* reports that, a long time ago in the bad radical sixties, a black man took a punch at the Praline mammy's head and hurt his hand on her coconut skull. Next day, he apologized. Now isn't that nice?

The other day, my friend Chuck passed by an angry demonstration by racially mixed folk in front of a Metairie savings and loan. They were carrying UNFAIR signs. He was told upon inquiry that it wasn't a discriminatory matter, but simply a matter of form: the bank had been rude to someone who happened to be black, and they were picketing it. And there you have it: racism is but the invisible shadow of the real monster—lack of manners. That's the only thing we don't cotton to.

I was severely chastized one time, in front of some true connoisseurs, when I refused to have lunch at the New Orleans Slave Exchange, a little restaurant on the site of what used to be a real slave exchange in the old days. I was sure I'd gag on my po' boy and upchuck gravy all the way to the Mississippi. But no, my companions insisted, when the food's great it's rude not to eat it.

The other evening I was having a drink on the terrace of my favorite hotel and I'd barely taken my first sip when a whole crowd of blonde belles in Victorian hoop skirts followed by gents in Confederate uniforms started second-lining down the steps as the sole black saxophone player in a sweaty tux led them down the stairs. Not one to spoil the festivities, I remarked to my companions how odd it was to see white folks in antebellum drag doing a black funeral dance, when one of the dancers dropped an Elvis doll and a pair of pink handcuffs on and around my drink. Pardon me, she said, most mortified. Oh, you're excused, I beamed, and true happiness reigned in the night. Next time, I said, but she didn't hear me, you oughta get a mammie doll for your Elvis. That'll keep him from dropping in a stranger's drink, thank you very much.

The Jazz Age

They called the twenties the Jazz Age, and in many ways New Orleans is a town of the twenties. Two blocks from where I live is the house where young F. Scott Fitzgerald allegedly wrote his first book, *This Side of Paradise*. His old apartment looks over the Prytania Cemetery, where Anne Rice, the gothic writer, set the residence of the vampire Lestat. Cemeteries, paradises, vampires, heat, long nights, and jazz—that's the city that makes me dream. New Orleans *was* the twenties, but then, in most ways, it still is. Where else do you see tuxedoed gents and barefoot southern belles in evening gowns stepping into limos in the wee hours of the morn, holding slippers filled with champagne and looking as if they'd just disembarked from the Titanic? And music streams from everywhere: the walled patios of the French Quarter, the overlush gardens of Uptown mansions, the hot front steps of the old black neighborhoods.

Under a freeway underpass, a young man practices the saxophone. He's listening for a special sound. The air of New Orleans is saturated with sound: blues, jazz, Dixie, swing, Cajun, zydeco. You can lean on a wall on a hot afternoon and feel the sound that's keeping the old bricks together begin to seep into your body. You vibrate in tune with the other creatures of the evening, past and present, including young F. Scott and young Tennessee Williams, his heart full of jazz and melancholy. The Jazz Fest, an annual party that the city of parties throws itself every spring, is drawing out the lovers of sound from everywhere. Like pale moths emerging from eternal darkness, northerners of all stripes are released into the bright sound of New Orleans and bathed in music. I wandered the grounds of the fest the other day feeling a mixed range of emotions, many of which, I am sure, were not mine. People were swaying to the blues, dancing to zydeco, weeping to smoky voices, swooning to Gospel, swelling with brass. It was all flowing through me the way words flow through a song. I felt that I could stop the flow at any moment and write down whatever it was that needed writing down. Writing is jazz, too. It is best when it joins the music and it just happens, from deep down. There are passages like that in F. Scott and Tennessee and Faulkner that couldn't have been written anywhere else. In fact, they weren't *written*: they were riffed and let loose.

Fantastic Fast

I decided to stop eating for a few days in solidarity with Cathy of the comic strip who's been trying to fit into swimsuits for about two weeks now. Seeing her in the newspaper struggling day after day with the chief summer agony of the middle class made me lose my appetite. On the other hand, I could stand to lose a few pounds. Living in New Orleans is like drinking blubber through a straw. Even the air is caloric. The atmosphere is permeated by rays of roux and bubbles of cornbread. Gumbo gives off a cloud of cayenne-flavored fat that envelops the passerby. Fish fries and shrimp are breaded all around the innocent. Stopped in front of restaurants, hypnotized tourists discuss menus without noticing that they are already being fed by the invisible emanations. We will not even talk about the humans inside, who, oblivious to all but the architectonics of their shrimp and the peaks of their mile-high pies, are being remodeled to look like wine casks. One can see through the windows of these restaurants people literally tied up in angel-hair pasta motioning pitifully for help that will not come.

Fasting under these circumstances is one of the bravest things a man can do, and this week I am that man. Light-headed and sharp-witted, I pass quickly and thinly through the rotund crowds. I am close to the mystical state vouchsafed to the desert fathers: visions of complexly pleated loaves of bread filled with oysters and shrimp pass before me. I dodge the hypnagogic enlargement of a bouquet of steak fries blocking my path. I avert my eyes from the many HAPPY HOUR signs posted on taverns with offers of free Buffalo chicken wings, asparagus tips, and baby back ribs. I ignore the painted pot of jambalaya with each grain of rice vividly reliefed on the window sign of the corner store. I see now that those who complain about America are in a tough spot: after you dodge all the food, real and imaginary, that attacks you from everywhere, what can you do but watch TV? Of course, New Orleans isn't America—but it's close enough. Sing that demon pie away!

Pre—Mardi Gras Blues

I didn't think much about Mardi Gras this year. All around me, people tried on new masks. The debutantes got crowned somewhere. At Liberty Fabrics in Metairie overwrought teen beauties drove their mothers insane before glittering fabrics. At fancy balls in gilded salons the courts of the parade monarchs met for bouts of formal drinking. In the French Quarter the exhibitionists began quietly arriving by the planeload. There was even one across the street, on a balcony, stark naked, snarling the traffic. They took this one away for premature exhibitionism in the wrong neighborhood.

I missed most of the early parades, but I did catch a strange one last night. It poured rain on the Freret Parade as it went oddly glittering by. First came the plastic-coated marching girls with light shining through them, looking like water fairies. They were followed by the St. Augustine Band with rivulets flowing off their drums and dripping glistening brass, weird water gods in Roman helmets driving forth the wet plastic fairies. Soaked floats with shiny, oversize heads, grotesque eyes, and fat, puckered lips, glided forward full of masked goblinesque critters throwing gold and silver doubloons and beaded jewels through the already jeweled strands of rain. I caught several strands of pearls on top of my umbrella. Everywhere I looked there were pearls, rubies, diamonds, and gold coins landing on the black domes of bumpershoots. Hands would now and then dart out from under the domes and catch a fleeting amulet before it landed. The bright reflector lights at the heads of the floats and the rotating colors atop police cruisers turned the street into something by Monsieur Seurat. In fact, that's the one thing every year that I notice about Mardi Gras, whether I pay any attention to it or not. Everything looks as if it should be or already was painted, photographed, filmed, reproduced. And for all that, it's still real, three-dimensional, and unfailingly bizarre. And just when I thought that I'd missed the spirit, I got wet enough to enjoy it all over again.

Mardi Gras Again

Yes, folks in snowbound lands, this is the time of the year when my house, my city, and my life become a commune. When friends I haven't heard from in years and friends of their friends of whom I haven't even heard camp on my floors and on my porch, coming and going, going and coming, bearing the bizarre or being borne by it. Three of the people on the floor are from my son's college: he knows one of them. Good enough for me.

This is the time when night becomes day and day becomes night, when some rise while others sink, never at the same time but always in reverse order from how they usually rise and fall in those faraway places that are not New Orleans.

This is the time when my stern antimaterialist friend Jack the Ascetic is overcome by bead greed. Swept away by glittery things, he glides on the wake of a carnival float like a middle-aged moth with shiny eyes not well hidden by a leather mask. There are others like him, because this is the time when normally sober people are drunk and normal drunks become Rabelaisian, which is drunks with an epic mission.

This is when people dangling pearls from balconies become cruel aristocrats exacting an exhibitionist frenzy from their pedestrian peasant subjects. They will do anything, these peasants: the tone-deaf are suddenly capable of singing, the color-blind see rainbows. Anything, everything, cosmic, humiliating, or funny: Throw me something, mister! This is when normally buttoned-down folk feel the urge to wear nothing but jewelry. When the mild-mannered put on masks of fierceness while the fierce become loveable animals. The pretty become prettier while the plain become fantastique. The clumsy dance, the dancers soar. This is when you find intimacy in strangers and strangeness in your intimates.

It's time with an edge, ladies and gentlemen! Watch that ladder full of children fall while a horse bolts—but the thousand-armed crowd catches them! Watch the spiked high heel come down hard on a hand scooping up a doubloon. Step right up to the big hissing gumbo pot because you need the hot, hot.

This is the time when the music that seems to come from your head actually comes from the street. When the music you hear from the street comes from your head. When the music you hear in your head lodges itself in your dreams. And the music that was in your dreams comes from the street. This is the time when the part of you that is music overcomes the part of you that is silence. This is when music rules the fools. It's Mardi Gras in New Orleans, ladies and gentlemen, and the good times roll, and you might as well roll with them because there is only music to hold on to.

The Krewe de Vieux Carré:
The Korpse of Komatose 1991

The rabble gathered in front of Café Brasil. There was a giant dressed in cardboard with one bare foot, the other shod in a boot too big for it, a housewife out of work, an Aunt Jemima look-alike with a sign that said OPPRESSED DOMESTIC, a stockbroker without a shirt and with a pistol in his pocket, a man wheeling a papier-mâché corpse, a trashy Jackie Onassis who was actually a man, and the Queen herself atop a shopping cart filled with urban discards. The Mystick Korpse of Komatose was ready to march.

It was a warm and lovely evening. The Krewe de Vieux Carré, of which the Komatose was part, began wending its way through the crowds in the French Quarter dispensing political acid and beads. Being one of the paraders was quite different from being one of the crowd, which is what I always was—until now. Instead of proffering adoring hands to the masks streaming down, I was the one hands were being proffered to. I distributed my wealth of beads, doubloons, and medallions with Mecaena-like grandeur. Flirting young and old women batted their eyelashes and wiggled with sincere eagerness lined only slightly with parody. Little children with paper bags stood wide-eyed at the very edge of the parade wearing pouts, smiles, frowns, and various urgencies. Their gratitude flowed like warm molasses when I pressed doubloons into their sweaty little greed graspers. The women I regaled with strands of fake pearls and plastic strands sent mock kisses into the velvety air, their eyes half-lidded with faux abandon. For years now I'd been a begging atom in the mass, subject to pleasant humiliation and despair. But no more: I now flowed through the increasingly bigger crowds, an object of desire and a horn of plenty.

Until, that is, I ran out of loot. In my eagerness I'd spent my wealth at the beginning of the march, and I was now empty-handed just at the point—on Royal Street—where the crowds were thicker and neediest.

Their demands were more imperative also, and my remoteness—the dignity of a ruined aristocrat—only sharpened their greed-turning-to-anger. I somehow made it past Canal Street, but I now know the other side: the rich better be prepared.

1992 Mardi Gras:
Death Was the Theme

The Krewe de Vieux Carré, the first one to march, chose Death as its theme this year. We paraded funereally through the French Quarter: black chiffon angels, executioners, coffins, wreaths, and a guillotine. This isn't all that unusual in this town, where death enjoys respect and familiarity, where people take their picnics to cemeteries, bury each other with jazz bands, and live as if there were no tomorrow. Which could pretty well be the case if the Mississippi River levees break.

But this year's parade was unusually mortuarial, even given the town's proclivities. The Krewe de Vieux's official newsletter, *Le Monde de Merde*, listed various recent deaths under the headline POSTHUMOR-OUSLY YOURS. The greatest was the death of several old-time parades, Comus and Proteus chief among them, because they wouldn't go along with desegregation. Some of the Krewe's officials found these deaths tragic, while others thought that racism deserves to die, so good riddance. Consequently, while some sub-krewes laid wreaths at the door of the Boston Club, headquarters of the defunct parades, and called for a moment of silence, others blew whistles and threw rubber eggs and plastic turds at the hallowed locus. Other than that, the Krewe of the Mystic Inane, Krewe of Space Age Love, Krewe of Underwear, and especially the Mystick Korpse of Komatose, mourned or celebrated: the death of education in Louisiana, the death of New Orleans by casino, and the demise of Republicanism. Statements were issued by the Transylvanian Liberation Front against vampire discrimination and by the Mystic Korpse of Komatose against discrimination of any kind. It was also announced that the "Shroud of Turism" was discovered in New Orleans. The parade proceeded without incident almost to the end, when a sudden wind picked up the guillotine and destroyed a tourist. A cold rain fell, but by then most marchers were full of firewater and the music never stopped playing.

Bayou Babylon Café

It's a smoky place, of course, though in deference to the increasing
masses of ecopurists there is a no-smoking terrace, where among the
cascading bougainvillea you can hear but barely see. Welcome to Bayou
Babylon Café! As you sip your absinthe-mimosa-hurricane-bitters the
resident anarchist lights his cigarillo with his bomb fuse and holds forth
for a moment. It's the Anarchist Moment with Dr. John Clark, author,
coincidentally, of *The Anarchist Moment*. Under a blue spot the café's
cook demonstrates self-cannibalistic cooking by delicately removing
parts of his body for filet-ing, spicing, breading, and broiling. In a dark
corner a groupicle of trance-mongers hold hands over a round table
without nails calling forth dead New Orleans writers who show up, one
by one, and speak. Kate Chopin: "I can't believe the price of real estate
on Esplanade!" Or Faulkner, either to the assembled, or to F. Scott:
"Pass the corn whiskey!"

At long last, it's time to make an exquisite corpse at Bayou Babylon Café. A drawing is held. The winner strips bare and steps on stage
under the now purple throbescent spot and the audience, armed with
Magic Markers of various colors, streams up to the lucky nude and
writes all over him or her lines of sublime poesy. Or draws spiders on
the eyelids, etc. When the work is finished the "exquisite corpse," as
the nude is now known, is loudly read either by someone with a very
good voice (me) or by everybody at once. If you are reminded of Cabaret
Voltaire in Zurich in 1916, hold on. This is New Orleans, not Zurich.
We also have voodoo with chicken claws going against the bad and for
the good, bayou musicians and street musicians and dancers, and grave
dirt in the potted plants. And the year is 1993, not 1916, and the
word *Babylon*'s enough to give anyone the shivers. Preachers preach
against the biblical Babylon, militant reggae musicians call America

"Babylon," and on the site of old Babylon stands present-day Iraq. And for all that, there is only one place to see contortionists to the sound of New Orleans jazz-blues, and it's right here, at the Bayou Babylon Bar and Café.

Cult Extra!

There was a shrouded corpse on a cart, lying in full view in the courtyard of Sacred Heart Academy, and the well-lit crowd pressed on to see. I crossed the street to avoid the spectacle because things like this make me queasy. I like to take my evening walk in peace.

I turned onto Prytania, a lovely old street with melancholy mansions dripping with whispered dramas from another time, and made for the Lafayette Cemetery to sit and think. It's a pretty old boneyard, run down and vandalized by time, moonlight, and pranksters, but it bears its age gracefully. A sliver of Turkish moon was coming up over the river, but I was surprised to see more light than the moon and the streetlamps would normally give off on this sort of evening. Angels! I thought, Wouldn't that be delightful! But as I cautiously approached, I saw that the entire cemetery was bathed in cobalt blue light while spectral figures ran shouting between the crypts and fallen graves.

Stop it! I felt like shouting, Enough is enough!

What malevolent force had risen out of the depths of ignorance to ruin my peace? Alas, I knew only too well.

I was not surprised to pass the Bultman Funeral Home and to see that a body was being wheeled under bright lights into an artificial shadow of roses and skulls, while debutantes holding champagne glasses leaned against limousines with their shoes off. They were "star watching," a popular sport lately. Sadly, it has nothing to do with the stars above.

If you haven't guessed by now, the spooky doings I have been describing are the work of a cult that has increasingly taken over the mind and soul of America. I speak of Hollywood, the roaming monster of illusion, which is taking its hydra-headed heads on the road and sucking character out of places like so much marrow from brittle bones.

One after another, the old cities fall to this scourge, and few rise up against it!

It's a peculiar thing about charm. The people who live in it take it for granted. When outsiders notice it, they begin to see it, too. Then they start selling it. But, alas, charm can never be used exactly the way it's found, especially by Hollywood. The oaks need more moss, the mansions need more spookiness, streets should bear other names, the people aren't quite right, either. Very soon, houses are fixed, street names changed, moss added, real people replaced by actors. At last, the place is perfect! But it's a stage set and nobody can live in it. The monster belches and lurches on, to look for more "real" charm.

I count my steps.

Robbery Approved

In New Orleans, it's okay to be robbed on the streetcar. You can be deprived of your most precious assets by official ordinance. This is what the *disclaimer* over my head says: "Upon boarding this vehicle you hereby grant to RTA and others permission to photograph and record you visually and orally for various TV and/or film productions. You grant universal rights for any reproduction of your image, likeness, or voice."

Ho, there! Am I no longer a free man once I step into this public conveyance? Can anybody steal my image and my voice and do with it what they will? Violate my privacy? Without reading me my rights? It would seem so, but as I sit quietly fuming in the rattling wagon I see little concern in my fellow passengers. Should camera crews from outer space board the streetcar at this very moment nary one of 'em would raise a fuss. They seem utterly resigned to the loss of their liberties and property. If pushed, one of them might countenance that tourism is good for the city and streetcars in their picturesqueness are flypaper to the photo-mad tourist. Balderdash! I say. Tourists are the bane of civilization. They are bad enough all clustered about the obvious, but they should be severely censured when they stray from the path.

All over America, decent people are rolling over for tourists because it's good for some abstract entity called "the good of the city," which is just another name for ad men, con men, tourist bureaus, backroom deals and assorted rackets. On the other hand, the authorized theft sign above my head may not be referring to tourists but to film crews, which, lately, have been finding New Orleans a charming backdrop for the bloody carnage they feed America out of TVs and shopping malls. If so, that's even worse because that's out-and-out theft without even the excuse of stupidity. It's bad enough that you can never find a cop when you need one because they're all stopping traffic while a dog-food commercial rolls, but now they're ripping off the populace.

I would like to be there when the first be-camera'd freak tries to steal my voice and picture. I'll read him his rights so quick his camera'll have a hell of a time rolling away from the streetcar.

Oddnicity

After a year-long foray in the transparencies of rediscovered ethnicity I am returning to my true nature, oddnicity. I didn't mind being an ethnic—for a moment—but like a "beatnik" an ethnic is mostly an invention of the people watching. Or listening. The year just prolapsed was like a long ethnic joke, so long that nobody stayed around for the punch line. What didjew say happened to that Romanian-Pole-Estonian? Yeah, well, never mind, here is another one: There is this Arab-Jew-American. . . .

Okay, maybe history's a long, pointless ethnic joke, but there are other things going on. Why, right here in New Orleans, where everybody's of uncertain oddnicity, we had this tattooed naked guy walking around an art gallery with nothing on but a ten-gallon hat right after he purchased $60,000 worth of paintings. And he goes up to this well-dressed art-goer lady and asks her for a date. She says no, but when she walks out of the gallery she sees that he's driving a Lamborghini. And she *changes her mind*, rushes back inside, accepts the date. It's true, I met her. "Why did you change your mind?" I asked her. "He had a beautiful body," she replies with all the brave sincerity of a slightly ruined cynic from the city of oddnicity. "And his Lamborghini reminded me of it." "And what happened on the date?" I insist. "He had another girl with him," she says. Ah, but that's not all. Fearing my judgment of possible frivolity—she doesn't know me very well: I condemn the world for its paucity of frivolity!—she adds, "It wasn't just his body! He was a manufacturer and exporter of fine precision machinery from Switzerland. We just don't have that around here!"

There you have it, ladies and gentlemen! You can have all your Romanian-Pole-Estonians floundering drowningly about in the uncertain punch lines of ethnicity, but there are more significant things in the world: beautiful bodies welded to precision machinery in the mind of a New Orleanian mademoiselle! That's oddnicity without a punch line, just like the world.

Alligator Sauce Piquante

I talk funny. I know it. But then so does everybody else around here. I say, "Put it in the oven," and they say, "What ward you from, cher?" The other day I was explicating to someone how the food's just as funny as the words, take squirrel balls, for instance, or alligator piquante. Well, a man at another table overheard this and he said, in an accent that sounded just like mine, "I'll cook you the best gator you ever ate!" It turns out he was a Romanian from Transylvania just like me who operated a Cajun fast-food restaurant on Florida Boulevard in Baton Rouge.

Sure enough, I went over there the next day and he'd cooked a spicy batch of red brew with tender chunks of gator in it that tasted both heady and exhilarating, and it made me a little tipsy, if you know what I mean. He served this on white Louisiana rice with a side of greens, regaling me all the while with the wild tale of how he got from Transylvania to Louisiana, which was part of the enjoyment, and required in these parts. Telling a story to go with the meal is *de rigueur*, cher, it makes the food more memorable, and both meal and story get better when you sip that ice-cold Dixie beer. When I was done, my landsman wrapped a huge bag of fried alligator strips to take over to a party I was going to later that evening—there were three parties, actually, but I'd chosen just one after an agonizing soul-search. The strips were a big hit, and they provided me with the chance to retell my strange countryman's story. He had been the manager of a collective farm in Transylvania when he met a Swede one day. The Swede drew him a crawfish on a matchbook. My friend got children to catch boxes of them to ship to Sweden. When Romania ran out of mudbugs, he came to Louisiana to get some more, but discovered alligator instead. The Swedes didn't want it, so he started cooking it first for himself, then for his neighbors, then for me, and now for everyone at the party. And soon for everyone who hears this story. It's the Gospel truth, cher.

Dishwasher Fish

On my way to Mardi Gras in Mamou, which is as close to nowhere as a
motorist will ever get, I stopped at a tiny country store for fresh boudin.
Boudin is a spicy liver-and-rice sausage that you suck out one end of
the skin until you've got every grain. Good boudin is like currency
hereabouts, and places claim themselves to be "boudin" capital just like
others say they are "jambalaya" or "gumbo" capital. Mamou, for instance, makes a gumbo from hundreds of chickens caught by Mardi Gras
riders from dawn till sunset, and it's such famous gumbo, bowls of it get
shipped to addicts all over the world. If you're a boudin or gumbo fancier
you can spend your life in an area of several hundred square miles armed
with a hot sauce bottle and an attitude.

They make other things around here they tell nobody about, things
like dishwasher fish. You wrap your catch in spices and flour, seal it in
a plastic bag, put it in the dishwasher. When your gumbo bowls are
clean, your fish is done. You can substitute a dryer if you're having a
party at a Laundromat—everybody just takes their fish over and watches
it spin with the clothes. You taste and compare when you fold. But that's
rare even for New Orleans, though it may catch on. What's a lot more
common is finding yourself before a perfect stranger wearing a T-shirt that
says, SUCK DA HEADS AND EAT DA TAILS! They're referring to crawfish, or
mudbugs, the tiny red little mountains of lobster look-alikes that people
dump on newspapers in front of themselves and chomp down till the sun
goes way down. After a few Dixies even the most squeamish do suck da
heads and eat da tails just like the stranger's T-shirt says, only you're
not strangers anymore after you've wallowed like this in bits of flesh,
spices, shell, and suds in front of one another. In New Orleans, no food
is just food.

Gone Fishin'

Happens every year. My friend Keith calls and we go fishin'. It happens, that is, because it almost doesn't happen. First, Keith has to fix the boat hitch on his truck, which every year develops this hitch problem. But then he does, and we are off. My son Tristan, who's been walking around the house with his fishing rod every day since told that we're going fishin', and very nearly blinding the entire family with it, has a little problem getting up at 5 A.M. He has this little problem every day at 8 A.M. when he's supposed to go to school, but that's understandable.

It's a fine drive in the soft, cool dark through the Louisiana countryside. Birds are waking up in the marshes, the wind ruffles the pampas grass, and the Spanish moss on the cypresses. Leaning shacks and houseboats come out of the lavender dawn on the shores of bayous. Country stores with hand-lettered signs advertise alligator boudin, crawfish, shrimp, and possum.

There is a place called Fisherman's Wharf at Bayou Gauche where we tie the boat. You pay two dollars at the bar for the privilege, and you get to look at wood-carver and taxidermist C. de Jean's work on the walls: a huge snapping turtle with his mouth open, an alligator with a turtle in his mouth, foxes, deer, and armadillos. Some are real, some are wooden, but Tristan wants to set out right away. He wants fish, not art.

It's far from civilization in the old bayou as we come to a halt among leaning willows, sleeping ducks, and swamp chickens. Tristan finally gets to use his oft-fingered fishing rod, but not before he gets me to put a minnow on the hook, an activity he claims is a little difficult for him because of "those eyes." I'm not too keen on those eyes myself, but I thread the hook right through with all the hard-nosed indifference of forty years of living on this cruel planet, but mainly because I don't want him to think otherwise.

"I've taken so many fish outta here," declares Keith, "it embarrassed me to count 'em." It's true. Fish are leaping into the air all around the boat and our lines, snapping at dragonflies, spiders, and warm air. Bluegills, bass, and catfish teem in the water. Every few seconds our minnows and worms get bitten hard, and we reel in the lines to put more worms and minnows on the hooks. "It's a savvy bunch around here," mumbles Keith, hinting at some dark knowledge of our coming, transmitted seconds before we came, by fish telegraph. And Tristan pretends to grumble when they elude him.

No matter. It's a good day for tales, beer, and soda, and after a while we've told more fish tales than there are fish in the bayou, and that sits with him just fine, though he won't admit it. On the way back, he's fast asleep in the back of the truck. "Funny thing," says Keith, "it's like this sometimes."

Sure enough. And we like it plenty, just this way.

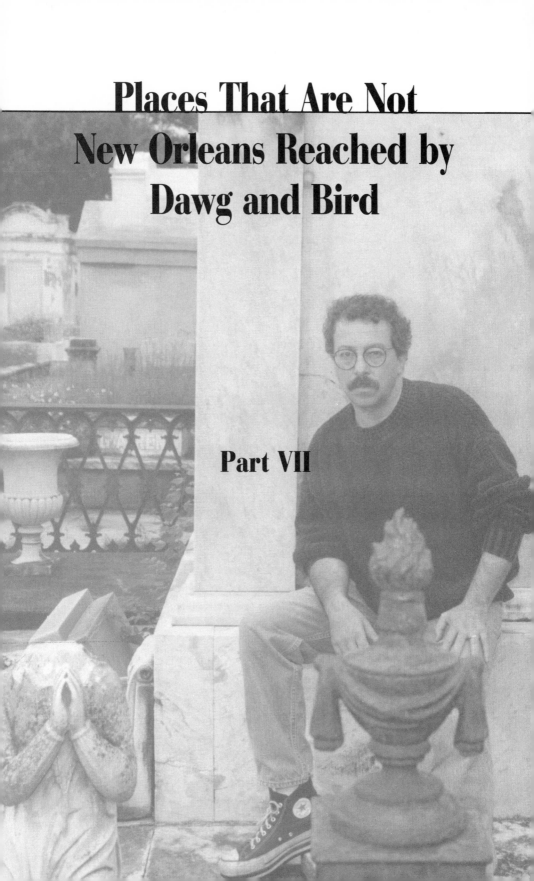

Places That Are Not New Orleans Reached by Dawg and Bird

Part VII

Life Without Greyhound

Years ago when I started riding the Dawg I knew that if the Dawg went on strike I could always take Big Red. Back in those days, people even got uppity when the service wasn't up to snuff, like a four-hour delay or a rude driver. Don'cha worry! they would say. I'm taking Big Red next time! And that was a big thing for people because people who ride the bus aren't the kind of people anybody hears: they are poor, they don't vote, and you never see them on TV.

That's the reason why not long ago the Dawg swallowed Big Red and there wasn't a peep out of Congress. Here we are, a huge so-called competitive nation with a bus monopoly! Where are the antitrust laws? Does it make sense to have a single lousy nationwide bus system that can be bought and sold by anyone lucky enough to land their chip on it on the Monopoly board? When we had two lousy bus companies we at least had a choice. Never mind the fact that every civilized country and many not-so-civilized countries in the world have a bus system ten times better than ours. Did you know Greyhound prices go up on holidays just so poor people who go see their kin can get there even poorer than they are? You can't go almost anywhere by train anymore because we've let all that rot and deteriorate. They did a study here to see if a passenger rail between New Orleans and Baton Rouge was feasible. Not safe for people, they decided. No, sirree, but it's safe enough for transporting quantities of deadly chemicals that could make the people of the state scarcer than Greyhound buses. "Look at it this way," a cop told me, "it keeps the scum out of town. No buses, no weirdos coming in cheap." Presumably, the weirdos who can afford a plane are okay. When the Dawg swallowed Big Red I wrote an outraged comment to that effect, and I promptly got a call from the PR guy for the president of Greyhound asking for a copy. I thought he sounded like a guy who makes cement bathtubs, so I sent him one. After hearing all the recent hoopla, I'm sure that he's not the only one at Greyhound who's in the cement business. Their scabs have been ramming right through the pickets outside the station here, nearly killing everyone. Scabs like that must be first-draft choices from the Hell's Angels. Must have been slim pickings after Eastern Airlines and air-traffic control got theirs. As for myself, I've thrown myself upon the kindness of strangers for rides. And I've changed my phone number.

Greyhound, Continued

Here is another tale from the unending pool of grief and bitter hilarity known as the Greyhound Company. For those unfamiliar with the evil Transportation Megamoth of Norte America, I will only say that the Greyhound Company is like the Ottoman Empire in its last days: unfocused, disorganized, foul-smelling, and bureaucratically rude. The Ottoman Empire eventually relinquished its hold on the unfortunates of the earth. One day, Greyhound will too.

In any case, there I was, miraculously seated—not a seldom occurrence—and the bus was about to pull out of Baton Rouge nearly on time. I could hardly believe it, and I soon had reason to be right. As the coach lurched backward there was a rap-rap on the door and a frantic citizen in hair curlers and slippers demanded attention. "My family's going to a funeral!" she cried. "Wait for them to buy their tickets." The bus driver, an obliging fellow, waited. Ten minutes later the funeral party boarded the Dawg, led by an exceedingly large human with a child folded under each arm. The driver suggested to this person that she might layer her brood on two seats to the back since in front all the rows had at least one person in them. The funeral-goer refused and plopped her flesh and the flesh of her flesh next to, or rather on, a Dutch tourist girl, who disappeared completely. "Madam," the bus driver insisted, "you must move so as not to give our country a reputation for rudeness in Dutchland!" "I'm going to a funeral!" shrieked the blob. "So are we!" shouted several people on the bus. Half the riders, it turns out, were going to funerals. It was a typical Greyhound crowd. The other half were going to mental hospitals. To make a long story short, the funeral party abandoned the bus and staged a crying period of mourning in front of it. The honor of our country was upheld in front of the Dutch. We were one hour late. Nobody got to their funerals. But the mental hospitals were still open and they gave me pen and paper to write this.

Crazy Bob's

The other day at Crazy Bob's Café at the Greyhound bus station in Baton Rouge, I heard a woman say to a bus driver, "I'm headin' south on account of the owls." "Yeah," said the bus driver, "Lotsa people headin' out these days on account of fish, too." It turns out the woman was from a place in the Northwest where the spotted owl was bankrupting the lumber industry. And the bus driver said that the fishing industry was gone in places where it wasn't legal now to catch more than two fish a week. "Can you imagine," the woman said, "it's even illegal to own a spotted owl. You can do time for it." "Like kidnappin' a baby or sump-thin' " laughed the bus driver. "And two fish," marveled the woman, "What can you do with two fish?" "Nothin', unless you're Jesus," the driver said.

There was a pause, during which I thought to insert the thought that maybe owls and fish have a right to live, too, but I thought better of it when the woman said, "They worry about owls. How about babies? What's gonna happen ten years from now?" "The owls will reproduce," said the bus driver, "and the babies will all be on welfare." "I saw a bumper sticker," said the woman, "I FEED MY OWL EXXON OIL." They both laughed. "Them preservationists," laughed the driver, "they all have offices and houses and fish for a hobby. Maybe two fish is all they need. They buy the other two from the deli." There was satisfied silence between them as they basked in agreement. They'd identified one more way in which the little man gets screwed. At this point, Crazy Bob, who owns Crazy Bob's and who charges ten cents for matches and eighty-six cents for a foam cup of coffee, switched on the Gospel station on the radio, and a preacher came on so loud I jumped and nearly scalded myself. "The Devil," shouted the preacher, "lives in the air. The Devil lives in the second heaven of the airwaves. That's where he is, controllin' Baton Rouge and the surrounding areas!" "Amen," said the woman, "and the areas surrounding *those*." "I drive through them Devil lands alla time," laughed the driver.

After that they called my bus and I got on with the rest of the loudest Silent Majority I ever heard.

The New Eating Tribes

There are an equal number of churches and barbecue houses in Jackson, Mississippi. After the churches let out, clean pastel-dressed families stream through the heat into the barbecue joints and eat expertly, rarely getting sauce unto their Sunday best. There is little traffic on I-55, which is the main drag in town, slicing carelessly through neighborhoods, dragging Wendy's, McDonald's, and Taco Bells in its wake.

The menu for the Mississippi ACLU's twenty-first anniversary dinner wasn't particularly southern, but it was chicken, the official food of the state. There were also little American toothpick flags in the apple, orange, and cheese slices on the hors d'oeuvre table and everyone wore a little American flag on the lapel. If you didn't know like I did that this group contained some of the fiercest, most embattled, and toughest civil libertarians in the country, you would have thought you were at an American Legion meeting. The Mississippi ACLU has gotten little rest in the Deep South since it was founded, and it is getting even less now that the golden age of demagoguery is upon us, bearing down on the Constitution in varied and multifarious ways. There are flag-burners to defend, musicians to bail out, artists and art dealers to protect, electric chairs to unplug. Two presidents have now publicly made the ACLU their enemy, but not only is it still in business, few take it lightly. Said Marc Marquardt, the chief tough in Mississippi, "We get what we want with a just a phone call sometimes. . . . That ACLU, they say, they don't mess around. . . ."

As for me, I felt positively subversive wearing my ACLU T-shirt in downtown Jackson after church. Nobody said anything, but I felt eyes riveted on my person, making me overly conscious of the barbecue sauce that demands great skill to keep off in the best of times.

Nonetheless, I was ready to mouth off. In fact I felt like doing something real bad, like putting 100 flag toothpicks in my hair. After all, I'd just met about 300 lawyers waiting for something.

Nouveau Plateau

Men and women achieve new plateaus in their endeavors every day. Records are now broken that were once thought impossible. If our grandfathers could see how fast we are now running the mile, they would put down their pipes in wonder.

I went to a fashionable nightspot in New York the other night called Nell's. My publisher was having a party there for his latest book. I handed the bartender a twenty for two drinks and I got back two dollars. That in itself was a shock to my provincial soul, but the real revelation came later when I considered purchasing some simple grease to cut through the expensive bourbon. There on the wax-spattered menu was the following: *French fries: Six dollars.* As I gazed in mute wonder at this phenomenal equation, I felt that certain tingle that comes in the presence of the absolutely new. I was sure that here was a record. The rest of the document wasn't so shabby, either. *House wine: Five dollars. Coffee: Four dollars.* A New York friend, familiar with the research, explained that this was a club for mostly rich Europeans who wanted the American experience. Those french fries were part of their initiation: what they were paying for wasn't just fries, it was education. I don't want to belabor the obvious, but I had just spent at least six dollars on the half-block stretch from the cab to club, on about twenty homeless wretches who were freezing in cardboard boxes all over the sidewalk. Had I decided to feed them instead, I wouldn't have had enough french fries for all of them, even at one fry per head.

Such quiet but significant records often pass unnoticed. It may well be that my six-dollar french fries are not even a record. Somewhere in the fashionable bowels of another neighborhood this achievement may have been surpassed. Has it? If so, let me know. Write to me here at St. Martin's Press if you can top these six-buck fries.

Man Tales

"Is that Mount Saint Helens?" the man asked, a slight look of disdain on his rough, bewhiskered face. He pointed to a snow-covered crater nestled between peaks five miles below us. "I don't know," I honestly said, impressed equally by the mountain and by the expression on his face. "You know mountains, then," I tentatively asked. "Yup. Fly over them every Monday when I go to work on the North Slope," he said.

I was going home from a poetry reading in Longview, Washington, near Portland, Oregon. My seatmate was flying from Anchorage to Dallas. The closer we got to our destination, the more disdainful he got. "You people in the Lower Forty-Eight are in trouble," he said. "You'll be drownin' in your garbage soon." "Alaska pretty clean, huh?" I encouraged him. "Yup. Went fishin' the other day, caught a ninety-five-pound halibut." "How did you get him in the boat?" "Shot him through the head. Pretty much have to or he'd sink you." He then went on to tell me that he shot caribou, black bear, and ducks, too. Had four freezers full of meat and fish. The week before he'd feasted on king crab, salmon, and huge shrimp boiled right on the beach. A polar bear was watching, no more than two feet away. "Pink salmon," he said, frowning, "we feed that to the dogs." "Taste pretty good to me," I said timidly. "Yeah," he said. "I caught a thirty-pound pink salmon when I first got to Alaska and the ole sourdough who ran the camp kitchen wouldn't cook it. 'That's for the dogs,' he said." "Seems like a waste," I opined. "No waste," he said gruffly, "I eat everything I shoot and fish. 'Tis a shame, though. People shoot black bears now for their gall bladders. Sell 'em to the Japanese for aphrodisiacs." I asked him about opening the Alaskan wildlife refuge to drilling for oil. "Won't harm the animals," he said. "They'll just live with it. It's the Lower Forty-Eight that got to watch out. Our birds don't go to California no more. Too many toxic pits. Ducks are winterin' at home. They're not stupid." "Gets pretty cold, huh?" I said, philosophically. I'd watched the weather channel in Portland and knew that temperatures had been at minus eighty that day in Anchorage. My seatmate didn't reply. I felt stupid. Of course it gets cold. But after a weighty silence, he turned to me again. "What did you say the temperature in Dallas was?" "Sixty-five." He nodded doubtfully. "The steel in this plane," he said, "it just went from eighty below to sixty-five above." I saw his point, felt tiny cracks right under my seat, felt the distance right down to my bones.

Buffalo: City of No Illusions

When I got out of the car a blade of frigid wind whipped my face with the fury of a pack of wolves starving in the snowy deeps of Siberia. "I can't believe you people live here!" I howled *contra venti* at my friend Deborah Ott, who was flattened by the gale against a wall of the University of Buffalo. "It's nothing," she said, "wait til next month!" Luckily, I wasn't going to. I was going back next day to my scented bower of camellias, azaleas, wisteria, magnolia, and birds, where winter is only a dream, and our only fear is not finding a table at our favorite outdoor café. Nonetheless, in spite of or maybe because of the weather, Buffalo is a city full of poets. Here at the university they have a chair for Robert Creeley, the man who recently wrote:

> *The world is a round but*
> *diminishing ball, a spherical*
> *ice cube . . .*

And here was where the giant, Maximus, aka Charles Olson, spent many years writing and talking up a snowstorm. In the cooled inner recesses of the Buffalo Poetry Collection, Robert Berthoff, the librarian, shows me the original notebook that became *Ulysses* by James Joyce, and the typewritten and crumbling manuscript of William Carlos Williams's *The Farmer's Daughters*. "Williams bought some cheap paper in bulk somewhere, and it's falling apart!" growls Berthoff, who could be Mephistopheles, and probably is. A fiendish pursuer of the archives and books of American poets, he stays up in the long winter nights of Buffalo bidding for souls. In the backyard of Jack Clarke's house a similarly phantomatic mixture of cold and poetry hold sway. We have come outside to see the sharp, bright stars. Quickly moving snow clouds move under them. A cat darts out from under a frozen tree. Chilled to the bone, we move back inside to where the wine and the music are. I am beginning to remember the pleasures of deep winter, the common front people make against the cold with soup and warm bread. . . . Neah, I'll go back to my bower of birds and ease, where I'll wear only my new T-shirt: BUFFALO: CITY OF NO ILLUSIONS.

Whence Inspiration?

What inspires people to do amazing things? In Detroit, Michigan, a city that looks like Dresden after the bombs, a young artist named Tyree Guyton has been transforming the slum where he lives into an explosive world of color. There are brightly painted dolls, shoes, bicycles, and toys climbing up gnarly winter trees. There is a crucified bicycle ringed with lights to which a dolorous path paved with lost shoes winds its way, an urban Golgotha. And there is a grave there, too, where are interred the souls of two houses that Tyree and his girl, Karen, transformed. Two houses that the city of Detroit tore down in the middle of the night.

Yes, Detroit fears Tyree and art. It tore down his houses, and it curtailed hours at the art museum. Meanwhile, crack houses and burned-out hulks full of rats keep unmolested vigil over the industrial nightmare. There are shoes on Tyree's road, too, hundreds of shoes. "They are lost people," Tyree explains, "people looking for home, for food, for love." And there are even more now. Michigan cut thousands of people off welfare rolls. And the day after I talked to Tyree, GM announced plans for 27,000 layoffs by 1995. Tyree remains undaunted: he'll keep going. It's his mission to transform bleakness into color and feeling.

He lives in a little house with Karen and with Grampa. Grampa is well past eighty. He keeps warm by the gas jets on the kitchen stove, seated at a table piled high with his drawings, which he keeps making as we speak, one after another. And he philosophizes as he works, quoting the prophets in the Bible. A neighborhood kid, about nine, drops in and, wordlessly, starts making drawings too. He's made a dragon-man with fire in his eyes. "Do you like it?" he asks me. I do. Tyree pats him on the head. "We've got a lotta kids here after school," he explains. I see the bright fire dragons of a lot of kids keeping them from becoming lost shoes on Detroit's roads to nowhere.

Divine Justices

There is a little display case in the village of Volcano in Hawaii full of stones that tourists took back with them and then mailed back with notes that said, *I lost my job and my cat died. Please give the goddess back her stone.* It appears that Goddess Pele, who rules the volcanoes of Hawaii, doesn't want her stones removed. Bad things happen if you do. Bad things also happen to people who steal pieces of pottery from pre-Columbian sites in Mexico. Someone I know found a little ceramic foot belonging to some kind of Mayan demon and took it to Baton Rouge. On the way home from the airport there was a toxic spill and he nearly died. He mailed back the foot pronto. Everyone knows about the archaeologists at King Tut's tomb who dropped dead one by one without any apparent reason.

One would be hard put to figure out how ancient stones and artifacts take revenge on people who disturb them. There was a recent incident, however, that is perfectly understandable. After people abandoned their houses around Chernobyl, thieves walked in and stole contaminated icons from the walls. These icons are now turning up all over the world in the houses of art collectors. It is clear, in this case, how modern evil gods operate. Maybe the ancient gods operated the same way. Filled with power and bloated with worship, they held sway until they collapsed or were conquered one day. Nothing remained of their former glory except the afterglow of their radiance. The unwitting tourist picks it up and brings it home. Which brings me to my real subject, tourists. These dislocated creatures wander the planet now, more and more numerous, a quickly reproducing tribe that leaves no stone unturned, no sight unphotographed, no native undisturbed. I see them pass by my house every day, intent on stealing whatever their inattention lands upon. I'm tempted to spray something on their cameras. I can see how one can become an ancient evil god. The power of the old icons may have been only a defense against tourism.

Stupidity

I went to a neo-post-après punk bar in Washington, D.C., looking for some of that soul-healing stupidity that used to give the scene such charm. Several ruined bodies were collapsed in their scuffed leathers and chains at the marbletop bar. But instead of rotgut red they were drinking espresso and brandy. "Say," I accosted my neighbor, an angular anorexic androgyne with a proper glaze over enlarged pupils, "What's happenin'?"

"Listen," he said, "I come here after my dramatic improvisation group. I work with computers all day, but I don't have one at home. I studied music at Juilliard, and I'm looking for someone who makes panpipes and knows as much as there is to know about ancient Greek music and versification." I regarded him indignantly. "Listen, man," I said, underlining "man" to underscore the generational and intentional border that separated us, "I come here to be stupid. You wouldn't know where I can find that ineffable substance?" "Stupidity?" he said, "That's the hottest commodity on the market today. Costs more than cocaine. About a thousand dollars' worth of plane tickets to a new industrial village in the Balkans, I'd say." And even there, I thought, nobody's really stupid, just exhausted. I had the sudden and heartbreaking vision of a world devoid of the basic right to shut it out. It is only in stupidity that one can ask once again the basic questions and make them new. Stupidity isn't natural. It's an artificial commodity people produce to keep the world at bay. Nobody is naturally stupid. It's hard work.

The media produces a kind of artificial, informational stupidity that is a large ingredient in real stupidity, but it's an unstable mixture and it takes an ungodly amount of TV watching to make the real thing. I loved the punks when they first came on the scene because I thought that here, at long last, was a generation that would create a real barrier-reef against the world. But alas, as I cast about, I saw only the children of professionals pretending they just landed on the planet, while secretly reading art and architecture magazines. There are even voters among them. I downed my espresso in a single bitter gulp and headed for the library.

Sunny Day in Boston

It was a beautiful sunny day in Boston, and every Bostonian was out running alongside the Charles River. The girls from Cornell in red boats with red and white oars streaked past the men from Yale going the other way in black boats with black oars. The ducklings by the swanboats on Boston Common looked recently disembarked from the famous childrens' book about them. The old bookstores along Newbury Street smelled full of old books in good shape. Time stood still for a while in the Brattle Bookstore while an old atlas turned pages. The clock started ticking again outside, but it stopped again in the Avenue Victor Hugo Bookshop. A mad cabdriver laughing for no reason drove insanely to Cambridge. On Harvard Square the dyed mohawks of thirteen-year-olds on skateboards stood sharply against the sky. Their frowning punk countenances clouded but did not hide many sensitive features inherited from their Harvard prof parents. They smelled like torn denim, cigarettes, and insecurity.

A little farther up the street, at the Harvard Club, one could see the turtlelike heads of their venerably ancient grandfathers buried in newspapers. They exuded an aroma of leather, cigars, and authority. "It's a good day to be a Brahmin," someone remarked casually to someone else, as the wheels of their handmade New England baby carriages rattled over the cobblestones. At the Thai restaurant there was a line of people gesturing in air redolent with lemongrass and spicy shrimp. Cumin and allspice issued in a brief burst from a subterranean Arab shop. A middle-aged man descended into a Spanish Civil War–vintage coffeehouse below the street looking for the copy of *Being and Nothingness* he had left there twenty-five years before. He found, instead, several friends from other cities who thought it very natural that they should meet like this after a very long time. Everyone wore glasses, talked fast, had an excellent book under a firm arm, and did not smoke. Evening was quickly descending on Boston, and the clouds of talk rose higher. At Grolier's bookshop they were all out of Codrescu's books, which are very popular and get stolen regularly. Certain things never change in Boston.

The Media and the Hermit

Near Boston at a place called Braintree they are building a waste-incinerator. Not far from the future incinerator in a car cemetery lives a hermit and folk artist named Bill, or William, as one of the junkyard workers, a young muscle-builder with jail tattooes, respectfully calls him. William has made a little world of icons out of car parts: there is a Virgin Mary floating on hubcap clouds, a Jesus with antennae, and dashboard altars with wire flowers. Every part of William's world is transformed: his dashboards have words written on them, a wooden plank warning trespassers to stay out is painted with squiggly, heavenly blue lines. An old mailbox has been padlocked shut and the mail slot is closed. Bill has made it clear: don't come near, don't even write to me.

I was not surprised when Bill came out to tell us to go away. We were five. The director, the producer, the cameraman, the soundman, and I. We were making a movie. We were at Bill's because of the incinerator. "Here lives Bill the Hermit," I was supposed to say, "They are gonna poison the air/All around the one who thought/He'll get away." So here we were, five strong, the media, ready to bug Bill to tell the world that it's hard to be Bill nowadays. Bill was a black man in his forties or fifties—kind of young for a hermit, I thought—and he wasn't very good at making us go away. I wanted to leave, but the director said, "Hey, it's a public street, can't let a hermit ruin a perfect shot of a hermit." The producer thought Bill might come out with an art-rifle of some kind to back up his demands so she said we should do whatever we do real fast. The cameraman was of the same opinion, but the fading light concerned him more than Bill. "How can we," I shouted at the director, "stand here and praise the solitude of a man whose privacy we are destroying?" "Let's just do it once," he said, "to see how it works. We are the media . . . we invade everybody." We stood by Bill's holy fence carrying on when Bill reappeared. He was dressed for the occasion.

He wore several toy police badges, a cowboy belt without pistols, a hat with medals on it. He strutted belligerently forward. "What's the matter with me?" he said, in a fierce but less-than-threatening tone. "Nothing is the matter with you!" screamed the cameraman, "but the light is fading!" Bill ran back to hide somewhere inside his religious empire. We shot the film. The light faded, first from the future incinerator, which was on a rise, then from the junkyard where William lives.

An Old-Fashioned Party

A few of us, artists and writers from New Orleans, went to Boston over the weekend to visit with some Boston artists and writers. It had been decided that no two cities are more unalike than Boston and New Orleans. Bostonians eat lobsters and burn witches. New Orleanians eat crawfish and worship witches. It's always cold in Boston and it's always hot in New Orleans. Bostonians are eggheads. New Orleanians are sensualists. And so on.

Based on these differences, the two groups made each other some ritual gifts. The Bostonians sent us a two-ton block of ice with essential items, such as plastic mouths full of white beans, imbedded in them. The ice melted pictorially as we ate oysters off the Boston ice at the reception party. There were candles in the ice, and someone suggested holding a Black Mass on it around midnight but we couldn't find any virgins.

In exchange, we set out for Boston carrying five suitcases full of Mississippi mud mixed with grave dirt and filé gumbo. Imbedded in the mud were found items such as a denture with gold teeth and the disk containing the complete text of my latest novel. We delivered the mud to The Space, the downtown art gallery where our counterparts were based. The digging of the items out of mud was accomplished with great aplomb by one of the Bostonians.

We then adjourned to a lavish dinner prepared by one of our hosts at his renovated Victorian mansion and had lobster in red bell pepper sauce, followed by an ancient colonial stew of salted cod and white beans, which some of us laced with Tabasco hot sauce from the bottles we carried in our pockets for just such an emergency. After the custard dessert made with honey from a neighborhood beehive, the hosts put on Cajun music, which, being unfamiliar to the natives, caused several of them to fall and break valuable vases, antique dishes, and clay sculptures. Around midnight, it was decided that there wasn't much difference between Boston and New Orleans, so we officially exchanged the names of our cities, promising to refer henceforth to Boston as New Orleans and to New Orleans as Boston. Next stop—Minneapolis.

Return to Minneapolis

Years ago I went to Minneapolis and declared the city "dirt free." Last week I went back and they asked me if the city still looked clean to me. "Cleaner than ever," I said. On Sunday morning, I turned on the television and there was a preacher on every channel except one, and on that one they were talking about day-care centers. The Sunday paper had in it a great big editorial from a gay activist about the necessity of protecting cruising in the city parks, an activity described as a historical and traditional form of gay expression.

The people I met were also very nice and very careful to point out the positive points of everything. It is true, one of them said, I have a very melancholy disposition, but I have had very liberal parents who encouraged me to express everything. In fact, *expression*, *potential*, and *healing* were words very much in use. "We meet to heal each other, not to criticize," a writer told me, only half in jest. And indeed, healing, even among curmudgeon writers, is *de rigueur*. The poet Robert Bly leads large groups of men into the woods to get in touch with their maleness. There is some kind of subtle difference between this and cruising, but I have to look up my Joseph Campbell to tell you what it is.

At a lovely party in a tree-shaded suburban home where we stood about eating small cracker, roast beef, and mayonnaise sandwiches, someone told me that, in Minneapolis, "everyone knows the Twelve Steps." Those, in case you're a barbarian, are the steps leading from hell to health in Alcoholics Anonymous. Nobody smokes, drinks, or swears in this beautiful northern city, and even the artists that I met go to bed at 10:30 P.M. These artists, incidentally, have more money to "express themselves" than just about anybody else in the country. There are large cash grants of all sorts, many "nurturing" institutions, philanthropic capitalists, generous citizens of all stripes. Social services and buses work, there is generalized interest in sports, and the children look unbelievably healthy. Bad things like cigarettes and booze cost a lot of money, and they come with a brochure detailing the Twelve Steps. For all that, there are still some bad things in Minneapolis because no matter how good the people get, they are still given four months of winter every year as punishment. It's unfair and everyone knows it, and tries harder to be good.

Extra: Minneapolis's Lazear Tries to Calm Down New Orleans's Codrescu

My agent wrote a book, it's called *Meditations for Men Who Do Too Much* by Jonathon Lazear. He sent it to me about two weeks ago, but I haven't had time to read it. I finally got around to it yesterday, and it cleared up at least one mystery for me. I now know why I can never get a hold of him by phone. He's out following his own advice, things like "By letting go, it all gets done; The world is won by those who let it go!" which purports to be a quote from the Tao Te Ching, written no doubt before they had telephones.

Jonathon lives in Minneapolis, where everybody is an "olic" of some kind, alcoholic, sexaholic, workaholic, support-groupaholic. People there work very hard at this. Anyway, it's interesting that he sent me this book twenty days before the deadline for my book, which is in worse shape than George Santayana, who said, "Our dignity is not in what we do, but in what we understand." Heck, I understand everything. Now, where is the Little Red Hen? Twenty days before deadline and my agent sends me this comforting little bag of soothing quips for workaholics. He almost got me, too. I lay there for almost an hour watching TV after I read that "four out of five people are more in need of rest than exercise." Dr. Logan Clendening, whoever he is, said that. I would have been very successful at it until I noticed that all there was on was Chelsea Clinton's cat, Socks, on every channel.

I went back to Jonathon's book to find out if there was anything between extreme boredom and workaholism, a kind of middle state for authors under the gun. They don't call them "*dead*lines" for nothing. I found this radical statement by William Saroyan: "The greatest happiness you can have is knowing that you do not necessarily require happiness," which sounds okay until you remember what an unhappy, mean bastard Saroyan was, and then you're not so sure about the happiness of being miserable. I like John Ciardi better, who said, "The day will happen whether or not you get up." Of course, he wrote that down, and it's the only way we know that his day happened. I appreciate this, Jonathon, I really do, but I've got many typos to go before I quip.

Selling Selling

I went to the McDonald's Museum in Des Plaines, Illinois, and admired the life-size plaster statues of early McDonald's employees dispensing the first dollops of what soon became a mighty river of burgers. I admired the early plastic fries, the primitive milk-shake machines, and the not-yet-merged neon arches. McDonald's was a triumph of private enterprise that seduced America and now parts of the world without any seeming help from the government. And why should the government help a successful business that does better than the government? Well, that's what I thought—until I read in the morning paper that McDonald's got $465,000 from the Department of Agriculture last year for ads, paper tray liners, and counter displays promoting Chicken McNuggets around the world. Campbell Soup Co. got $450,000 to push V-8 juice in Japan, Argentina, Korea, and Taiwan. Burger King, M&M Mars, Hershey Foods, Del Monte, Welch's, Ocean Spray Cranberries, Nabisco Foods, and Quaker Oats Co. also got a bundle. Sunkist Growers got $10 million to promote citrus, Gallo got $5 million to push vino, and Pillsbury got nearly $3 million to sell cookies to the heathen.

What's going on here? At a time when cities like Detroit are dying on the vine, when the state of Michigan cuts one-third of its welfare recipients off the rolls, when food-stamp allocations issued by the very same Department of Agriculture are being reduced for families who can barely afford an orange or a Big Mac? Wouldn't the Department of Agriculture be better off subsidizing *Americans* to buy burgers, oranges, and oatmeal? The government is giving away our money to companies that already take a big chunk of it, including food taxes. Does McDonald's, which made $20 billion last year, really need our welfare money? This is a case of multiple robbery by double taxation, welfare for the rich, and waste. You don't see McDonald's, Gallo, Pillsbury, and Sunkist giving anything away, do you?

Art Food

In Seattle the other day, I picked an item called "crab enchiladas" out of the menu and a strange work of art appeared on my plate. A glutinous rice pancake was wrapped thickly around a core of mayonnaise-infused crabmeat with chunks of ginger in it. Surrounding this assemblage were halved blue potatoes. Yes, blue. When my eyes rolled almost involuntarily out of my head the waiter smiled an ineffable, "yes, I *am* Gregory" smile and explained that these potatoes were indeed blue, naturally blue, and that the establishment, the neighborhood, and the city of Seattle were mighty proud of the fact. Disregarding my low-class doubts, I tried one of the damn things: they were not only blue, they were *raw*.

Next day, I carefully avoided the elaborate and cheerful eateries of downtown Seattle, where lavish muffin creations beckoned from artistic windows, and went to what looked like a generic Mexican restaurant. I ordered from the blissfully ordinary menu the "number one" combination, enchiladas, chile rellenos, and one cheese burrito. When the food came, I thought that some mistake had been made. The food was entirely *white*! The enchiladas were *pancakes* wrapped around something reminiscent of chicken salad. The rellenos lay invisible under a white blanket of melted cheese with flakes of pimiento in it. Instead of tortillas there was a basket of *cheese bread*! The number one looked like the stuff they feed inmates at mental hospitals. I sat there drenched in cold sweat. The town had been entirely taken over by *art food* like the Village of the Damned. A square meal was nowhere to be had.

Since then, I have been to other muffin cities where "art food" has taken over: Minneapolis, where items of dubious ethnicity and even more suspect consistency surround even the most unassuming plate; Washington, D.C., where arugula grows unhindered under every entrée; and, notably, Boulder, Colorado, where yuppie panhandlers stand under the whole-wheat rain begging the passerby for five dollars for a double cappuccino and a pack of Gitanes.

There is a good reason why most national cuisines have a limited number of dishes. By experimenting over thousands of years, they have eliminated thousands of ideas. Nouveau cities, I beg of you, do not invent food! We do not have thousands of years to spare!

I Saw a Man Dancing with
His Wife in Chicago, Chicago

Last time I looked at the Chicago Tribune Tower in Chicago I was moved
to write a poem. Imbedded in the sides of the massive castle are chunks
of the world's most famous buildings, from the Great Wall of China to
Stonehenge. I wondered then, as I do now, how the builders had gotten
away with taking home large chunks of cathedrals, Shinto shrines, Mongolian dojos, and sacred battlefields. But there they were, testimonies
to a time when raw, crude American power could pack the world in a
suitcase. Chicago buildings still give me that peculiar chill that comes
with standing before the shameless arrogance of a time before taxes and
civic humility, when money yielded a kind of grandiose power scarcely
imaginable these days. The Wrigley Building on the other side of Michigan Avenue stands likewise unabashed and ostentatious.

There are a great many new buildings in Chicago since I was last
here, notably the new deco-flavored NBC skyscraper with its gold pea-
cock glinting imperially in the gray of a frozen November day. On the
other hand, the Sears Tower, once the world's tallest building, is for
sale. If the Japanese don't buy it, I will. It has enough rooms for all my
friends. We can have the largest commune in the world in there. Looking
up at the fantastic cloud-covered apartment buildings swaying in the
wind from Lake Michigan, I imagined for a moment the sensation of
living there. It would be like standing perpetually at the prow of a ship,
feeling nothing but power and wind. A friend of mine went to dinner up
there on the sixty-seventh floor and the china shifted as the building
swayed. And after dinner, the host ran the length of his considerable
living room and hurled himself bodily against the wall-size plateglass
window my friend felt too dizzy to stand next to. It didn't break, but the
queasiness hung in the air for a minute as if the laws of nature had been
broken.

There is something here, in the heart of the Midwest, that stands for both the best and the worst in the American character. On the good side it is solid, powerful, daring, seemingly limitless. On the other, it's crude, arrogant, flaunting its wealth in the face of the world like a filet mignon burp. The cutting arctic air from the lake gave me chills. But they weren't entirely from the cold.

Denver

Denver is like New Orleans—a nice city. And like other nice cities, it is being abandoned by many people who can't find work. The economy's stagnant, the jobs are scarce, crime is bad, but the artists love it. There are cheap rents, available studio spaces, and a layered charm that bespeaks an interesting history. My friends, the Lodo Art and Boxing Team, would rather the secret didn't get out. Lodo stands for Lower Downtown, where their huge brick studios are located, and they'd hate to see Lodo become Soho, which would necessitate the creation of Sodo, Nodo, and Dodo, as new frontiers before the ever expanding onslaught of chic and cash. As in New Orleans, however, there is little danger of that occurring as we speak. The chambers of commerce in both our cities give lip service to art and artists, but little else. Spending a few grand on buying a favorable story in a major magazine gets you visible results. Giving artists a tax or zoning break has uncertain results at best, and could even be a dangerous thing these days, when taxpayers everywhere are up in arms about art crucifixes and photo-homosexuals.

In Denver itself, public outcry about a wonderfully sweet sculpture by Red Grooms of a frontier wagon with a dueling cowboy and Indian caused the work to be removed from a central spot to an obscure corner of the art museum where nobody can find it. The citizens, it appears, were shocked by the cartoon description of what they no doubt think of as a noble and solemn history unfolding like movie credits to the sacred rhythms of "Home on the Range." Here in New Orleans, we are more tolerant of our checkered past, partly because it's hard to keep a straight face about the unbelievable procession of allegiances, flags, betrayals, and eccentricities that constitute it. The Denver Lodo Art and Boxing Team has now joined Exquisite Corpse in New Orleans for a defense of cheapness. We want to keep our cities cheap and friendly. We need room to be bad in.

On the Set

I went to the Sundance Film Fest in Park City, Utah, to peddle my great film *Road Scholar*, which I wrote and I'm the s-t-a-a-r of, if you know what I mean. This is not about the greatness of the movie, though it's the greatest movie as far as movies go. I'm a word man myself, so don't expect me to push it. I think images are the narcotics of the masses, not bad as narcotics go, but in the long run . . .

Anyway, there I was in this pop-up skiing town in the mountains, snowdrifts up to the eaves of Bavarian schlosses, trying to breathe at thousands of feet up, having just come from below sea level in New Orleans, and there were hundreds of people everywhere who cared only about movies, movies, movies, as if the rest of the world was but a stage, lights, camera, action, etc. For seven days I climbed icy paths to darkened movie theaters, went to thousands of parties, shook off the chill in my Jacuzzi, and didn't see a newspaper or hear the news. The world, for all I knew, had shrunk and was gone, nothing left but a projector and a screen. Met real movie stars, too. I won't tell you who, but they are not like us, that's for sure—they are taller. I was introduced to a man who asked me how I liked Park City. "Splendid," I said, "just like a nineteenth-century TB sanatorium where Nietzsche and Kafka spent time." "I developed most of it," said the man.

And that wasn't the only faux pas. I made dozens of them, and slipped accordingly, facedown on the ice; I have the bruises to prove it. The movies weren't bad, though they all seemed to last about nine and a half hours, not counting the credits. The parties were pretty long, too. After a time, I saw people's words in balloons over their heads, and I was so tired I had no idea what they were saying. Trudging back to my Jacuzzi one star-pierced night, I became convinced that Park City, Utah, is where they keep Christmas year-round so that people who can't get enough of it at Christmastime can come here and for a few thousand bucks keep being in the spirit. I mention this because it occurred to me on the spot that this would make a great movie, *Eternal Christmas*, or something. Next day I sold it. Only kidding. I only sold ten movie ideas, and *Eternal Christmas* wasn't among them.

Memphis: The City of Dead Kings

Memphis in Egypt was the City of Dead Kings, and so it is with Memphis, Tennessee. Our Memphis boasts two dead kings, Elvis, king of rock and roll, and Martin Luther, king of the poor. Between these two kings there stretches the outlandish spectacle of the American mind, which swings like a yo-yo between frivolity and concern.

You get to the house of King Elvis after you pass the giant rat on top of Atomic Pest Control, the Little Guns Motel, a huge milk bottle, and a Graceland Dodge dealership. You turn off Bellevue onto Elvis Presley Boulevard, and then you're there, at Graceland, where they unload a bus tour every three minutes to take gaggles of folk with awestruck bouffants and greased ducktails through the mirrored chintz of a white American nightmare. It's a good place to pick up decorating hints for your trailer. There is shag rug on the ceiling, window curtains gathered over a pool table, and one to three TVs in every room, including the dining room, where Elvis would have dinner with up to twelve people and never miss his favorite shows. One whole room, the proud guide says, was bought by Elvis right off the showroom floor of a downtown furnisher. That's the one with the mirrors, the huge neo-Hawaiian hairy chairs, and the waterfall. And then, in a connected building, are endless rows of gold and platinum records interspersed with trophies, movie posters, honorary deputy badges, and even an ID card proclaiming the stoned-looking Elvis in the photo a captain of the Memphis police. There are full-size dolls of Elvis and Priscilla in their wedding clothes, and a plaque from the local Cadillac dealership with thirty-one names inscribed on it to commemorate the famous "night of the Cadillacs," when a generous Elvis gave away thirty-one of these to friends and relatives. There are his numerous guns, and the bullet holes in the door Elvis used for target practice, right next to his father-in-law's office who, wisely, stayed inside during the fusillade.

Elvis is buried in the backyard between his mother and father, and some of his family lives upstairs, peering through drawn curtains at the 3,000 to 5,000 visitors who stream through every day at about ten bucks a head. The graves are in a semicircular walkway past a statue of Jesus with his arms in the air, and the visitors read the names on the tombstones carefully, moving their lips. One such gravesite visitor asked the guide, "Is this a relative of Elvis? Where is Elvis buried?" "That *is* Elvis, ma'am," said the guide politely. Several visitors expressed the same kind of doubt. It seemed impossible to them that the actual Elvis, not an impersonator, was buried in there. For them, Elvis was an idea and Graceland only the temporary stopping place for this idea. But they love Graceland, because it's their idea of how to live it up if they became kings somehow. Many of them are worried that Lisa Marie, who stands to inherit Graceland when she turns twenty-five, might decide to redecorate. That would be neither more nor less than messing with the interior furnishings of the American mind itself.

Later at the Groundhog Café, I ordered Elvis's "favorite," the peanut-butter-and-banana sandwich. It came grilled, oozing a blended substance the consistency of baby doo-doo. It was one of the most vile things I ever laid a tongue on, but there was something about it at the same time, something *eerie* and *total*, as if I'd touched an electric icon (a sore on the Devil's eyelid, to be more precise), and I realized that I had reached an apex, the Grand Sum of White Trash Cooking. Elvis had these sandwiches made for him by his mum and flown to his stoned dressing room in Vegas where a legion of aides labored to pull him into his performing suit. They were, these baby-doo-doo sandwiches, his last sad link to reality.

The Lorraine Motel, on the other hand, is an abandoned shell with a heap of rubble in front. The sun beats mercilessly down from the cloudless sky on the abandoned asphalt and cement of downtown Memphis. There is a sign on one of the few doors left among many gaping holes on the second floor, a sign that alerts the passerby that this was Martin Luther King's room. From the balcony hangs a wreath. This is the spot where King stood when he was shot. A high, wire fence surrounds the desolate ruin. Camped in front in a small tent is Jacqueline Smith, the last tenant of the Lorraine. She has vowed not to move until the city builds a free civil-rights learning and cultural center there. But the city, which owns the expensive real estate, envisions a paying "museum of civil rights" displaying Martin Luther King's trophies with tour buses coming and going every three minutes. No way, says Ms.

Smith, handing the rare visitor a sheet with Martin Luther King's last sermon, which says, in part: "I won't have the fine and luxurious things of life to leave behind. But I just want to leave a committed life behind."

I browse through the few but essential clippings and newspaper photos that Ms. Smith has laid on a makeshift table. The hot sun is melting the plastic on the cheap frames. Her seemingly hopeless battle with the city has not made her bitter. She sees herself continuing Dr. King's struggle, her cause no different from her daily chores. Between answering questions, she goes in and out of her tent with a pan of water for her tea. Even ten years ago she would have had many friends and supporters around her, perhaps a whole street full of tents. But it is 1990 now, and this lone protester's cause is about something that makes us all very uncomfortable. Graceland, on the other hand, makes us feel safe and cool because it, too, is about something, namely money, pathos, cruelty, and bad taste.

Graceland has an army of keepers to keep the business going. The Lorraine has only Jacqueline Smith. Memphis has two dead kings. America has two minds.

Dice

I was stuck in the snow in Reno, Nevada, for two and a half days, and I have come back to warn you of the demon of gambling. I didn't know how I felt about it before, whenever I heard talk of legalizing gambling to raise revenue in Louisiana, but I know now. Don't do it: people like me will everywhere fall into the deep pit of their darkest self, there to turn the sweat of their brows into quick oblivion. Of all addictions, it has to be the worst. At least with sex and drugs you get a little relief while you're high, but there is no relief in gambling. Win or lose, you keep playing. You play until morning when the muscles in your back are so sore there are wings of pain sprouting from it; you play until only you and the three deeply wrinkled cowboys with their hats pulled low over bloodshot eyes are left, the four of you a devil's quartet thirsty for that last blackjack that will clean you out completely and irremediably.

There is undoubtedly something religious about it: everyone believes that they are special, that they are chosen, that they have a special relation with fate. Here is the test: you turn over card after card to see in which way that is true. If you can defy the odds, you may be saved. And when you are cleaned out, the last penny gone, you are enlightened at last, free perhaps, exhilarated like an ascetic by the falling away of the material world. The only trouble is, you never have enough. You go to the bank wall for your savings, you make your kin wire you their savings, you sign away your soul to a dude in a black hat. Or so would Dostoevski have done. Me, I was doing fine at blackjack, losing twenty, thirty bucks here and there while snow fell mercilessly outside. I felt safe and anonymous in the warm, clockless womb of the chiming, clicking casino. Unbeknownst to me, in the parking lot outside, casino attendants had captured a hungry mountain lion who'd come down looking for food. It did not occur to me that these pleasantly chiming plastic chips represented things in the real world, like food. In my most anonymous, dream-filled voice I said, "Give me another card," and the indifferent dealer said, "I hear you on the radio all the time!" And that was the end of my anonymity—and of my money. I lost hand after hand while the dealer told me story after story. When my 400 bucks was gone, the snow stopped, and airplanes started taking off again. It was Mardi Gras in New Orleans when I got back. Plastic chips rained on the crowd. They sounded and felt the same and, once more, I felt anonymous. "Turn over another card," I said, to no one in particular.

Dali in Vegas

All the blackjack dealers at Bob Stupak's Vegas World wore bow ties that said, STUPAK: HES POLISH. From the twinkling night-sky-ceiling, rockets plummeted, satellites orbited, astronauts rocked while on earth cherries tumbled, plums rolled, bells clanged, dice clacked, cards slapped. Everything else clinked and chimed. Stupak himself inspired grins or guffaws whenever he was mentioned. He ran for mayor, it appears, and when he lost, he punched a reporter on live TV. That's Vegas for you, still rough desert under a light quilt.

My friend Lamar Marchese once photographed all the lights in Vegas for a historical project. He pointed out the STARDUST sign floating in the desert sky, a masterwork of shimmer. As we drove downtown he made me close my eyes on a dark street. When I opened them we were in Glitter Gulch, and I went nearly blind in the neon cocktail. Lamar is even nostalgic about a certain cherry red that can't be made anymore because it made people sick. "There was a cocktail glass with a cherry in it," laments Lamar. "It was perfect." We pass the neon arches of the world's glitziest McDonald's. In the parking lot snazzed-out teens sway to their boom cars. The most normal looking building on the block is the Desert Inn at the top of which Howard Hughes hid from the world. At Caesar's Palace a Roman soldier gets photo'd with the tourists, while a Japanese man prays quietly at Caesar's Buddhist shrine, where candles can be lit for cash. The gun stores are doing a booming business, as do the tarted-out wedding chapels. Above one gun store, a lewd nymphette with an assault rifle betwixt her legs promotes machine-gun rentals. Other joints rent machine guns too. Honest gangsters presumably do their work and return their guns. Or else the desert is full of limping rabbits.

A woman's been standing watching the front of a wedding chapel for two nights. "Would you get married there?" she asks passersby in bewildered distress. The survey does not bode well. "Sure!" they answer. One place has "Prime Rib, Lobster and Bad Girls Show" for $9.99, while another sports "Nudes on Ice." But there is High Culture in Vegas, too. HUGE SALVADOR DALI SHOW, announces one marquee, right next to another touting a live appearance by Roy Orbison, a feat possible only in Vegas. The Dali Show, true to its name, displays stacks of dubious late Dali prints factory-style for popular prices between two and five grand. He's just another Surrealist here. Excalibur, the new Walt Disney World Lego castle going up next door, is the real Surreal McCoy.

The *Nouveaux Riches* of Hungary

You see them everywhere, seated at the expensive cafés along the Danube, making deals in the lobby of the Atrium Hyatt, handing their Mercedes and BMWs to tuxedoed parking attendants. At night they go to places like the Nautilus Nightclub and Restaurant, which is made entirely out of fish tanks, where they have whiskey surrounded by tropical fish that swim under their feet and over their heads, and eat such things as blinis with caviar and octopus Provençale from gold plates. They pay with large-denomination *deutsche marks* and speak English with the waiters, dipping into Hungarian only when it's absolutely necessary, like in the marble toilet where the attendant speaks only the vulgate.

They are the *nouveaux riches* of Hungary, and they've been sprouting like mushrooms overnight in the frontierlike feeling that's overtaken Budapest since the communists fell. New glass-and-marble buildings are going up, ancient Empire restaurants are being restored to their former glory by New York chefs, outdoor stands groan with exotic fruit, taxis are everywhere, and prices are comparable with Paris and Tokyo. Hungarian women are dressed both fashionably and provocatively, sporting anything from flesh-colored Lycra and black brassieres to designer outfits straight from Rome and Paris. A friend of mine, a historian, once a popular intellectual with a large readership, told me that her entire office has been following with great interest the fortunes of her brother-in-law, who started with a vegetable stand in 1990 and now owns two minimarts, two fruit stands, and a Laundromat. In the two short years since the grocer got rich, the once famous intellectuals who helped bring down the communist government have gone from esteem and sufficiency to neglect and shabbiness. Their salaries, like those of other professionals and workers in state-owned factories, are barely enough to live on. They watch, with increasing ironic wonder, the pathetic sales of their once influential books and the shrinking of their audiences. This isn't exactly what they had in mind when they overthrew the regime. They knew that some people would have to be sacrificed, they just didn't know it would be themselves.

Honey

A consummate traveler like myself knows what to pack. I went to Hungary for a week with my fit-under-your-airplane-seat bag stuffed with the absolutely essential two pairs of jeans, three T-shirts, the one dress shirt necessary in case Important People Invite You to an Expensive Restaurant, and five books weighing five pounds each—unfortunately— plus the necessary hygiene-cum-cosmetics kit that makes one fresh and pleasantly scented throughout airports, streets, and aliens. The hope, as always, is that the jeans and T-shirts could be used in rotation while being washed. Everything worked according to plan, even though Budapest has a lamentable lack of Laundromats and a pollution index that makes everything filthy gray in two hours. A friend told me that if one took a dog to a certain passage in the city, the dog would be dead in five minutes because of pollution. The original test dog had apparently been in excellent health. I stayed out of that area and handed my wardrobe to a hotel maid, who brought it back starched and ironed, which is more respect than these clothes ever got in America.

The trouble began when I went shopping for presents, a nightmare activity that I try to accomplish as soon as possible while I still have my wits about me. There was nothing either interesting or affordable among the rows of embroideries and fur hats being displayed by faux peasants along the Danube, and I was starting to feel the familiar despair of the untalented shopper who has but two choices: the hidden disapproval of his loved ones or suicide. It was at this point that I came upon a lonely vendor of honey jars reading a book in a small alley. These jars of reddish Hungarian honey had the honeycombs still in them and they struck me as the perfect presents that would convey at once a message of sweetness, and a certain practical sense. I mean, who doesn't like honey? And the exotic bees who made it were conducive to dreaming of foreign summers in sleepy fields of poppies and rye. I packed the honey jars tightly between my starched haberdashery and traveled about the country only to find—after a day of rough train rides—that one of the jars had broken and all my jeans and shirts were smeared with honey like some surreal sartorial toast. No effort at removing the stuff seemed to work, so I came back to America smeared with the essence of my poor shopping and gift giving. On the plane, I attracted strange small insects, and anyone who had the misfortune of brushing against me was instantly attached and had to struggle for freedom. I also became glued to my seat, and it was only with difficulty that two stewards managed to lift me off with the seat-fuzz still attached. There is no moral to this sticky tale except that I now understood the U.S. government injunction printed in my passport, not to bring any "foreign foods" into the country, especially honey, which in addition to being food is cloying and sentimental.

Columbus, the Pyramids,
Tristan, and I

My son Tristan became interested in Native Americans because he'd
been reading the Don Juan books by Carlos Castaneda. He was all set
to find himself a teacher among the shamans that abound in the parts of
Mexico described in those books. I tried to tell him about more pressing
contemporary Native American issues like land disputes, fishing rights,
setting straight the teaching of history, alcoholism, poverty, casinos, and
keeping Kevin Costner from claiming that he invented them. That was
all fine with him, but he was after shamans. I read in the newspaper that
Native American runners from North and South America were planning
to meet at the pyramids on Teotihuacán near Mexico City on Columbus
Day for a ceremony of mourning. I hustled some tickets from a friendly
airline magazine and off we went, to spend Columbus Day with people
who wished he had never been born. Personally, I don't feel about
Columbus one way or another. He wrecked paradise sixteenth-century-
style, and if he hadn't someone else would have. Besides, I like Chi-
canos, and especially Chicanas, and if no Columbus no Chicanas. Olaf
somebody might have done the job and I'm not so sure about an Indian-
Norwegian race. Anyway, that's my own feeling.

It was a rainy day at Teotihuacán but the descendants of the Aztecs
were out in force, selling mud-turtle flutes and fake pre-Columbian heads
to the buses full of tourists from Mexico City. They were impressive, the
pyramids, a whole immense city of ceremonial buildings whose mysterious purpose remains mysterious. The ancient Aztecs found these pyramids just the way they are now, looking just as mysterious. Tristan took
off like a bullet to look for a shaman, and I climbed to the top of the
Pyramid of the Sun to look for the Native American runners. I spotted
them, sitting in a small circle on ceremonial grounds about two miles
away. Eventually, we found our way to the circle. It was sweet and
wistful. Representatives of tribes exchanged ritual staffs and chanted the

names of their tribes. A medicine woman burned incense in the middle of the grounds. A few hippies gone native walked about with babies in papooses smoking peace pipes. We could have been in California at some gathering of the tribes, but we were not. We were at the center of the Aztec civilization, it was Columbus Day, and it was raining. Later, we took a highly personalized public bus back. Jim Morrison was singing from a boom box, La Raza was talking loud, laughing, and smoking, and the driver had the Virgin of Guadalupe, Quetzalcoatl, and flowers above the dashboard. "He's the shaman," I told Tristan. Don't know if he believed me.

Sixteenth-Century Vacation

I took a vacation to central Europe in the sixteenth century. People there are not like us at all. Their teeth hurt all the time. They have terrible eye problems. The bitter smell of herbal infusions, concoctions, compresses permeates everything. Boils are lanced without anesthetics. The air is one long scream. Executions are public spectacles that vie for ingeniousness. Simple decapitations and hangings won't do. There are bonfires for witches, quartering for thieves, impalement for rebels. If the aristocrat who puts on the pageant is particularly miffed, the victim *du jour* might be boiled, fried in a hot-iron seat, skinned, flayed, or hung by one foot over a flame pit. The castles are damp and freezing cold in the winter, damp and unbearably hot in the summer. Children die like flies. Torture is the chief aristocratic entertainment. Any infraction, no matter how small, even misplacing the mistress's comb, leads to the torture of the responsible maid whether she confesses or not. Hot needles are inserted under her fingernails, she is publicly whipped and humiliated.

There are so few objects, every single one is counted and recounted, dusted and polished every day. Loss, theft, or misplacement is met with bursts of anger, gales of temper, and, of course, torture. There is little connection between crime and punishment. Punishment is meted out continually without any regard for the offense. True crimes are committed only by the powerful, who commit them in order to see how far they can go before they, in their turn, are punished. There is always somebody powerful enough to punish criminals. Only the king and a handful of feudal lords are above all laws, and cannot be punished. They are the greatest criminals. There is little or no morality to speak of. Everybody hates monks and churchmen. Everybody fears the Devil, which is why they do everything to get his attention. Everyone is filthy, scrupleless, ready to steal, rape, murder, and fornicate in church if there is an opportunity and a chance to escape punishment. Eventually, everybody is tortured. The few that escape are victims of egregious bodily pain and discomfort. No one lives long, everybody is totally burned out by the age of thirty. It's not a fun time. Don't go there. If you have to time-travel, go to the end of the nineteenth century. It's much better.

The Tedium of Self

The editor of a travel magazine asked me to write some stories about places I go to. Sure, I said, but I can't do 'em in the first person. There is a character inside me who's a much better traveler than I. His name is Pen, and he is a better observer, a sharper wit, and a classier dude all around. For instance, last year at Marienbad, the Pen found himself face-to-face with a maître d' who disapproved of his blue jeans. The Pen drew himself up to the uppermost point of his nib and demanded to see the owner of the establishment. The owner, a sour dwarf in an Armani three-piece with several jangling gold chunks on his fingers and around his neck, was illiterate but guilty about it. When the Pen explained that he was the author of several highly regarded volumes of difficult verse, he was given dispensation and seated by the window with a view to the pale green Mediterranean. It was an overcast day and the *bouillabaisse* was overrated. Still, it was better than what one might find anywhere else. The mussels held the fresh flavor of the Mediterranean sun within the tender firmness of their pulp, and the other *coquilles* were matched perfectly to the garlic and the extra virgin olive oil. The Pen considered this dish to be the epitome of the Franco-Italian spirit, that civilized hybrid of sun, olives, and poetry.

The Pen doesn't have a mission. In fact, he doesn't even have any business. His purpose is to be amused. "The word *amuse* contains the muse," he often tells those of his acquaintances sporadically seized by curiosity. "And the muse is the force that drives this Pen," he concludes grandly. The Pen travels because he is curious. He is arch though quite tolerant, he finds human foibles endearing but is unforgiving of pretention. What a crank!

The Pen, of course, is not alone, I told the editor. He keeps company with all sort of portly, unmusical, and lazy characters in me. Together they keep the tedium of self at bay. *I*, as Rimbaud said, *is another*. And another. And one more.

Flying Times

I was quietly reading Geza Roheim's book on Vogul mythology, and I'd just gotten to the interesting part where the Vogul hero kills both his early and his late chieftain and then stacks them up by age to establish priorities in the afterworld, when the gent in the window seat exclaimed mournfully, "Conventions! They are all the same!" I lay down the Roheim and inquired what conventions he had in mind. "Managers of VA cemeteries," he said. "We are meeting in Denver. There are eighty of us taking care of one hundred and seventeen cemeteries." "Isn't that spreading yourself a little thin?" I asked. "Well, no," he said, "I used to work in Alaska and there wasn't much to do there. . . . We dug one hundred graves in the summer. Covered them with plywood. Filled 'em up every winter." He laughed. "That's life." He was a pretty cheerful fellow, a disposition I'd noticed before in people of his profession. I picked up the Voguls again, but before I read a line, the fellow in the aisle seat started up. "Can't wait to get back home," he said. "I been hunting mountain lion up to my hips in the snow." "Kill anything?" I said. "Yeah. Got him. Followed him for five hours. He got up on a tree right on top of me. Not before he hurt one of my dogs. Tore up his nose. My buddy stitched him right up. Gave him a quarter of an aspirin. Knocked him out." "Where is the lion?" asked the cemetery manager. "Getting stuffed. I'll get him in six weeks. Good deal, though. The hunting license was only fifty-one dollars. Two hundred dollars to stuff him."

I noticed with some distress that both men had somewhat identical physiques. Huge beer bellies, round faces, unduly happy double chins that quaked as if they were about to be shaken by imminent laughter. I feared that if the plane was going to crash now we could all end up in some kind of cosmic lounge with stuffed heads on the wall listening for eternity to some country singer wailing about people all dressed up with no place to go. I picked up my book, then put it down again. What's the point? The Voguls are among us. I mean, around us.

Geography

I was never good at geography. In tenth grade, when the teacher, exasperated by my inability to distinguish South America from Africa, asked me to point out north and south on the world map, I pointed to south for north and to north for south. And I can't tell left from right, either, which is why I don't drive. Consequently I've become such an anarchist that not only do I not recognize the borders of nation-states, I refuse to recognize the boundaries of *continents*. My punishment for this geographic insubordination is to travel constantly everywhere at greater and greater speeds in order to experience huge and terrifying contradictions. For instance, one week I will be in Rio de Janeiro in the Southern Hemisphere, where it is winter, but winter there means that the beaches are full of deeply tanned, bikini-clad people. The week after that I'll go to the mountains of Utah, where it's early spring at the end of June and there is still enough snow on the slopes to ski. This year I caught spring in several places going south to north, and then I caught spring sideways going east to west, but maybe it's the other way around.

I looked at my recent travel journal and it sounds written by a madman. "Camellias in New Orleans. Pussy willows in Ohio. Ice breaking in Maine." A poet I know, Maureen Owen, once wrote a book called *The No-Travels Journal*, which was a detailed journal of imaginary travels to exotic places. She described the spices, the tastes, and the people, and managed to sound for all the world as if she'd been there. If not for the title no one would have been any wiser. Her *No-Travels Journal* sounds much more believable than my real-travels journal. But that's a literary complaint, and my travels are really a literary punishment. In Copacabana the passion fruit, guava, and lime drinks taste like the maracas of samba. In Utah the gritty snow makes me want to lie down on it and melt down into the runoff racing to the valley. In Ohio the bitter smell of pussy willows fills me with childhood. In New Orleans the heat makes me sleep and dream. Who cares what the map says? I know what places feel like.

Escape

If you want to run away, now there is a book full of places to run away to. It's called *Intentional Communities: A Guide to Cooperative Living*. It's a book of communes, hundreds of them, all over the United States. I was surprised to see that there are so many active communes still left. The conventional wisdom is that after the sixties everybody was poured into a suit behind a desk and forced to live with a mate in front of a TV set. It certainly seemed that way to me, because all the communes I knew back in those mythical days broke up on the jagged rocks of poverty, jealousy, and whose turn it was to wash the dishes. Not so, according to this directory. If your taste is for the simple life and you like plants, for instance, you can join the Adirondack Herbs community where you can gather medicines, work with bees and greenhouses, and eat vegetarian food. If you think feeding the homeless is a good idea, check out Casa Maria in Milwaukee. For the Platonic groves of philosophy there is the Krotona Institute in Ojai, California. If you love the pleasures of the flesh, check out the Kerista Society in San Francisco. They practice orthodox polyfidelity. Whatever that is.

Almost all of these utopias and would-be utopias are located in or near paradise. Looking at the map, I see that every state has communes—except Utah. I'm sure that there are communes in Utah, but maybe their lifestyle philosophies are too startling to be listed here. There is also no word in the book on what any of these places do about washing dishes. But it's reassuring that they are still around. It means that not everyone in this country is in the army, in school, or in prison. State communism may be dead, but the communal urge is not. A friend of mine, once a commune addict, now a software designer, told me wistfully, "It's not the high principles I miss . . . it's the smell of soy and cayenne . . . and the pitty-patter of many naked feet in the morning." In other words, the comfort of family. He has something there.

People in Paradise

Me and paradise are on uneasy terms ever since I lived there. That was in California years ago. I lived in my mother's womb, too, but I barely remember that paradise, if that's what it was. It might have been more like being in a stormy sea because she wasn't too happy at the time. Anyway, I went to Rowe Camp in Massachusetts to meet a group of people desirous of poetry on an autumn weekend. The signs were all there: a few bright golden and red trees flaming fiercely in the Berkshire Hills. Apple trees with bright orange apples and no leaves standing on meadows like the illustration to the original fairy tale. Bright blue lakes rippled by otters. Canada geese spelling the letter A in honor of my first name. Rowe Camp itself, nestled like one of God's more relaxed moments, between two mountains.

I was intrigued but not entirely convinced by the remarkable collection of wackos, radicals, saints, and scholars that lead weekend workshops at Rowe. They have Noam Chomsky one week, a crystal healer witch the next. R. D. Laing was supposed to come but died instead. So they asked me. Armed with this kind of attitude, I wasn't going to be softened by a bunch of heartbreaking nature, which, after all, has no choice but to be beautiful if there aren't any Dow Chemical smokestacks in it. But I'll be danged, to use the idiom, if I wasn't completely charmed, taken over, recast, and inspired. The motley crew of poesy-loving humans was as distinct and special as a perfect day of Indian summer. There was a folksinging hobo, a pre-Raphaelite idealistic young couple, two businesspeople with socially conscious poetic souls, a number of New Yorkers with wit you could sharpen your fangs on, a high school teacher, a man with a puppet, and quite a few rather pure dreamers who'd had lives but had not let them get in the way of an impossible yearning for the beautiful. To this you may add fresh bread, garden-herb-flavored stew, and homebaked goodies at communal tables, initiated by a bit of Unitarian hand-holding and singing. Maybe it's because I've never really been to camp, but this stuff touched me. And when later, by the fragrant heat of a woodstove, over some wine jugs, we made poetry . . . what can I say? People are pretty wondrous creatures when you come right down to it. Set them up with a few trees and leaves, and you have the kind of paradise even I can stand.

The New Uses of American Space

The Infinite Column by Constantin Brâncuşi is one of the most famous sculptures in the world. Its spiraling thrust suggests infinity, universality, and hope. Brâncuşi, the Romanian-French sculptor who created it at the beginning of our century, took its shape from a humble detail of a peasant house in the mountains of Romania, a carved wooden porch support. The humble origin of Brâncuşi's universal symbol is important. Romanians, like other people under the merciless gun of history, have never put their faith in big, official buildings where the power of the day resided. They preferred instead to stay close to the earth and to make their own statements about the purpose of space.

I have been thinking about Brâncuşi's column again after reading a book called *The New Americans* by Al Santoli, a collection of interviews with recent refugees and immigrants who are changing American space and challenging its conventional uses.

By the middle of the next century Americans of European extraction will be a minority in the United States if the recent emigration trends continue. So say demographers, with a mixture of concern and bravado. The concern is that American cities will all look like the futuristic Los Angeles in *Blade Runner*, where racially mixed gangs roam the streets speaking a vaguely oriental mélange of martial Japanese and obscene Spanglish. On the other hand, recent immigrants are saving our decaying cities by transforming urban war zones into vibrant ethnic villages. The Vietnamese have created a "little Vietnam" in uptown Chicago; there is a Korean city in midtown Manhattan, and a "little Odessa" in Queens. There is even a Hmong tribe fishing village in Minnesota. These are fairly dramatic examples, but the big view tells only part of the story. There are also the humble details. Josef Patyna, a former Solidarity organizer from Poland interviewed in Santoli's book, lives in a "two story white house on a quiet tree-lined street . . ." in Providence, Rhode

Island. "Their living room is graced with a bright painting of Pope John Paul II, which is reflected in a large mirror above the fireplace. On the mantel is a glass beer mug, inscribed with the Virgin Mary of the Passion, the logo of the Silesian coal miners' guild. A single red candle is set on top of the television."

One feels that all these details are important to the Patynas, but there is something about that red candle on top of the television that really gets me. It is as if the Patynas, who are about to be engulfed by America as it pours out of its TV mouthpiece, are trying to contain and resist its onslaught. They have joined the living light of their symbolic candle to the cold light of the electronic eye in order to make peace between the two worlds they know, between past and present, Poland and America. Like Brâncuşi's *Infinite Column*, the Patynas' TV-cum-candle is a humble detail with a universal echo. It is the first ripple from which wider circles of change transform American space.

Epilogue

Toward the end of the movie *Road Scholar* I am hurtling down Lombard Street in San Francisco, "the crookedest street in the world," and I say: "It's nice of San Francisco to have a street that's a metaphor for a poet's life." As we hurtle toward the end of the millennium, that gets to be truer and truer, not just for me but for everyone else. In a short time after this book was finished, I attended the "Rosa Luxemburg Conference" in Chicago, a gathering of what's left of the American Left, and felt quite keenly the pathos of ravaged American idealism. The (mostly) older people attending had bright eyes, bottomless curiosity, and a passion for improving the world. They also smoked cigarettes! In a conference room! In 1994! Three days later I found myself speaking at the annual gathering of the Boston Consulting Group in Naples, Florida. The BCG is an organization of CEOs of Fortune 500 companies. I had a (smokeless) dinner in the company of Chicago First National (and spouse), the America-China Venture Company ($10 billion), and the head of BCG, dean at the Harvard Business School. For the attendees of the Rosa Luxemburg Conference, the men of the Boston Consulting Group were, very likely the very enemy. The funny thing is, I said exactly the same thing in both places: the world is a perilous, crooked street these days. Newly revived fascism is everyone's enemy. Passion for change and money for investment have the same purpose these days: increase liberty for people who don't yet have any and fight those who'd take it away. That's the good news. The bad is that people with passion have no power and people with power have no passion. That's where the poets come in. People, give your poets their say.